My Sweet Danish Rose

Tina Peterson Scott

My Sweet Danish Rose

My Sweet Danish Rose

Tina Peterson Scott

Mesa, Arizona, USA
foutfablesandmore@gmail.com

Copyright 2015 by Tina Peterson Scott

All rights reserved. No part of this book may be reproduced in any format or in any medium without the written permission of the author.

This is a work of fiction. The characters, names, and dialogue are products of the author's imagination, and are not to be construed as real.

Cover Design by Eden Literary
http://www.edenliterary.com

ISBN 13: 978-0-9891581-2-1

Thank you to the many women of the American Night Writer's Association for their collective wisdom and for their willingness to share their knowledge. A special thank you to Jennifer Griffith for her editing expertise, to my children for their love and support, and to my dear husband who encourages my writing and who thinks I'm brilliant.

Tina Peterson Scott

"And after their temptations, and much tribulation, behold, I, the Lord, will feel after them, and if they harden not their hearts, and stiffen not their necks against me, they shall be converted, and I will heal them."
D&C 112:13

My Sweet Danish Rose

April 1863

Angry voices coming from the parlor awakened me. Who could be here at this early hour? I pushed Grandmother's quilt aside and sat up. Then, scrunching it to my face I took a moment to remember her. It didn't ward off the strange feeling growing within my breast—flitting anxious butterflies and squeezes of anxiety. I needed air and tried filling my lungs. It didn't help.

This had been the longest month in my fifteen years of life. It wasn't fair to realize I wanted a future with Jens Larsen just as time drew near to leave. We were immigrating to America in the morn, and then traveling to a place called Utah to be with the Prophet Brigham Young and other members of our new Mormon faith.

But how could I leave Jens? Or Denmark?

When I first agreed to immigrate, it sounded exciting, adventurous even. We had prayed as a family and decided it was the right thing to do. But that was a year ago. Things had changed since then. *Breathe, Berta, breathe.* My heart hurt. I clutched it. Could I die of a broken heart?

Mama would think I was full of pure nonsense. Shaking my head, I slipped out of bed to dress.

Though she dreamed of living among the American Saints, Catherine, my older sister was staying to wed her longtime beau. Perhaps I should stay as well. We could each marry, save for a year, and leave together. I glanced over at her. She still slept, although I didn't know how she could.

Not immigrating hadn't even been an option. Until now. How

would I live without her? We were the best of friends and close confidants. We had shared this bed since I was two.

More angry voices startled me. I crept out of the room to see what was going on. Why had Papa raised his voice? A shiver went up my spine. I had never heard him this angry.

"This isn't right," Papa said. "We agreed on twice that amount."

I inched closer.

"What's going on?" asked Catherine, startling me.

"Shhh," I whispered.

She led the way, and we crept toward the parlor entryway. She peeked around the corner, and I tried to see.

"It's out of my control," said an unknown man. He was shorter than Papa, thicker around the middle, and had thin graying hair that reached the collar of his shirt. Since he had his back to us I could not see his face.

Mama and Papa were expecting Mr. Ilse. This must be him.

"You have every control, and certainly more than you should!"

"There's no need to raise your voice. Let's be gentlemen about this." He sounded calm and self-assured.

"Ha!" Papa scoffed. "A gentleman wouldn't wait until the eve of our departure to say he can only come up with half the remaining payment. If you'd even told us a week ago, I could have sold farm tools and furniture to help make up the difference."

"We can't cry over spilt milk. Do you want my money, or don't you?"

I looked at Catherine. If we didn't have enough money to immigrate, what would become of us? She put a finger to her lips before I could ask.

"You know very well that we're leaving tomorrow," Papa said. "We've already paid our passage to America. I need that money to make a new life for my family."

"Then I'll require your signature, here."

"My oldest daughter, Catherine, is staying in Denmark. She

won't be leaving for her aunt's until noon tomorrow." Papa still sounded angry. "Don't take possession of the property until the following morn."

"Let me see," I whispered. "I want a peek."

"Nej." Catherine pulled me back. "It's best if Papa doesn't see us here."

She headed toward our bedroom, and I followed her while trying to block the angry words from my mind. I closed the door behind me. We rushed to our bed and threw the covers over us, huddling beneath their protection.

"Do you think we'll stay?" I asked.

"Nej. Do not worry. Papa has enough."

I nodded, but worried anyway—not that we couldn't leave, but that we would. "What do you think will happen to us in America?" I asked.

"It will be wonderful," Catherine muttered wistfully. "You will be in a place where everyone believes as we do."

"Will I ever see you again?"

Catherine remained silent to my question for a long time. I didn't see why because tears filled my eyes, and I pressed my arm to my face, blotting them with my sleeve.

"With the Lord's help we will meet again one day," she whispered.

It was all the assurance I could ask for. I lunged over and hugged her tight, making the cover slip to our shoulders. We gazed into each other's faces and smiled through our tears.

"I love you," she said.

"More than a thousand dancing fairies," was my choked response.

We both crawled to the edge of the bed. "What shall we do today?" I asked.

"We'll need fresh water."

"Ja, ja." Mama would be pleased to see that I gathered it without her asking. While Catherine dressed, I crept back to the kitchen, slipped on my clogs, and went out to the pump. As my bucket filled, I wondered how this turn of events affected my family. Would we truly have enough money to make it the whole distance to Zion?

I didn't ponder long on the unknown. Instead, I thought of Jens at our last social. He had escorted me gently to the dance floor. I'd tingled with delight when our hands touched as he offered me refreshments. His eyes glistened in merriment as we talked.

The sound of water splashing out of the bucket and onto the ground brought me back to the present. I pushed the pump handle down and lugged the overfull bucket to the house, spilling water with each step.

Mama met me in the kitchen. Mary and Ana, my little sisters, pulled at her skirts anxious about something.

"Get your sisters dressed. Go out and milk the cow. Take your sisters with you." Strands of Mama's beautiful brown hair hung around her face. She blew a puff of air, moving the stray locks aside.

"Ja, Mama." I took the girls' hands and hurried away. It would be a long day indeed with Mama stressed so soon this morning. I'd overheard Mama and Papa worrying all month, fearing that Mr. Ilse might not bring the rest of the money he owed. They didn't trust him, yet his was the only offer. It seemed now they were right to worry.

After helping the girls dress, Mary handed me the brush. I groomed and braided their hair. Then I pinned it up off their neck.

Ana toddled and picked up her bonnet. "Me do it," she insisted.

I smiled and nodded. "Go on and give it a try." She was growing more independent every day. By the time Ana turned three, which was only five months away, she would probably insist on dressing herself.

I gave them each a hug. "Get your shawls, it's still chilly out."

"Are we 'Mericans now?" Ana asked as I led them outside and toward the barn.

"Nej, princess." I knelt and hugged my baby sister. "It will take a long time to get to America." I blinked moisture from my eyes and stood gazing around the inner courtyard. Would I ever feel at home anywhere else? "The Lord will take care of us," I assured my sisters. Though I didn't feel sure.

Mary tugged at my hand. "Can I milk the cow today?"

"I will let you try for a moment but then you must let me finish." Mary's hands, at six, weren't yet strong enough to do a good job of milking the cow.

Inside the barn, Mary got out the stool and Ana held the milking pail. "Wait right here," I cautioned. "She might kick if she gets nervous, and I don't want you to get hurt."

The cow came easily under my lead and I tied her to the post. "Bring the stool," I urged. "Ana, give me the pail."

Mary tried to milk her first but wasn't able to get more than a couple of drops into the pail, so I finished the chore. Not only did the Larsens own the finest flour mill in the region, Jens's family also had a dozen Danish Reds. Their cheese and dairy products were local favorites. If I stayed, would I one day milk beside him?

"Hold onto my skirt," I said. "And watch your step." There wasn't any real danger, but I didn't want to take a chance on one of my sisters getting hurt. Not today.

The milk was heavy but I lugged it all the way to the house without stopping. "Here's the milk, Mama." I heaved the bucket onto the kitchen table and saw that only one of our ceramic milk jars was there. "What will we do with the extra milk? Are we leaving it for Herrer Ilse?"

"Never. We will pour some into a dish for the cat. The rest will water the rose bushes. I'll not leave any more than necessary for that man."

"Ja, ja. I overheard Papa talking with him." I ladled the milk and poured it through several layers of cheesecloth and into the jar. "Will we have enough money?" My heart leapt with hope that something would happen to keep me and Jens together. Perhaps we'd have to stay another year. By then Jens might ask to marry me.

"This is not your worry." Mama frowned. "The Lord has blessed us sufficiently," she said, and then her eyes gleamed with inspiration. "Go to the Andersdatters's. They've always admired our butter churn. If they come right away, we will sell it to them for a song."

I nodded and gulped back my dread. Sofrina Andersdatter and I had fought each other for Jens's attentions since I was ten. When we became old enough to join the young person's guild, our rivalry continued, each hoping for Jens as our partner for the year. He had been my partner this year. I clasped my hands, worrying my palms together. Now, only months later, I was leaving him.

"First go and gather the eggs for our breakfast." Mama smiled then turned to mix the biscuit dough. "We shall be settled in Zion before we get fresh eggs again."

Zion! Could I do it? Could I leave my home and the man I loved for this unknown place? Anxiety shivered through my soul. I breathed the word as I hurried to the back door where we kept the egg basket. I grabbed it and ran through the inner courtyard and out to the chicken yard where Papa gave our chickens just enough room to be happy.

The hens had a nice house there for laying eggs and for staying in during the cold winter months. They were fenced in and away from the horses, and also separate from the goats' pasture—but the goats had already been sold, so their pasture was empty.

The ice on the pond at the far end of our property had long ago melted—or what was once our property. Gazing there, I saw several geese gliding along the surface. Beyond the pond, a startled partridge fluttered and then flew into the thicket that marked the end of our land. Did they have partridges in America? My stomach growled at the thought of Mama's roast partridge. I hoped so.

Our family had lived on this property for more than a hundred years. And after tomorrow, we wouldn't. I unlatched the gate, pushed my way into the chicken coop, and gathered the eggs. There were twelve. Mr. Ilse, the horrible man, would have himself some good layers.

Tomorrow our family, along with hundreds of other Danes, would start our pilgrimage by going first to Germany and then to England. After traveling by rail across the country to the harbor, we'd sail all the way to America. There we would buy handcarts and walk double—triple the expanse of Denmark through a wilderness assuredly fraught with peril, to that place in Utah that was known to Mormons as Zion.

My legs ached at the mere thought, and I chewed the inside of my lip. If we made it there alive, our lives would be forever changed.

I opened the kitchen door and set the basket near the stove. "Here's the eggs." Seeing a bowl of water there, I washed them off and placed them into a pot of boiling water that Mama had ready. "Shall I go to Andersdatter's now or wait till after breakfast?"

"All is well and good. I sent Catherine."

I hadn't worried. Not really. I swallowed my displeasure and helped put breakfast on the table.

Catherine came in just as we were sitting down. "Herrer Andersdatter said he would come right away," she said.

Papa nodded. "Perhaps there is more he would like to purchase."

Mama's eyes grew large. "Berta's chest?"

"Nej, not my precious chest!" I'd have rather left it behind not knowing what became of it than to know Sofrina had it.

Papa and Mama had both worked hard to provide us girls

each with a chest of fabrics for making clothes once we wed. Papa had made the chests and hand-carved beautiful designs on each of them. They were elegant like something from a royal castle. Mama had taught us and helped us card, spin, and weave our own fabrics for years to add to our chances of marrying well.

"We can't take it." Mama's eyes softened. "I've packed as much of the fabric as I can, but we can't take the chest. Better the Andersdatters have it than Herrer Ilse."

I nodded and stared down at my plate. If I had a reason to stay, I could keep my chest.

We finished eating and were cleaning the kitchen when Mr. Andersdatter came to the door. Mama curtsied and let him in. "We have several things including our Berta's chest and some of her fabrics." She indicated the chest near the entry. I could not bear the thought of Sofrina having the beautiful box that Papa had carved for me, and I hurried past them to the front door.

While trying to make my escape, I nearly bumped into Sofrina. "Good day," I muttered, trying to get past.

"Oh Berta, the day is simply divine." Sofrina linked arms with me and stepped into the house. "I mean, it's poor fortune on your part that you can't take your chest and fabrics, but your papa is an excellent carver, and I shall make good use of them." She blinked up at her papa with hopeful eyes. "I can have them, can't I?"

"You shall have it all if you like."

She squealed with delight. "You are the best Papa."

I clenched my free hand in my apron pocket. This was not right.

Mama and Mr. Andersdatter walked through the house. Mama pointed out the other things that might interest him. I hated this. I felt like we were beggars trying to sell our wares.

"I need to go water the roses," I said in an attempt to leave.

"Herrer Ilse can water them tomorrow if needs be," said Mama.

Sofrina opened my chest. "Is this all the fabric you've made?"

She tsk-tsked as she rummaged through my remaining pieces of cloth.

With my tongue held firmly between my teeth, I was assured of not displeasing Mama by saying unkind words to Sofrina. My chest had been full yesterday.

"Oh, look at this piece of lace. And this blue fabric! I shall make a blouse out of it and add the lace to it." Sofrina held a piece of homespun wool to her chin. "Jens Larsen loves blue."

My heart skipped a beat. I'd used that lace-making project as an excuse to be near Jens. His mama had helped me make it. I fought the urge to snatch it from her hands. Mama must have overlooked it in packing and had only taken my finer pieces that she had helped me with. I clenched my teeth together, not willing to allow Sofrina to see how her comments bothered me.

"I thought you were seeing someone else," I said with an air of disinterest.

She smiled serenely. "Things change."

I stepped away from her. She would have my chest, my fabrics—my Jens. Tomorrow morning Sofrina would inherit my whole life. I turned and followed the sound of Mama's voice to Catherine's and my bedroom. Mama held my Sunday dress in her hands.

"It's fairly new," Mama said. "She outgrew her other one."

Hoping Mama hadn't seen me, I spun on my heel, my insides screaming in rebellion, and hurried past Sofrina and through the kitchen door. After closing the door softly so as not to anger Mama, I leaned against the frame, gulping breaths of air and dabbing at my eyes with my handkerchief.

Why had I thought this would be easy? Until this very day, I'd kept my feelings separate—my excitement regarding my family's religious pilgrimage stayed neatly in one area of my heart, my secret love for Jens and the desire to never leave him tucked neatly in another.

I could do it no longer.

At this very moment, the areas of my heart safeguarding my three loves—family, religion, and Jens—crashed together. They waged a war that could not be won without pain. Lots of it. Keeping my feelings secret had not spared me one speck of grief. If I left without seeing Jens, he would never know how I felt. And worse, I would never know how he felt about me, not really. Did he care? Would he have proposed?

Peering down at my wooden shoes near the doorstep, I grabbed them up before Sofrina could claim them. While holding them, and with my shawl around my shoulders, I stormed across the length of our inner-courtyard. Then I slipped through the open area between house and barn where Papa brought the cow in at night.

The horses were in the field grazing, the thick grass a soft cushion to my feet. In my opinion, Papa had the best horses in our region. They were the stocky, bred for cold weather Faroese horses. I made a kissing sound and the mare I called Caja pranced over and nudged me with her nose. I'd asked for Jens's help in training her though I didn't need it. I'd used it as an excuse to have him near.

"I need one more favor, girl." Pulling some grass, I fed it to her then grabbed her mane and lifted myself onto her back. "Take me to Larsen's." Deciding to worry about my consequences later, I tapped her gently with my foot.

I had to see Jens.

Chapter 2

While I leaned against her warm neck, Caja sped away knowing our destination instinctively from going there so often in the past. The rhythm of my heartbeat raced with hers and I relished the feel of my horse and me together. Papa had let me claim her since I'd been there to witness the miracle of her birth. But Caja couldn't come with us to America.

I had thought I had faith, thought I could trust myself to the Lord's care, thought I could live without Jens—until seeing Sofrina pawing over my things while hinting he would be hers. Why couldn't she have remained quiet? Why didn't Mr. Ilse just pay the money he owed? Sofrina would never have come to our house if he had.

The countryside rose and fell in their gentle hills and I pulled Caja into a walk. Would Jens be glad to see me? My heart skipped a beat. Would he scoff at my presumptions? Although I had made every excuse to see him in the past and he always made me feel special, he had never made his intentions clear.

A sudden urge to turn around and speed home in all haste nearly overcame me. It was a feeling of acute danger. I scanned the countryside. There was no danger. I saw no wild beasts about. No travelers on the road. I urged Caja forward. I'd come too far to turn around. It was my nerves.

A mixture of dread and anticipation prickled up my spine and I stopped. He was in the field near a fence post—repairing it, I assumed. I said a quick prayer of gratitude at not having to go all the way to his house.

"Jens!"

He looked up.

Forcing a smile, I waved and then galloped the remaining distance.

His puzzled frown turned into a smile just as I hoped it would. "Berta?"

"Ja, ja, it is me." Sliding off the horse, I rushed to him then stopped short and glanced away, embarrassed with my bold behavior. I needn't have worried because Jens immediately took me in his arms and kissed the top of my head. I took a deep, relaxing breath, smelling the familiar scent of him. I was amazed that he calmed my nerves so easily.

"I had hoped to see you one more time before you left." Jens stepped back a pace. "I have a parting gift—something for you to remember me by." The corners of his mouth quirked up.

I loved Jens's smile—I loved the way my hand fit into his—I loved him. Smiling up at him, I followed as he led me to the top of a short incline.

He sat on the moist earth and pulled me into his lap. "All this land will be mine one day." Jens waved his hand, indicating their farmland. "My dream is to share it with someone I care about."

I cherished the intimacy as together we viewed the rolling countryside, the smell of sweet grass and rich soil greeting my nose. Only in the far distance could I see the thick line of trees that separated his property from his neighbor's.

"Your leaving to America poses a problem, ja?"

Unsure of my voice, I nodded in agreement. A tear rolled down my cheek, and I leaned against his chest. It brought great relief knowing Jens cared for me. He wasn't generally forthcoming with that type of information.

As he wrapped his arms around me, I wondered about a solution to our dilemma and wished I didn't have to go to America—everything and everyone I loved was here in Denmark.

"Catherine is staying." I glanced back at him timidly.

Jens slipped from underneath me, and sitting cross-legged

he faced me, taking both my hands in his. "How can that be so? I understand Herrer Ilse has purchased the lease on your land and now owns it and all that is on it."

"This is true." I gazed down as he rubbed his thumbs against the back of my hands. "Catherine will stay with Aunt Thora in Vejstrup."

"Too bad it is not you, for I am accompanying father to Vejstrup next Friday." Jens lifted my hand to his lips and kissed it. "I would bring you home to live with me."

Was that a proposal? I gulped and peeked at him through my eyelashes. "Mama needs my help, but if I could…" Did I dare say the words? Did I dare stay? I peered into his eyes, and gulped. "If Papa allows it, I will be in Vejstrup with Catherine." The words whispered from me, and in my soul I knew they were true.

"If you stayed, I would come for you." He brushed his fingers across my cheek. "Why does your sister go to Vejstrup?"

"Mama asked her to help care for Aunt Thora until she marries Isaac Thompsen next year."

"If they love each other, why do they wait?"

He and Isaac's brother were good friends. I shook my head. They would talk and Catherine had told me in confidence. "It is not up to me to say."

"But you know the reason?"

I looked away with my bottom lip securely between my teeth. Catherine would not want me to tell.

"It doesn't matter." He peered at me—his eyes nearly the color of periwinkles they were so blue—and sidled up next to me, putting his arm around my shoulder. "Perhaps it is a secret between sisters." His voice sounded teasing, but his eyes seemed serious. "Maybe she is not so anxious to marry the son of a banker, or maybe she has a secret beau in Vejstrup where your aunt resides and she is hoping for a better proposal." Jens leaned back on his elbow and picked a blade of grass, tossed it into the air, and watched it fall.

"That's not it at all. It's only Isaac that she loves." I grabbed a handful of grass and threw it at him, hoping to change our conversation.

"There must be some devious plan in the works that would keep two people who love each other apart for so long—especially with you and your family leaving."

Did he not think I was sincere about staying? I turned away, holding back the tears as Jens brushed the grass off of his vest and breeches.

"Is it something to do with your new religion?"

"What if it is?" My tears disappeared and I frowned in response.

"Surely your church won't keep them apart." Jens sat up, his mouth forming a thin line.

"It's not our church keeping them apart—she is merely hoping that with time, Isaac will convert." My heart sank a little at confessing Catherine's secret, but he needed to understand.

"Isaac is willing to overlook your family's religion and marry her anyway." He grimaced. "But he'll never convert."

"You can't possibly know that. Once he finishes the Book of Mormon, he'll understand how important our religion is. This is why she stays." Clenching my teeth, I dared him with my eyes to challenge my words.

He didn't.

Jens pulled at a grass blade down by the root. He chewed on the sweet and tender end for a moment before throwing it back to the earth with a sigh. Turning to me, he breathed deeply once more, his face taking on a serene appearance.

"Is that why you are leaving? Are you anxious to leave your home to find a Mormon beau?"

His words cut me—he had to know how I felt about him. I was here, pushing myself on him, telling him that although Mama needed my help, I would stay. For him. All after I'd felt the burning in my bosom regarding our immigration. Had he thought that I really needed his help to train Caja as a foal? Had he really believed that I needed his mother to show me how to make lace? I'd done it all for him.

The corner of Jens's lip turned up.

Thinking that perhaps he mocked me, I stood and walked away. The dream of marrying Jens was frustratingly beyond my grasp. We had scrimped and saved as a family for a whole year, fasting and praying and hoping that one day we could join the Saints in Zion—and then Mr. Ilse came with an offer to purchase our animals and the lease on our property.

Since that time, Jens had shared stories of ships being lost at sea, of immigration ships where nearly everyone died from the measles and because of the filth. The only reason Jens could possibly have for telling me these horrible things was that he wanted me to stay. So why didn't he come right out and ask? Why didn't he fight for me?

"I'm sorry. I've upset you." Jens walked up behind me and put his arms around my waist. "I am merely jealous thinking that it will be some other man who gives you your first kiss."

Frozen with the fear of his implication, I didn't turn around as he probably hoped I would. After a moment of uncomfortable silence he released me.

"I need to get home," I said. How could he talk of kissing here, so close to the road? Anyone could see. I walked down the slope of land and away from him once more.

I'd gone only a short distance before I felt something tickling against my neck and stopped. A dainty little ring on a simple chain danced in front of my face—silver with a drop of amber. My hand automatically reached up to grasp it, but as soon as I did, it danced away from me and out of sight. Jens dangled the golden jewel like a carrot before me but I couldn't care that he was teasing me with it—he had bought me a ring!

I turned and saw his mischievous grin. "Say you forgive me first."

"I forgive you. I do." I jumped up to get it and in one fell swoop, he dropped it into his vest pocket, grabbed me in his arms and twirled me around and around.

"Stop, stop!" I laughed.

When he finally put me down, I started to sway. To keep me from toppling over, Jens held both of my shoulders until the world stopped swirling.

"Now, if I may?" His eyebrows lifted and he pulled the ring out of his vest pocket. I nodded. He took it from the chain and placed it on the pinkie finger of my left hand.

"It is so beautiful." I rubbed the small golden gem with my thumb. Jens must truly care for me. There wasn't a petrified insect suspended in the translucent resin—something common in the more expensive pieces—but it was beautiful nonetheless. He put his arms around me, squeezing me tight and kissing my shoulder. His affections made me nervous, so again I stepped away.

"Berta, don't run from me." Jens moved behind me and nuzzled my neck.

I turned and considered him questioningly.

"May I have just one kiss from my sweet Berta before she sails out of my life forever?"

My heart thudded in my chest. I'd never kissed a man before—not on the lips. I'd hoped to share my first kiss with the man I would marry. Yet, had we decided to stay in Denmark, that person would most definitely be Jens.

How could I deny him?

My head went down in doubt, but I didn't move away. Jens lifted my chin with his warm hand, peering once again into my eyes—my soul.

"May I?"

His question made it doubly hard for me, as I didn't know what to do. Should I stand on my tip-toes—and where did my nose go?

"Berta."

With the pleading whisper and the catch in his voice, shivers ran up my neck. I glanced into his eyes, taking in the deep blue with flecks of gold and how they shimmered—and how strands of sandy blond hair lay across his forehead—his nose, so straight—his lips so perfect and eager for mine. His face broadened into a brief smile as he leaned forward, his kiss soft.

My heart leapt, my breath quickened, and then it ended.

I took in a breath, acutely feeling his absence. He met me with another kiss—warmer and gradually more intense, and I felt myself melting into him. I could see myself growing old with Jens on this very mound as our hearts beat in rhythm. But as he continued, the energy of his passion scared me. I pulled away, touching the heat on my cheeks with my fingertips.

My eyes watered, blurring my vision, and as much as I hated to, I walked toward Caja. I needed to get home.

Jens matched my pace easily and slipped his hand around mine. "Will you speak to me?"

Shaking my head slightly in response, I tried to continue my pace, but when he stopped I felt myself moving to face him as he gave a gentle pull. Not wanting him to see my tears, I looked away, but it was no use. He took his handkerchief out of his pocket and dabbed at my face.

"Are those tears for me?"

I nodded. Why did he have to be so wonderful? Why did he have to kiss me and make leaving all the harder?

"Will you miss me now? Will you think of me when you are in America with an American beau at your side?" He wiped the stray hairs from my face and kissed my nose. My face was a wet mess. With the ends of my shawl in each hand, I tried wiping it dry.

"You can come with us," I said, suddenly hopeful.

"I cannot leave. You know that. Father depends on me." His voice almost reproachful, he gazed at me with an expression I didn't quite recognize. I wished I could read his mind.

"America is huge. Your parents can own land there." I hated the way my voice sounded—childlike and begging.

"Dear, dear Berta." He shook his head with a sad kind of smile. "I will stay here and inherit what is rightfully mine.

Perhaps it is your family that should stay—you said your sister is staying."

"Nej, we cannot all stay." Somehow we had started walking again but I didn't realize it until Caja nudged me. I patted her soft velvety nose, wishing that I could stay longer and convince Jens to come with us to America. Yet I knew Mama would be angry at my absence. I needed to get home.

"This is good-bye?"

At his words, the tears flowed down my face, and I couldn't find the strength to mount upon Caja's back. I buried my face in her side, wetting her coat. After a moment, Jens pulled me to him, holding me to his chest and rubbing my back. When Jens rested his chin on the top of my head I sobbed all the harder.

"Don't cry. Berta, please." He shifted, and touching his forehead to mine, dabbed at my tears once more. Then his lips found mine. Eagerly I transported myself into a world where only Jens and I existed—a world where there were no goodbyes. My hand automatically went to his hair, fingering the sandy blond curls at the nape of his neck, and I accidentally knocked off his cap.

With me still securely in his embrace, Jens straightened. I clung to him desperately, my feet dangling, and not wishing to ever leave. Yet, against my will and every desire, he pulled away.

He placed me on the ground and touched his fingers to my chin. "You had better get back home." He lifted me easily onto Caja's back, gave her a swift pat on the flank, and Caja began walking away.

My vision blurred, but I stared back at him wishing that although his father owned land and was important in our community, that Jens could leave his family and come to America with me.

Jens waved twice then put his cap on and went back to work.

Hugging Caja's neck, I sobbed into her mane, mourning the loss of him. This could not be the end of our love.

Chapter 3

"I hope you have that out of your system?" Mama met me at the gate. I acknowledged her with a shrug. "Your papa and I have been worried sick. Where did you go?"

"Saying goodbye." My voice quavered so I didn't say more.

Mama's locket glistened around her neck. Papa had given her the exquisite memento when they wed, with a priceless image of each of them snug inside. The awareness of Jens's ring burned against my calf—could this be my priceless token? I'd concealed it in my stocking and wondered if Mama could see it—but forced myself not to peek.

"Why do you insist on making things hard on yourself?"

Glancing at her, I wondered if she knew where I had gone. I took my handkerchief from my apron pocket and wiped my eyes and then my nose. I sniffed back one last sob and then slid off Caja and into Mama's arms.

"It is too hard, Mama. Leaving."

Mama pulled me into a hug. "It seems difficult now, leaving all that we know. But in a year's time when we live in Zion, we shall look back on this moment and be glad that we made the right choice."

"Is leaving the right choice?" I rested my head on Mama's shoulder, enjoying her comfort.

"It is, princess. And you will remember soon enough." Mama took me by the shoulders and pulled me upright. "Are you finished with your packing?"

"Nej, Mama." I hung my head, not wanting to see her disappointment.

"Then you had better get right to work." Mama gave my behind a swat. "You must be packed before supper, and there are still plenty of ways for you to help."

"Ja, Mama. Just let me put Caja back to pasture first."

"You've had enough time to say goodbye to the horse. Get on into the house and take care of your responsibilities."

Mama motioned me away with her hands and I hurried toward the house before causing her more displeasure. But I couldn't help replaying the events of the morning. I never knew someone's lips could be so soft. In remembrance of Jens's warm lips, my fingers went to mine.

"Where have you been?" Papa wore the frown of disappointment on his face. It dismayed me to cause them such grief, but had they known, their grief would not be lessened.

"Riding my horse one last time," I said.

Catherine glared in disapproval from across the kitchen, and I knew she had an idea of where I'd been.

"Well, it is time for you to help." He continued placing things into a wooden crate. "We've got a long enough day tomorrow without having to arise earlier to accomplish tasks that should be completed today." He stood and played with the hair at his neck. "I was hoping my daughter would give me a haircut after supper. Ja?"

"Ja, Papa. I will be happy to cut your hair." Papa said no one could cut his hair better than I did.

In the bedroom I took the small bag reserved for the few belongings I was allowed to take and placed it on the bed. My beautiful Sunday dress was no longer in the armoire. I clenched my teeth together and pulled out two equally dull skirts with two plain blouses and laid them near the bag. Traveling long distances required sturdy work clothing, nothing frilly or soft.

Walking and cold weather both required thick woolen stockings—they went to the bottom of the bag. A change of underclothing went next followed by one skirt and blouse—I would wear the others.

Sheep from the Faroe Islands grew exceptionally thick and warm wool for cold winter nights. My Faroese blanket went on top.

I placed my foot on the bed and felt the ring through my stocking. I wouldn't take it out, wouldn't let anyone see it, not even Catherine. Leaving Jens was my sorrow and mine alone. I couldn't bring voice to my pain and still be expected to immigrate. It would crush me.

My hand smoothed across the wooden headboard and the little painted flowers that Mama had added later as a Christmas surprise. I still held a shadowy memory of my excitement of that first day when Papa brought the bed indoors. Just like Ana, I was anxious to grow up and sleep in a regular bed.

The room wasn't large, so Papa had made the bed adjustable. The side pulled out at night for both me and Catherine to sleep comfortably. It pushed into a narrow bed during the daytime, making more room for play when the weather was bad. Catherine and I had shared it since she was six and I was four.

The soft mattress was made of cotton ticking and goose down. We folded it in half during the day. Grandma's quilt graced the top. I touched the stitching—each one sewn with loving care. None of it could go with us. Not our table or the chairs, not the desk made by Grandpa Jensen, not the little rocking horse made to celebrate Ana's birth. We would walk across America, with our belongings and Papa's tools, in a handcart.

I fastened the bag and set it in the corner and then flopped on the bed, pictures of Jens mixing with those of family, friends and home. I frowned. Why hadn't Sofrina also taken my quilt? Then she could have my whole life and tend Grandma's grave as though it was her own grandma's.

"Maybe you could come help, ja?" Catherine stood in the doorway interrupting my thoughts.

"Ja, ja. All is well and good." I jumped up and followed her. My troubled thoughts resurfaced as I walked through our home. The butter churn in the kitchen was gone, as were all of Mama's irons. The space where our precious chests had been was vacant except for Catherine's. Knowing that our things were at the Andersdatters' instead of waiting for Mr. Ilse to pawn them off did not help me mourn them less.

It didn't matter that Mr. Ilse had cheated him. Papa wanted as much of our remaining things packed and ready for Mr. Ilse as possible. And regardless of how Mama felt about the man, she wanted everything spotless. I scrubbed the parlor windows clean and swept the floor and then went into Mama and Papa's room to start the process over.

Hours later and exhausted, I stepped into the courtyard, pumped a bucket of water and took it into the house. The beginnings of an evening fog already hovered near the earth.

"Mary, Ana, let's wash for supper."

The girls came running. With a towel in my lap and soap in my hand, I dipped the washrag into the water then wiped the soap on it and scrubbed my little sisters' faces and hands.

They turned to rush away, but I suspected the job was not yet completed and snatched hold of Mary's skirt, holding her back. "Give me your hands again. I want to check under your nails to make sure I got all the dirt off."

"They're clean." Mary inspected her fingers and turned to leave once more.

"Wait." I grabbed her arm and pulled her closer. After studying her fingernails, I dipped them into the water. Submersing the rag, I took to the underneath of her nails trying to force the dirt loose.

"Ouch! That hurts!" Mary tried jerking free, but I held tight to her arm.

"Would you rather Mama do it?" I scrubbed again and Mary remained still. "It's not my fault that you and Ana dig in the dirt."

"We wanted to bring some of Mama's flower bulbs with us."

"You can't bring flowers to America." I frowned and shook my head.

"Mama said we could. The bulbs won't die." Mary made a face, but I ignored it and inspected Ana's fingernails. They were dirty as well.

"Come on, you little goose. Let's get those fingernails clean." I dipped Ana's fingers in the bucket and nodded to Mary. "Go help Catie set the table."

Our home filled with the wonderful aromas of food as Mama took it from our earthen oven and placed it on the table. She had prepared a special feast of *flæskesteg* for our last night together. My nose tingled as the heavenly scent of roast pork with the fat side cooked to crispy perfection, mixed with the nutty aroma of multiple-grained rye bread. We also dined on the last of our previous summer's potatoes and *rødkål*. The slightly sweetened potatoes matched well with the tangy red cabbage. All were Catherine's favorites, but I loved them too.

I slathered a piece of warm bread with homemade butter knowing I wouldn't have any more for the longest time. Immigrants weren't served such finery aboard ship and we wouldn't have a cow we until settled in Zion.

It would be strange being Mary and Ana's eldest sister once we left. Could I possibly do the job as well as Catherine? How I would miss her! To lose both her and Jens at the same time—I dashed from the table and to my bed, the tears flowing freely.

"Berta! Supper is not yet finished," Papa called.

After composing myself, I came back out and sat once again

to the table. I hadn't realized that leaving Denmark would be so hard. "Where's Catherine?" I shoved my last bite of bread into my mouth.

"She has gone to the barn to talk with Isaac Thompsen." Mama's lips pursed with disapproval.

I remembered Catherine's private meeting, and Mama's frustration over the impropriety of Catie's greeting Isaac in the barn. Catherine had insisted on having this private moment and reminded Mama that if they got worried, she could come out and check on them.

After clearing the table I put water on to boil for washing the dishes and went into the parlor.

"Papa, I am ready to cut your hair." It was too dark outside, so I had Papa sit near the dining table.

"I am glad. It will be a long time before we land in America." He settled under the sheet I wrapped around his neck.

"Cutting it aboard a ship would be a tricky thing. Ja?"

"Indeed." Papa grinned. "With one large ocean wave, I might end up minus an ear."

"Oh, Papa!" I tapped his shoulder playfully. "I wouldn't cut off your ear."

"Don't forget that our elves need to finish their task tonight."

"Ja, ja, Papa."

Mama had the idea to sew our money into our petticoats and into a lining for Papa's breeches. This would keep our money with us and away from pickpockets as we traveled. Mary and Ana weren't old enough to keep secrets, so we worked on it each night after they went to bed.

When the haircut was over, I swept up the mess and then turned my attention to the dirty dishes and the hot water. Mama and Papa became ominously quiet as they continued their preparations for our departure. The fog had seeped further into the courtyard and I washed the dishes while staring at the window, wishing I could see through it and into the barn.

Catherine had given Isaac her Book of Mormon to read, and he said that he would. I wondered what he thought of our scripture. I had been totally convinced of its truthfulness before even having to pray about it. Catherine's conversion had come more cautiously.

Mama left to put Mary and Ana to bed, and Catherine still hadn't come in. My stomach began twisting in knots. Had I heard something outside? I took the dishtowel to the window, rubbing it and trying to see.

Several thuds and crashing noises were followed by a male voice raised in the unnatural sound of shouting. My insides shivered, and I rushed toward the door, intent on going out to the barn. A movement in the parlor startled me, and I looked up to see Papa with his hunting rifle. My eyes widened—what would Papa do? I hurried to his side. Somehow Catherine was in danger. I needed to help her.

Papa held me back. "Stay inside." He opened the back door, and I saw his jaw clench determinedly. I could hardly breathe as I watched him disappear into the murky night air.

Without thinking, I chewed on my fingernail, listening, waiting, wondering. It seemed like hours passed before I heard the sound of horse's hooves, agitated and galloping away.

Oh, my dear sister—what had gone wrong?

Unable to stand the tension any longer, I stepped outside, yet I didn't dare venture farther from the door for fear of displeasing Papa. He soon appeared through the thickness with my sobbing sister embraced in his arms.

"What happened, Papa?"

He shook his head, frowning, and stepped past me toward the bedroom. All the while Catherine sobbed and asked, "What have I done?"

I followed behind, hoping to discover this for myself, and

watched as Catherine left Papa's arms and crumpled onto our bed. Then he put his arm around me, leading me away from the room and closed the door behind us. I wanted to stay.

"What has happened, Papa?" My world felt shaken—Catherine and Isaac loved each other.

"Isaac Thompsen is not the man we thought." He turned to leave, but I took hold of his hand.

"Can't I go in and talk to her?" Clearly Papa would not tell me more, and I wanted every detail.

"She'll come out of her own accord when she's ready." He then retreated to his bedroom and stopped at the door. "If you wish to help, go to the parlor and finish up our project."

He wanted me to finish sewing the coins into our clothing. I rubbed at the calluses on my fingers and hoped they'd hold up until I finished the daunting task alone. I didn't want to immigrate with my hands wrapped in bandages.

Intent on doing as I was asked, I walked past Mama and Papa's bedroom door toward the parlor, and heard Mama tsk, tsk-ing. The hairs on my arms stood on end. I couldn't wait a moment longer to learn what had happened to my sister. I turned and hurried into our bedroom.

"Looks like Isaac didn't love me after all." Catherine, lying on our bed, wiped at her tears with a corner of her apron.

I tilted my head with a frown. "What do you mean?"

"He didn't read it!" Catherine took a shaky breath. "And I told him I was leaving—I'm coming with you." Her voice squeaked and she began crying again.

"Are you sure?" Why couldn't he read it later?

"Ja, ja." Catherine wiped at her tears. "He made his opinions on our religion—and on my sanity—perfectly clear. I will not stay."

"Are you all right?" Climbing into bed beside my distraught sister, I put my arms over her and nestled against her.

She responded with more tears.

Mama came in soon after and shooed me out of the room. My fingertip went in my mouth again, but I took it out, and sure enough—I'd chewed the nail to the quick.

Papa was in the parlor. He met me with a mischievous grin as I approached. When I tilted my head in question, he lifted Hans Christian Andersen's book of children's stories and then slipped it into his vest. I rushed forward and gave him a hug, grateful for his thoughtfulness.

"I love you, Papa." He read us these stories almost nightly. It would be nice to have something familiar when we were in a new country.

"Ja, ja. I love you, too. Now you must finish the sewing. We have a long day tomorrow."

I hurried to the sofa. Mama had taken apart several of our old petticoats and fashioned Papa a pant lining with little pouches sewn up and down the legs, leaving room at the knee area, and stopping near the inseam. My job was to take the bag that Mr. Ilse had left on the table, put one coin in each pouch, and then sew it tightly shut.

Mama came in just then carrying a travel bag.

"She says Isaac does not love her and that she is leaving with us on the morrow." Mama shook her head and sat the bag by the door. "She refuses to discuss it further. I packed for her."

"It is well." Papa nodded. "For after this night, I could not leave her here."

"How will we tell Thora?" Mama fretted. "She will worry."

"The only way is to somehow leave word for the driver." Papa patted Mama's hand.

Catherine's coming along was a good thing, but tonight my heart was heavy. I felt sad for her and her lost dreams. As I sewed, Mama and Papa kept busy. The pile of last minute additions to pack into the wagon grew. Finally my task was done and I knotted the last pouch shut just as Mama added a sack with tomorrow's noon meal onto the top of the pile.

"All of this upset has caused us to stay awake much longer than prudent. Off to bed with you now." Mama gave me a stern look.

"Good night, Mama, Papa. I love you." I nodded my farewell to each, and then I walked silently to my room.

Catherine's tears had quieted, but her trembling shoulders and occasional gasping let me know she cried still. I slipped under the covers and placed my hand on her arm. "Do you wish to talk about it?"

She answered with a nearly imperceptible shake of her head, so I extinguished the lantern in hopes of falling asleep. I was exhausted both physically and mentally. However, it seemed that my mind would not cooperate. My thoughts were as tumultuous as was my day.

What had happened between my sister and Isaac? I wrung my hands under the covers, trying to warm them. Why hadn't Heavenly Father helped Catherine? I glanced over at her but she was facing the wall. Why hadn't Heavenly Father made it so that Mr. Ilse gave Papa all the money he owed? And then I thought of the tender way Jens had kissed me—the way his kiss had hinted that he desired more.

Chapter 4

Before morning dawned, I climbed out of bed worn to a frazzle—but with an idea. I didn't have to leave the only man I'd ever loved. Catherine was immigrating. This left me free to stay in Denmark. I could care for my aunt Thora in Vejstrup until I married Jens.

My heart fluttered with hope. Though I'd only met the elderly woman once, she needed help, and it would ease Mama's mind considerably to have me stay. I'd be doing them both a great service. And then after Jens read the Book of Mormon, he would convert, we would marry, Aunt Thora could move in with us—and my life would be beautiful!

But was I strong enough to stay behind?

I paced the floor while chewing the remnants of a fingernail on my left hand—the nails on my right hand were already down to the quick. Everyone bustled about in pre-dawn energy, dressing, helping the little girls, transferring bags to the wagon. I dressed, but I could not eat. My stomach jumbled and tumbled about.

For the hundredth time I weighed my options—stay for Jens, or leave with my family. My mind screamed for me to immigrate, but my heart begged me to stay for a lifetime of Jens's kisses. Our last meeting left no doubt of Jens's love. He would do anything for me. He had to. His parents were good, decent people and once Jens converted to the gospel, they would as well. Jens was nothing like Isaac.

"The Lord will guide our journey." Catherine took my hand.

"He will lead us to kind and honorable men."

The crack in Catherine's voice betrayed her emotion. Otherwise I'd have reminded her that I already had a kind and honorable man. Then I saw the petticoat draped across my travel bag and a jolt of panic pierced my heart. What would become of it? I couldn't keep it with me—it was laced with coins.

Catherine saw me look at it, so I stooped and picked it up. "I'm too nervous to wear this. Will you wear it for me?"

"What is wrong?" She took the petticoat. "You know you can tell me anything."

I couldn't bear discussing it with her and hurried past. Leaving Catherine was a great sacrifice, as was leaving my parents and younger siblings. Could I do it? Could I strengthen Jens by providing the ultimate example of "cleaving to my husband?" It would help him. Leaving my family would help Jens as he did the same thing for me. Once he joined the church, he would probably want to join the Saints in America.

While still certain of my decision, I headed out the door to talk to Mama and Papa. Last night's fog still lay heavy on the earth, the chill air moist with dew. I stormed down the step and into the courtyard clinging to my shawl, ignoring my sister.

"Is this about Jens? It is, ja?" Catherine followed behind. "Please, don't do this."

She wanted me to talk to her, but I couldn't even look at her. If I did, I'd never be strong enough to stay.

Papa's lantern was my guide in the pre-dawn shadows as I hurried to the hitched horses and wagon in the courtyard. Mama helped Mary and Ana into the wagon, Papa stood at the back making room for my things—but he needn't worry.

"Where is your bag? I've left room for it here." Papa patted the wagon. "It is time we left."

I hesitated, suddenly unsure. How I wished I could stay without breaking Papa's heart!

"Berta." Catherine caught up to me. "Don't be impulsive," she whispered.

But I'd loved Jens my whole life.

Mama left the children and came to stand beside Papa. They yawned and snuggled into their blankets. If I were ever to claim Jens as mine, I had to say something. I was a mature woman and I needed to act like one.

"Mama, Papa, I want to stay." I stepped forward hoping they would one day forgive me for this, but I could not leave. Not without the man I loved. "I will stay with Aunt Thora in place of Catherine."

The color drained from Mama's face, and she clutched Papa's arm. "How could you do this? There is no time to make arrangements."

"Nej." Papa crossed his arms over his chest. "It is not a good idea."

"But, Papa, you were allowing Catherine to stay."

Catherine moved to my side. "You have to come." She clutched my arm. "We will be together as a family. It will be good, ja?" Her words were panicked, her expression stricken.

But I couldn't go with them when my greatest desire was to marry Jens.

Would Mama and Papa agree? In their expression, I saw them considering my proposal to stay and care for Aunt Thora, just as I had hoped. Catherine must have seen as well.

"Nej, Mama. Nej!" Catherine shouted. "Don't you understand? She is only doing this because of Jens Larsen."

I stepped away from her. She shouldn't have told this. My face warmed with embarrassment.

"Is it true?" Mama turned to me, her face pinched in concern.

"I told you, ja?" Catherine muttered. "Papa, please don't let her stay."

"It is partly true," I confessed. "Jens will ask me to marry him if I stay. He told me as much yesterday morn."

Papa threw his arms up and frowned. Mama pursed her lips. They shouldn't have known this, and it made me frustrated with Catherine.

"Jens and his parents are against the Mormons," Papa scolded. "Learn from what nearly happened to your sister. Nej. I cannot allow you to marry such a boy."

"Berta, dear, we cannot leave you here in the hands of a wolf," Mama chided.

"Would you feel differently if he was a member of our church?" Jens had shown an interest when our family had first been baptized.

"Of course it would be different." Mama frowned. "But you know his parents will not allow it."

"It is true they put a stop to his interest before, but Jens is older now and can stand on his own." I clutched the side of the wagon. "He is old enough to be their example. And he will be."

I took a deep breath. "Mama, Papa." I took their hands in mine. "I shall not marry a wolf, and I promise you this day that I shall not marry anyone who believes differently than I." In order to quell my tears, I stopped for a moment and chewed on my lip.

I had never before been without my family's love and support. A great hole already tore at my heart. "Aunt Thora lives far away—but Jens loves me. He will join the church, and then he will come to marry me."

"Thora does need our assistance," Mama whispered to Papa. "She refuses any financial support, but she has agreed to let one of our daughters stay with her and help."

Papa walked to the front of our wagon and lifted Mary and Ana down, then he returned. Papa knelt and removed his cap. "Let us say a prayer. The Lord will know what is right."

Praying was good. The Lord would allow me to stay in Denmark long enough to convert Jens. It was a worthy desire. My staying would also be a blessing for Aunt Thora. The Lord would grant this.

I listened carefully to Papa's prayer. He expressed the desire to keep our family together and prayed to know what was right. What would he decide? After he said amen, I peeked to see what was happening. He stayed on his knees for a time, silent. When he stood and looked at Mama, appearing devastated, a knot formed in my stomach.

"Berta will stay and help care for Aunt Thora." Papa brushed the knees of his breeches with his cap before returning it to his head.

My heart nearly overflowed with joy! I would be allowed to stay. I had a mission to perform in Denmark before I could even consider leaving for America. The Lord had answered my prayer—my testimony was strong enough to endure whatever trial lay ahead in order to convert the man I loved.

I threw myself into Mama's arms and sobbed both for joy and for sorrow. Though I was excited for my future, I sorrowed for the cost.

With tears shining in her eyes, Mama put her hand to the back of her neck. She was unlatching her locket! I watched, confused, as the treasure slid into her hand. And then she pressed it into mine.

In awe, I slowly opened my fingers to reveal Mama's precious locket. I opened the clasp to view their picture. Suddenly I couldn't see. I wiped at the tears with my sleeve and choked back sobs. "Mama, I can't take your locket."

"I want you to have it." Mama folded my fingers back around the treasure. "It will help you remember who you are." Mama's lips trembled. "We will be on the other side of the ocean, but I am still your Mama, and I will pray for you every day. Should you choose to follow us to America at a later time, you can return the locket then."

"Oh, Mama, thank you." I hugged her to me and then kissed her cheek.

"Take my Book of Mormon also." Mama pulled the book out of her travel bag and handed it to me. "It is the only thing as dear to me as my family. Keep your faith in mind when dealing with Jens."

"I will, Mama. I will." My voice cracked, and I wiped at my tears. If all went as planned, which I knew it would, Jens and I could be on our way to America by the following spring.

Mary and Ana rushed forward, clinging to me. "Nej. Don't stay, Berta! You must come with us, please!"

Mama blinked at her tears, pried the girls loose from my skirt, and ushered them back into the wagon.

Catherine and I rushed into one another's arms. "I love you so much!" Catherine sobbed.

"How will I ever live without your comfort?" I wiped the brown tendrils of hair out of her face. "You are the best sister anyone could hope for. I will miss you dearly."

We embraced once more, and then Catherine pulled an embroidered handkerchief from her pocket and handed it to me.

What did this mean? "Grandmother Erichsen helped you make this," I whispered.

"When I was ten," she said. "It is now yours. Keep it to remember me." How could she part with this special memento? I would cherish it forever and tucked it into my pocket, pulling mine out in nearly the same motion.

"This is the first thing you embroidered yourself," Catherine said, wide-eyed.

"It was a challenge for me to sew around the corners," I reminded her.

"You had to take it out five times." Catherine fingered the floral design. "But look at the corners now." She lifted it and showed me. "They each lie perfectly."

"It is yours." I folded her hands over it.

She wiped tears off her cheek, and we embraced once more. "I love you," she said, and then she went to the wagon still shaking with sobs. It was almost more than I could bear.

I wanted to chase after her, to be by her side as she followed Mama and Papa to America. I wanted to live in Zion. One thought of Jens's kiss held me still.

"What will we do without you?" Papa said softly.

"I don't know what I'll do without you, Papa. I will stay in Denmark, yet I will think of you every day, and I'll love you always."

Papa took my hands in his. "A carriage was arranged for Catherine, but it won't arrive until mid-morning. You will stay here and wait for it, ja?"

"Ja, Papa." I rubbed my arms warming them against the morning chill, not knowing how I could ever be all right without my papa near.

"Take Catherine's chest. It is yours now. Herrer Ilse will have no use for it, and we have worked hard for the special fabrics that are now yours."

"Ja." I leaned against him. I would think of Catherine when I used her fabric.

Papa reached into his pocket. "This is travel fare to Thora's and will help with a wedding should you desire." He placed a small bag of coins into my hand.

"Nej, Papa. It is too much." He hadn't gotten the money he needed. I shouldn't take this.

"I only wish it could be more. If you need anything, if things don't turn out with Aunt Thora, or Jens, Herrer Petersen is a good friend and can help you. Ja." Papa glanced at the sun starting to peek above the earth. "I am not happy leaving you here." He wiped a tear from my cheek. "If you had even told us yesterday of your doubts, we could have made better arrangements."

"All will be well, Papa." I lifted my lips to reassure him. "You prayed." I nodded. "God will be my guide."

"Remember your faith. Remember who you are. We had this set aside for Catherine, but she no longer has need for it." He squeezed my hands. "We must go now else we miss the ferry."

I thrust myself upon him and wept. Then, gently pulling himself free, he turned and joined my family.

Chapter 5

The urge to run after my family hit like a raging bull. If I followed them I could live in Zion. I could enjoy the comfort of family near. We would live in the same city as the prophet of God—and hadn't I had the confirmation that immigrating was right?

But Jens had asked me to stay. He loved me, and that was the most wonderful feeling in the world. I would convert Jens and we could still go to Zion. With that realization, and the thought of our special time together yester-morn, I stood firmly on Danish soil.

It seemed, though, that as my family disappeared my soul filled with chilly morning air. What would become of me? I drew my shawl tighter and turned away.

My home, once so warm and inviting, now seemed cold and empty. I stared at it for the longest time, almost afraid to go in. The half-timber framing and the thatched roof were all made by Great-Grandfather Erichsen. Nevertheless, when I finally forced myself through the door, I felt like an intruder.

I needed to pack my things so they'd be ready when the driver came—I could take more of my things to Aunt Thora's than I packed as an immigrant, and Papa had honored me with Catherine's chest. I put my arms around the chest, trying to heave it out the door and to the road where the carriage would meet me. I was too small-framed and could not carry it that way. It hurt my arms and my back. I released it gently.

Standing behind the chest, I leaned forward and pushed

it to the door. However, though the chest wasn't heavy, it was awkward for me to maneuver by myself and if I took it to the street, I would need to make several trips back and forth. It would be easier to fill the chest from where it was. When the driver came, he could help me carry it to the carriage with no effort.

Mama had painted an intricate flower pattern on the top. It complemented the few designs Papa had carved there. The combined effect was beautiful, and I traced a few of the flowers with my finger.

Remembering my ring, I pulled it out of my stocking and held it for a moment. I thought of Jens's kiss and his promise to come for me. The tiny gem glistened in a ray of morning light. Knowing he meant to use this ring as a symbol of our betrothal, I tried to put it on my ring finger. It didn't fit. This was why he had put it on my little finger. He'd seen it was too small.

Which finger I wore it on was irrelevant. I slipped it on and stood. Jens was my life now. My family. I smiled down on the ring and kissed it.

The house echoed as I walked through, gathering things and placing them inside my chest—a few of Mary and Ana's toys for when I had children—Mama's special plates—Papa's tiepin. Had he meant to leave it? Catherine's hair ribbons. I set Mama's Book of Mormon on top of the chest to carry with me. The noise of my wooden shoes pounded in my ears and seemed to say, *go catch up, go catch up*. It tormented me, and I thought of riding Caja. She could get me there easily.

But it was pure foolishness, and childish. I wouldn't question Papa's prayer. Nor would I question my own. I walked out the front door and peered down the road—they were gone. My heart sank. Being on my own would be difficult. I forced back a yawn. Through hard work and determination I would achieve my goal and rejoin myself to my family triumphant. No, I would not chase after them like a silly schoolgirl.

My shoes clomped once again as I stepped into the house and closed the door. Wooden shoes were too noisy inside. I set them by the door before going to retrieve my partially packed bag. The armoire door was ajar.

Sofrina had my nice dress. I remembered her actions from yesterday morn and started to be upset, but instead, I threw the thought away and considered the positive side. Papa had been compensated for the dress and other things the Andersdatters had taken. Not having that fancy dress left me plenty of room for something else. I looked around while trying to decide.

The armoire still held last year's Sunday dress made of blue cotton. It was simple and worn, but I hadn't completely outgrown it. I folded the dress and added it to my bag. There was room for something else. When my eyes landed on Grandmother's quilt, I touched the gently worn cotton and knew I could never part with it. I snuggled down into the quilt, feeling exhausted.

I would rest for only a minute and still be able to arrive at the Larsens' in time for breakfast. Perhaps Jens would ask to marry me this very morn over a meal of fresh eggs and toast. I smiled and closed my eyes.

I rubbed my eyes and yawned. Something had awakened me, but what? My rest had lasted longer than planned. However, judging the location of the sun shining through the window, I still had time to visit Jens before my ride to Vejstrup. Sitting up, I stretched and yawned again. But then I heard another noise. It sounded as though someone had come into the house. My heart thumped.

Papa had instructed Mr. Ilse to stay away until tomorrow. He wouldn't defy Papa. The idea seemed preposterous. Then who would come here? It must be someone who knew we were leaving. Mr. Andersdatter? Sofrina? But, everyone knew.

The Andersdatters had their pick of things just yesterday. Why would they come again today? They wouldn't. Why would anyone dare enter a home unannounced? Would this person steal from us? Our candlestick was on the nearby table. I grabbed it, leaned against the wall, and pulled the quilt to my chin with candlestick in hand.

Surely the intruder wouldn't come into the bedroom. I waited, listened, and hoped whoever it was would soon leave. Something heavy scraped against the floor. They were indeed taking our things, and being rather noisy about it. No one I knew would do this.

I glanced at the window. Should I climb through? The brazen intruders sounded as though they were taking everything. I shouldn't stay here, I thought, and started off my bed.

My bedroom door opened and a young man walked in.

I screamed.

He stopped mid-step and appeared as shocked as I was. He stared as though he'd never seen a young lady before. "Who are you?" He regarded me with suspicion.

My heart hammered, and I held the candlestick high. "Who are you?" I tried masking my fear with irritation. "And what are you doing in my house?"

"This is not your house." He folded his arms across his chest. "You need to leave immediately."

I stepped off the bed and faced him while wielding the candlestick. "This is indeed my house—I am not some street urchin that you can order about!" My jaw set and my eyes narrowed. I would not be intimidated in my own home. "Who are you to think you can talk to me so spitefully?" I raised the candlestick like a club, ready to defend self and property.

One eyebrow went up and his lips formed a smirk.

I waited indignantly for some odious reply and tried thinking of a good response. For, although he was quite handsome with his light hair and smoky-blue eyes, his clothing and manner led me to believe he was without a home. I'd caught him rummaging through what he must have deemed a vacant house and he didn't have the manners to apologize and leave the premises.

"What's going on here?" A portly older gentleman entered the room, startling me. "Anders, why are you not working?" His eyes followed the arrogant young man's trail of vision and stopped abruptly at me. "Who are you, Frøken, and what are you doing in my house?"

"Your house? Nej, you are mistaken." I took a step back, and losing my balance, landed on the bed. My face warmed and I stood again, my jaws set.

"She says she owns this house, but look at her—she's a beggar!"

"I am not." I stood, ready to defend myself again. "These are my travel clothes."

"Ah, you must be Hans Erichsen's daughter, Catherine." The older gentleman stepped forward and snatched the candlestick from my grasp, his mouth pulled into a pucker.

"Ja, ja, that is me." I felt suddenly hopeful. "I mean, I'm not Catherine, of course, but I am Hans Erichsen's daughter. Berta." I curtsied. "And who are the two of you?"

"Herrer Jacob Ilse, obviously." He looked at me as though I was of simple mind. "And my servant, Anders Jensen." He indicated with an impatient hand. "Not that I need explain myself to a child."

He was of similar build as the man I'd seen arguing with Papa, his gray hair hidden under a cap. This was the man who had cheated my parents. My mouth opened and closed as I tried forming a response.

"What are you doing here?" he groused. "You were to be gone

before morn's first light."

"I—I took the place of my sister in staying behind to care for our aunt Thora." I chewed my bottom lip and switched my weight to my left foot. "The carriage taking me to Vejstrup won't arrive until later."

"Well, then." He gave me a pointed stare. "Keep yourself out of the way while Anders here empties the house." He turned to walk away.

And then I remembered yesterday's conversation. "Papa told you not to come until tomorrow." This man was an intruder. "I have not yet finished packing." I raised my chin. "I am taking my chest as well as a few other things to my aunt's house." I pulled the quilt off my bed and began folding it in preparation of adding it to my bag.

"You'll do no such thing!" He snatched the quilt from my hand and tossed it to the young man he identified as Anders, and then handed him the candlestick as well.

Anders took my grandmother's quilt and the candlestick, his expression even, and left the room.

"Stop!" I lunged after the quilt. After all, it meant nothing to this man—this monster. Mr. Ilse stepped in the doorway, blocking my path, and so I held out my hand. "I want what is mine."

"Nej! Enough of your quibbling. I paid your father a great deal of money for these things, and I'll not have you running away with them." He stepped forward and took my open bag, closed it, and handed it to me.

He had paid next to nothing for our things. Determined to acquire my quilt, my hands remained at my side.

"If you don't feel you need it." He lowered my bag. "Anders! I swear that boy moves slower than a pig on a wintry day." Irritated, he started to leave my room.

"That bag is mine, and I want it." I rushed forward and

grabbed the bag. It left his grasp easily.

"It is well, Frøken. I am not an unreasonable man. You may have what's yours—I am not a thief. However, neither am I an easy target for sweet young girls. You may not have what is mine, bought and paid for." He gave me a condescending half-smile. "And, now that I know it's your intention to steal from me, I must ask that you wait at the street until your wagon arrives."

My face burned with humiliation at his accusation.

"Come now." He took my elbow and began escorting me from the room.

"Sir, I cannot leave without two things that are mine." I pulled him to a stop. "My chest is by the front door, as is my Book of Mormon. If you'd waited until tomorrow to come—"

"Why wouldn't I be here?" He glared at me. "The sooner I take possession, the quicker I thwart would-be thieves."

"Ja, ja, of course you have every right to be here." Not believing a word that I said, I raised my eyebrows and smiled hopefully. "Nonetheless, I cannot leave without my chest and my book of scripture. May I please? I will be quick."

"Hmph! If I'd have seen your dratted book, I'd have burned it instantly." He started once more in escorting me toward the front door. "Nevertheless, I paid a fair price for the home and all the furniture in it. That includes your chest."

"My chest and my Book of Mormon are of no value to you, yet they are invaluable to me. Please, sir, allow me to keep them" A homemade wooden box with a few homemade treasures meant nothing to him, but they meant the world to me, and I could not live without my scriptures.

"Leave you to wander through my home so that you may find other things you desire to take—an heirloom table—a precious armoire—the bed of your childhood? When should my generosity end? Nej. You will have none of it, but I will take you to the front door and through it. You'll see that I am no fool—there is no book there. Probably never was one." He escorted me roughly to the front door, and true to his word, my Book of Mormon was gone as was my chest.

Anders came in through the back door then with another man and together they lifted the table to carry it out.

"He has it!" I pointed toward Anders. "He has taken my book." He had been the only other person in the house. I hurried to him. "Now give it back!" I felt angry tears welling but determined not to show weakness. "Please," I said more softly as I held out my hand.

He merely looked at my hand and then me. "Herrer Ilse, sir, I have no idea what this young lass is talking about." He spoke to Mr. Ilse, but his eyes never left mine. It was as though he dared me to contradict him. "You know that I feel the same as you regarding those Mormons."

But I hadn't mentioned Mormons or my Book of Mormon to him.

"Make him give it back!" Could neither of these men see reason? "He as much as confessed he has my scriptures."

"Dear child." Mr. Ilse secured his hand on my arm and led me away. "Let's not make a fuss. It is not becoming, and your conduct this fine morn would greatly distress your poor mother."

At his mention of Mama, I let him lead the way through our front door, my teeth clenched, my heart pounding. He sat me on the bench under the ash tree near the road and placed my bag on the ground beside me.

"This is a lovely piece of property. Very valuable." He smiled down at me. "You'll be a good girl and stay here until your ride arrives." He tipped his hat and disappeared into the house.

I waited for a time, watching these strangers remove every remaining memory of my life and family, being rough with it as though it had no value. My soul ached as I witnessed the scene.

Resting had been a dreadful idea. I didn't know when, exactly, the wagon would come. Did I have time to talk to Jens? He had to know that I stayed, else he might... I grimaced, unable even to form the words silently. I had to see him. I stood resolute, and crept to the side of the house. I'd take Caja to see Jens. If my ride came, we would pass each other on the road.

Once at the back of the house, I peeked around the corner to make sure no one was there. Caja was nowhere in sight, but I saw a half-full wagon near the outside entry to the barn, hitched to a strange horse. I'd somehow rescue my chest and probably my scriptures, and remain unseen. My insides shivered as I stole silently to the horse and rubbed his neck. "That's a good girl," I whispered. "Stay quiet for a moment and your burden will be lighter."

Mister Ilse and his helpers were in the barn. I heard them easily and hoped they would remain there until I'd gotten my chest and scriptures. Anxiety worried up my neck. Where was the best place to hide my treasure until I'd spoken to Jens? When I saw the currant bush on the other side of the barn, I began rummaging through the wagon. I could hide the chest under the bush. Jens would take it to his house after Mister Ilse left.

"Where is that boy?" I heard Mr. Ilse grumble. "If he wasn't such an accomplished horseman, I'd be rid of him."

Mr. Ilse had a foul disposition. Was he fussing at Anders? It seemed that Mr. Ilse ranted without ceasing. My heart skipped a beat. I needed to hurry. He would be furious if he caught me here. Maybe even call the authorities. I saw my chest, clutched it and tried lifting it out. I'd just gotten it dislodged when a twig snapped behind me.

"Someone isn't waiting for their carriage where they're supposed to be."

I whirled around, startled at Anders's nearness. He held fast to my arms.

"You had better get back out front." With ease, he turned me to face the house.

"Nej, this is mine. Please." I pulled from him, desperate. How would the Larsens allow me to marry Jens without my dowry of fabrics? "My papa made the chest and carved it. My sister, Catherine, made the fabrics. Papa gave them to me—and Mama gave me her scriptures. Take the other things out and please let me have the chest and my holy scriptures." How could I teach Jens the gospel without them? Worry settled in my stomach like an anvil.

"Herrer Ilse has already packed the chest in the wagon. It's his now." Anders put his hands on my shoulders and guided me toward the front of the house. "And you heard me tell him that I don't have your filthy book."

"Ja, ja, but you do have my book." I turned on him, angry. "You're a liar and a thief."

He glowered at me. It didn't matter that I resisted when I didn't weigh more than a newborn foal. This Anders, tall and slender with wispy blond hair, outweighed me by at least double. "The chest is mine. Papa intended it so." With my hands balled to fists and resting on my hips, I leaned forward. "The scriptures are mine as well, given to me by my mama." I gave a curt nod of my head. Why would he steal my book, and why would he pretend he hadn't?

He stopped at the front step. My bag, near the front door, seemed different.

"You've been riffling through my things!" I said, incredulous. "First you take my chest—leaving me no hopes for a good marriage. You take my scriptures—and now you try to steal my clothes?" I reached for the bag.

Anders slipped it from me and turned me to face him. "I have not been going through your things." He stepped closer then—uncomfortably so. "What would I do with women's work clothing and a woolen blanket?"

"Oh!" I gasped. "You have gone through them!" I stepped backward automatically, blinking back my anger.

He followed until he had me against the wall. His hands leaned against my home and pinned me there. "Let me tell you—what is your name again?"

I felt like a goose trapped in a fox's den and gulped at the panic that rose in my chest, refusing to satisfy him with my name. "If I scream, Herrer Ilse will come." I made my voice even to make my fear sound like anger. "He'll see what manner of man he has in his employ." I clenched my jaw and pushed against his arm wishing for him to release me.

"Screaming is not a good choice, ja." He quirked a smile. "My employer is an impatient man who has an affinity for pretty maidens. If you scream, it will be him who comes to your rescue." His voice was soft and playful. "And besides, I am not going to harm you." He leaned forward and I thought he meant to kiss me right there on my front doorstep.

"You wouldn't dare!" I turned my head. What would happen to me in my parents' absence? I shivered inwardly, my teeth clenched together hoping to keep my emotions at bay, but even with my eyes closed, still tears pushed their way onto my cheeks.

"It's just a stick caught in your hair." I felt a tug as he pulled it free. "What did you think I was doing?" He pitched the stick into the yard, and scowled. "You think that because I am not a Mormon boy that I will try to take advantage?"

In response, I blinked and gulped, my heart beating like a baby bunny's. Still, when he turned and strode through the house, I noticed that he smelled like Papa—of the earth and horses.

I hurried to the bench by the street and folded my arms around my knees, blinking back the tears. I was alone. By my own doing I was alone and my family was far way. Had I made a mistake? Should I try to chase after them? I looked up to gauge the time. They were probably on their way to the main island, Sjaelland. If I took the ferry, how would I get across the island and to the capitol? If I somehow made it to København and they were already gone—what would I do there?

My breathing came as long, broken sighs. My chest of fabrics was gone. My scriptures were gone. I opened my heart in prayer for the return of my Book of Mormon. As I did so, a mist of rain fell about my shoulders causing a shiver to worm its way up my arms and neck.

Chapter 6

I faced the heavens with my eyes closed and let drops of water splash on me. What if nothing ever went right again? The rain had stopped, and when I opened my eyes, a patch of blue Danish sky was peeking around the clouds. It was a sign. My life could only get better from here. I would not go to America until I had the man I loved by my side.

The carriage taking me to Vejstrup appeared over a short incline. I gritted my teeth in bitter disappointment. This meant there was no time to walk to the Larsens. We weren't going through town so I could purchase a stamp and send him word by mail. I crossed my fingers, hoping that Aunt Thora had paper and pencil and stamps. I didn't want to spend my wedding money, but I would. What if Sophrina got Jens to like her before he got word that I'd stayed? She was such a flirt.

I settled down and waited. It didn't take long. When the carriage arrived, I rushed to the house and picked up my bag. It seemed different—heavier or bigger somehow—and I shook my head at my foolishness in thinking so.

"Good day," I greeted the driver. "Will you please stop at the Larsens' when we get there?" It was not polite for me to ask, but I had to try. "It is down the road near town." I pointed the way. "I must tell them that I have not gone to America."

"Nej." He frowned. "I cannot do this thing." He put my bag in the back and then sat at his seat. "There is no stopping to chat with neighbors. We are already running late and must get to Vejstrup before nightfall."

I sat back on the bench with heavy heart. However, if I saw Jens, I would call to him. And the driver would stop for us.

The carriage, actually a large uncovered wagon with benches, gave me plenty of opportunity to memorize the landscape. Mama's rosebushes were green and beautiful—the tulips and irises planted near our home peeked from the earth, but were not yet in bloom. The chimney where our stork resided in the spring and summer still lay vacant. Who would she find living in our home upon her return? Would they welcome the stork as we had, or would they remove the nest?

Caja whinnied for my attention, chasing me along the fence line unaware she'd been sold to a wretched man. With trembling lips, I waved my farewell as though she understood. We passed over a hill and my world disappeared like a stone sinking into the sea. I covered my face with my shawl and wept.

After a short time, I peeked through my shawl and then tossed it aside waiting eagerly as we drew near the Larsen farm. Jens would be working in the field. I would see him as I had only yesterday morn—already it seemed an eternity ago.

I would call out his name. "Jens!"

He would rush forward. "Stop the carriage!"

I'd jump into his waiting arms. "Take my Book of Mormon. Read it and learn the truthfulness of our church."

"I will do anything for your love." He would take the book and slip it into his pocket. "I will come for you in a week's time and ask you to be my bride."

But my book was stolen from me. I threw my head back and groaned, and then I sat up worried that I'd miss him.

The field was empty. I searched repeatedly as we rode past, anxious and hoping that Jens would appear. He didn't, and I bit back my discouragement. When we neared his house, I stood. "Jens!" I shouted, hoping he'd hear. Wouldn't he be there chopping wood or working near the mill?

"Sit down, Frøken, before you fall and hurt yourself."

Jens had to see me, he had to know that I stayed for him. I didn't sit right away as I should have, but stubbornly held to the back of the bench and stretched on my toes, waiting for a glimpse of Jens, until the Larsen's home was a mere shadow on the horizon. Then I crumpled to my seat.

Hours later when I gained the strength to sit up straight and appreciate the countryside, two women had joined me.

"… She's a beautiful girl. Her hair is as light as spun sugar."

That was a similar description of my friend, Sofrina. Friend? I gritted my teeth at the term.

"Ja, ja, but he is handsome too. They will make a lovely couple."

Brilliant blue eyes came to mind, but I couldn't think of Jens. Not now. And not with her. I'd turn into a watery mess. I turned my attentions to the countryside.

On our journey, we passed one field after another. I could tell the ones owned by smallholders. Whole families worked a field too small to sustain them. Their clothes were ragged and worn. Like most smallholding families, they would probably end their lives in a poorhouse. Papa had explained to us about smallholders and poorhouses. I shuddered at the thought of spending my life in a place like that.

The residents of a poorhouse were expected to keep the place neat and clean, but sometimes infestations of bedbugs or scabies took over before they could get them under control. They also housed drunks and those who had gone mad. The men and women were kept separate by the means of high walls.

I shuddered again and turned my attention to a flock of swallows enjoying the light breeze. Hundreds of birds swarmed together, expanded out, floated, swooped, and danced joyously from one end of the field to the other.

My stomach growled, reminding me that I hadn't eaten since

last night's supper. I hoped Aunt Thora would soon greet me with a delicious meal.

Nevertheless, the sun had nearly found its way to the opposite horizon before the carriage stopped near her home. I drew my shawl close, my stomach roaring in anticipation.

Aunt Thora's home was in a neighborhood, and made of large, rough-hewn granite blocks. A row of berry brambles separated her home from the others; buds of green beginning to make them attractive once more. The rose bushes lining the front walk needed trimming. I would get to it on the morrow.

The grey granite of the home formed an archway on the left, and it was crowned with a red-scripted tile bearing the name, Kjar—her husband's family name. Through the archway, there was a small square porch, and then a large blue door symbolizing peace and friendliness to all who entered. I knocked.

A slender, slightly bent woman opened the door and stood on the step.

"Aunt Thora?" I dropped my bag and embraced her. She was now my only relative in Denmark.

"Catherine? I thought I sent word for you to travel with your parents to America."

"Nej. It is me, Berta." My aunt's back was bent with age. I felt tall standing beside her. "I have grown since you saw me last, ja?"

"You look like your mother."

She couldn't have given me better praise. I embraced her again and picked up my bag.

"Catherine did travel with Mama and Papa," I explained as we entered her home, "but I have come to help in her place." I stepped across the threshold, anxious to see the inside of a city house, and stopped. "Where shall I stay?" I asked, taking notice of my new surroundings. Concern churned inside me. Her home bore a layer of dust, and there was no fire in the fireplace. The evening sun cast long shadows in the living room.

"I did not expect you." Aunt Thora put her fingers to her mouth, appearing dismayed. "You say your parents have already left for America?"

"Ja, ja, it is well and good. No need to worry." I stepped further into my new home. There was so much to be done that I would not make myself a burden. "Show me your spare bedroom and I'll put my bag there."

Aunt Thora led the way to a small room at the back of the house. It, too, was filled with dust. Mama was right to let me stay here. Aunt Thora lit a candle, and I crossed the room to the interesting-looking bed. It had a thick mattress and a large metal frame that creaked when I sat down. I sat up and down on it several times, listening to the funny noise.

When I finally opened my bag, I gasped. A tear of thankfulness welled in the corner of my eye. Grandmother's quilt, stuffed into a small roll, lay on the top of my clothing. Anders hadn't been searching through my things—he'd been giving me this precious gift. His unexpected kindness did not completely pardon his taking of my scriptures. Unless... I quickly pulled the quilt out, poring through the meager contents for my Book of Mormon. It wasn't there. Nej. He was not forgiven. I spread the quilt over the bed and went to greet my aunt who paced about her kitchen.

"I have nothing for supper," Aunt Thora apologized.

"Nej, you are not to worry." I guided her to a chair. "I am not here to be waited on like a spoiled child. Now, where is the flour?"

Although the flour bin was nearly empty, I made biscuits and set them on the hearth. I found a few carrots in the cool-box and cooked them in a pan with a little sugar. It wasn't much, and as I noticed the empty wood-box near the hearth, I couldn't imagine how long it had been since she'd had a fire hot enough to warm her aging bones. Still, caring for her helped me feel close to Mama. I went outside and found a flattish rock and set it in the fireplace near the embers for later.

"Show me to the dishes, ja, and I will set the table." I curtsied.

"Nej, child, I am perfectly capable of getting them myself." Aunt Thora shuffled around and got plates, cups and silverware and set them on the table. "This looks lovely," she said when I placed a biscuit and some carrots on her plate. "I haven't had fresh biscuits since…" She closed her eyes and took in a deep breath.

When she didn't finish her sentence, I commented, "The food is good, ja?" I ate my last carrot, wishing I had pork roast and pie to complete the meal. Why hadn't she gone shopping for food before my arrival?

"Ja, ja. Your mother has taught you well." She ate her biscuit and remained quiet.

Aunt Thora was a funny old lady. I thought she'd be happier and full of life—like Mama. I wondered if she wasn't glad that I came. She needed help, though. Perhaps she was merely embarrassed and unaccustomed to company. I would prove to her that I was more than company.

"Do you have a stamp?" I asked. "Or is there someplace nearby where we can get one?"

"No one in this town will give me a stamp. I've asked several times." With a scowl on her face she turned and sat in the chair.

"What do you usually do in the evenings?" I picked up our plates and put them into the sink.

"Oh, child, I go to bed as soon as the sun goes down. It's warmer under the covers."

"The house is beginning to feel a little chilly." I rubbed my arms. "Don't you have a supply of firewood outside?"

"Me? I don't chop wood." She chuckled.

"Can't one of the neighbors chop it for you?"

"Ha. I wouldn't ask one of those busybodies to step on an ant for me, let alone perform a hard task like chopping firewood." Aunt Thora got up and poured cold water into the sink. She began wiping at a plate. I looked for a pot of hot water like Mama kept for washing dishes. There was none.

"You don't like your neighbors?" It didn't sound like the people of Vejstrup were very considerate. I stood beside her and rinsed and dried the dishes as she handed them to me.

"I liked them just fine until they started sticking their noses where they didn't belong, telling me to get a job. 'Go to work,' they said." She turned, indignant. "I've never worked in a store and I'm too crippled to follow a plow." She shook her head. "And those busybodies, they tell me to sell my house, but where would I live?" Her lip quivered. "What is to happen now that my Erik took off and left me?"

"He died years ago, Aunt Thora. He didn't leave." I put the towel down and hugged her close.

"Ja, ja." She nodded and rubbed her hands.

"All is well and good," I soothed. "Jens Larsen will be in town on Friday. He will help us." I hadn't been able to tell him I stayed, but he would look for me in hopes that I had. After our last conversation, I was certain of that. And they would help Aunt Thora and me by gathering and chopping wood.

After my embrace, she just stood in the middle of the floor appearing confused. She was tired. "Would you like to go to bed now?" I asked.

"I can stay up longer." She took a contradictory step toward her room. "Surely you're not ready to retire yet."

"Actually, I am very tired." I smiled and gestured toward her room. "Go get dressed. I warmed a rock for your bed."

Aunt Thora protested the whole way as she shuffled to her room to dress. I went to the service porch, found an old towel and wrapped the rock in it. I took it to Aunt Thora's room and knocked. "Are you in bed?" I heard a faint reply and entered. She was huddled under her covers. I lifted the quilt at the foot of her bed and slipped the towel-wrapped rock near her feet.

"You shouldn't have bothered," she said.

"It was no bother, Aunt Thora. Sleep tight."

The parlor lay in shadow and I realized there really was nothing for me to do except sleep. Hopefully I could. I went to my new room while wondering about my aunt. She seemed at a loss. Had it been this way since Uncle Erik passed on?

I pulled my hair from its braids wondering what was the right thing to do. Mama and Papa didn't want me to marry Jens until after he converted, and I'd promised not to. I'd never broken a promise before, but things were not quite right here with Aunt Thora.

The air was already chilly. I shivered and hurried into my nightdress. Then I took my warm blanket made of Faroese wool and put it over my grandmother's quilt. As I settled in underneath the covers, I remembered Anders's kindness in ensuring I kept the quilt. Upon remembering how his smoky eyes twinkled, and how I thought he'd wanted to kiss me, I pulled the covers over my head in a huff and forced my thoughts to return to Jens. His kiss and his eyes, the color of a brilliant blue wildflower, were all that mattered.

Sleep did not come quickly. Each time I moved, the bed squeaked. Did the noise disturb Aunt Thora? I lay in that strange and noisy bed waiting for sleep to come, worrying about the future, and planning. Jens would come to Vejstrup at the end of the week. Aunt Thora lived on the main road to town. I would see them when they drove past.

Chapter 7

The sky finally lightened, showing dawn was near. I arose from bed wrapped in my wool blanket and crept to the bedroom window. Lights shone in a nearby house. Who lived there, I wondered. Were there children? Did they have an older sister Catherine's age? I swallowed back a lump in my throat.

We always helped our neighbors when they were in trouble. Would these neighbors help us? A shiver of cold ran through me. I blew warm breath into my hands and rubbed my cold nose. Something must be done. The house would not get warm without some way to warm it.

After dressing hurriedly, I tiptoed to the kitchen in my stockings and began rummaging through the cupboards. What I discovered disturbed me. There were plates, cups and dozens of empty jars, but no milk. I found unfilled flour sacks and empty containers, but no more flour. Last night's biscuits were made from the last bit in the whole house. I found pots and pans and old kitchen towels, but not another vegetable or piece of fruit.

What would we do? Starve? My stomach growled. I searched through the kitchen again and found a small portion of ground oats hidden in one of the containers. It did not smell fresh, but would do well enough for our breakfast. Then what? I rummaged around again hoping I'd missed something else, but there was nothing. My spirits sank as I took a pot of water and added the oats.

There wasn't enough wood to heat water in the fireplace, but Aunt Thora's kitchen had a black iron stove with a chimney that went up and through the roof. I'd never used anything like it and had avoided the stove before, but it couldn't be too hard and maybe there was wood inside. Since the Larsens had one, I should know how to use it. A handle was on the front and when I pressed on the lever, the whole front-end of the stove acted as a door, and opened. I jumped back, startled.

There were only ashes inside, so I took the remaining kindling and sticks, placed them on the ashes and started the fire with the nearby tinderbox. Then I closed the stove door with trembling hands waiting for it to explode. It didn't. First I put a pot of water on the stove, but I needed a log to create enough heat to boil water and cook oats.

The stove's warmth felt wonderful, and I stuck my face near it to warm my nose. Then, gathering my courage and with the blanket tight around my head, I ran to the door and slipped on my wooden shoes before hurrying outside.

My breath came in frosty clouds as I paced the back yard searching for an axe and some wood. There was an odd-looking overgrown lump of morning glory rising up at the back of the house. Rubbing my arms for warmth, I walked there and began throwing leaves and pulling at the tumble of vines. Sure enough, there was wood underneath the mess. Some of the vines had attached themselves to the logs. I tugged and ripped them loose.

One log came out suddenly and flew out of my hands. I flailed about trying to gain my balance and nearly landed on the ground in a heap. As I righted myself, the log rolled onto my foot. "Ouch," I grumbled.

The log was decayed and would burn quickly. I needed more, so I tried closer to the top of the pile. As I pulled at the vines and tried to clear another log, I wondered who had put the wood here. Had it been cut by Uncle Erik before he passed on?

I got another log loose and carried them both to the stove. The handle was hot, and I grabbed a towel to open the door and put the logs inside. It didn't take long before they caught fire. I put the oats on to cook, and rubbed my hands near the heat once more before heading back outside for more wood, bracing myself against the chilly morning air.

"Good morning," greeted a boy of about ten or twelve. "Are you visiting Frau Kjar?" His breeches were worn and his stockings lopsided. Why was he in our backyard?

"Ja, ja. She is my aunt." I curtsied while eyeing the small bundle of sticks in his hand. "Are you from next door?"

He nodded. "Mother has me bring these sticks and set them on the lawn each morn. They are small enough for her to lift, yet if Frau Kjar knew we brought them, she would throw them in the street. She says she can take care of herself, but she can't."

"My aunt seems to have a hard time accepting help." I curtsied. "Thank you. My name is Berta Erichsen. My mother and Aunt Thora are sisters."

"I am Christopher Poulsen." He bowed politely. "We always wondered if she didn't have any family to care for her," he said as he spread the sticks in the lawn. "When Frau Kjar went walking, Mother used to bring her vegetables or fruit from our garden, but my little sister has been ill, and Mother hasn't come here in a week."

"Thank you again. If Mama knew how things were, she would never have left without her." This was terrible. How long had my aunt been a burden to her neighbors? I dared not ask.

"Your parents are gone?" He held the remaining stick in his hand and drew circles in the earth.

"Ja, ja, they left for America yesterday morn. I came to care for Aunt Thora until I wed."

"Will you leave soon?"

"My intended will be here on Friday. He will know what to do." I glanced over at the pile of wood and weeds. "I need to gather some logs for the wood box. The house gets cold at night, and my aunt has old bones." I started toward the woodpile.

"I can help until Father calls." He followed me. "This has been here forever. I didn't know there was wood underneath." He started working, and together we cleared and pulled.

None of it came easily, and I wished Aunt Thora had an axe. We had to tug and pull and yank at the weeds and vines to loosen each log. The sun had left the horizon and come up nicely in the morning sky when we heard someone whistle.

"That's Father. I must go now." Christopher wiped his hands on his breeches and started to leave.

"You are so kind for your help. Thank you again, and thank your parents." I curtsied.

"Ja, ja," he said and took off on the run.

Satisfied with the morning's effort, I carried the wood a couple of logs at a time to the back door and set them just to the side. There were eight logs in all. When I finished, I dusted off my skirt and blouse and then stacked four in my arms and carried them into the house.

"My, my, you've been busy." Aunt Thora met me near the door. "Here, I will take those." She grabbed at the wood in my hands.

"I've got it. Don't you worry." I pulled away but the wood started to topple. I tried keeping my burden from spilling to the floor, but spill they did. Several hit Aunt Thora on their way down.

"Are you all right?" I knelt down to pick up the logs.

"I'm such a clumsy old fool." She rubbed her arm.

"Nej, it is not your fault." I saw her torn sleeve. Leaving the logs on the floor, I stood and helped my aunt to a chair. "You are bleeding." I pulled up the tattered fabric. The skin near her elbow was scraped away. "Here, let me take care of that." I rushed to the kitchen, wetted a towel and took it to my aunt, pressing it lightly against her arm.

"Don't fuss over me so. I've had much worse." Aunt Thora took the cloth and dabbed her arm.

"Aunt Thora, I made us some porridge, but there's no milk. Does one of your neighbors have a cow?"

"Goodness, no." She looked up with a curious expression.

"Well, no matter. The porridge will be good enough without milk." I gathered the logs two at a time and put them near the hearth. When I finished, I came back and examined her arm. "It has stopped bleeding. Do you have any ointment to put on it?"

"In my room." She nodded. "Will you fetch it, please?"

My poor aunt. Her skin was so delicate. I rubbed my finger over the top of the thick ointment to soften it, then I dabbed it onto my aunt's wound and helped her wrap her arm.

"You're not wearing that dainty amber ring I saw on your finger yesterday. It's just as well with all the work you've been doing."

I looked down at my fingers, shocked. My ring was gone! "Oh my! What will I do? I didn't take it off, and now it's gone!" I dove to the floor and crawled around searching, but it wasn't there. I jumped up and ran to my room, throwing the covers up just in case it had fallen off during the night. The ring wasn't there either. What would Jens think when I saw him on Friday? He would hate me, I just knew it.

My heart ached at my foolishness. Never had anyone given me such a nice gift, and I hadn't cared for it properly. I came back into the kitchen and ransacked every cupboard and corner, but it was no use.

"It would be a pity if you lost it out in the yard," said Aunt Thora. "Where's some of that porridge you made?"

"Ja, ja, of course." How could she think of food at a time like this? I scooped the cooked oats into two bowls, brought it to the table, and then stirred it around to see if my ring had fallen there. "I would like to go outside and search for my ring first."

How could I ever eat again if I didn't find it?

"That ring isn't going anywhere. You might as well enjoy breakfast while it's warm." Aunt Thora grabbed a spoon and started to eat.

"May I say a blessing on the food?" I sat at the table.

When my aunt consented, I blessed the food as well as petitioned for the return of my Book of Mormon and my special ring. I also asked that my family be kept safe while crossing the great sea.

My toes tapped out my frustration as I ate the flavorless porridge. I wanted to search for my ring, but it wasn't kind to make Aunt Thora eat alone. She'd done too much of that since Uncle Erik had passed on.

A big lump of worry settled itself in my throat making it hard to swallow. My ring was gone, and I felt less certain things would turn out well for me. Aunt Thora was old. She was odd and a little grouchy, and I had no idea how to see that she got food in the house. Why hadn't she gone to the store for groceries?

What had she planned to do? I had searched the cupboards. Our two bowls of oatmeal were the last of the food, and it had most likely been provided by the neighbors. There was no flour, no milk, no vegetables.

Nothing.

What wood there was for cooking and warming the house with was under a mess of vines and old leaves. Then I reminded myself, I need only be brave until Friday. Jens would come then. He would tell me what to do. Everything would be all right. A rueful smile touched my lips. If I found my ring, I could be more certain.

Chapter 8

I tapped my finger absently on the table. What did Aunt Thora do with her pension money? I assumed that Uncle Erik left her money to care for herself after he passed on. I think Mama and Papa had assumed the same. She had to have money, else how was she here? Maybe it was just too hard for her to get to town and back. I was here now and that was no longer a problem. Aunt Thora put her spoon in the empty bowl.

"This oatmeal was delicious, ja," I said. "But you know there is no food in the house for our supper." I glanced at her expectantly.

"I thought the food would last me the week, ja, but you are young and you eat a lot." She pointed her finger at me. "What will you do now to make it up?"

I opened my mouth to offer an argument and then shut it again. If my aunt thought that what we'd had for supper last night and breakfast this morn was a week's worth of food, she could not be reasoned with.

"I—I—I don't know, Aunt," I finally stuttered. "What do you wish me to do?"

"Certainly your parents didn't leave you here without any money?" She stood and picked up her bowl.

I did have money, but it was for a different purpose. If I came to Jens with no ring, no money, and no chest of fabrics ... I blinked back my frustration.

She frowned and jabbed her finger accusingly toward me. "You are here to help, so figure something out," she said, and walked to the sink.

I followed her with my bowl in hand, my shoulders slumped. "I can wash our dishes, Aunt." I reached for hers, but she didn't pay me any heed.

"I've been washing my own dishes since before you were born, and I'm still perfectly capable." She put her bowl in the bottom of the porcelain sink and ladled cold water into it, took a few swipes with her washing rag and sat it on the counter.

"Wouldn't you like hot water for the dishes?" I put my bowl in the sink and went to the stove for the water I'd heated earlier. "Mama always heated our water. She says it helps clean things better."

"If I'd have wanted the water hot, I would have heated it," she snapped, and started out of the kitchen. "Young folk, they always think they know what's best, but the only thing they know is how to be a nuisance."

My heart thudded in frustration as I washed my dish and the oatmeal pot in the hot water. When I saw her shuffling into the other room, I quickly dipped hers in the hot water as well and then joined her in the parlor. "I can dust for you." I said a quick prayer for patience. "I would like to go search for my ring first, however." Things had to work themselves out by Friday, but I could not deny the miserable feeling in the pit of my stomach.

"Dust if you like." Aunt Thora sat in a chair. "There isn't any point in it, but whatever makes you happy."

"What I want, Aunt, is to make you happy." She tried my patience, but she looked too much like an older version of my mother to be disrespectful. Instead, I knelt in front of her. "I came to help you and to get to know you better."

Aunt Thora closed her eyes and it seemed that she went to sleep. I tiptoed from the room and went outside. I needed to find my ring. Starting at the back door, I bent and searched around the step and then walked slowly through the yard while retracing my steps. I took special care around the woodpile, remembering that I'd almost fallen there, but I didn't see anything that even resembled a ring.

Aunt Thora was nothing like my Mama. I had a hard time forgiving her sour attitude, so I stayed outside in the chill morning air contemplating what she'd said. Should I take my wedding money and buy something for us to eat? It seemed the only way. Should I try to get work in town? Is that how Mama and Papa wanted me to care for my aunt? She hadn't come right out and told me to, but it seemed like Aunt Thora expected it.

Perhaps I could find someone in town who needed help. Jens and his father were coming Friday. He said he'd come for me and take me home with him. I wished I could go, but at the very least he would know how I should help Aunt Thora. My heart skipped as I thought about the ring. Surely he would understand.

It would be hard talking to him about the missionaries, but he would be so happy that I'd stayed, he would listen to them. I heard talking and looked up.

Several people were outside at the neighboring house. Since I'd met Christopher, and he'd indicated that their family was responsible for helping my aunt, I walked over to talk to the woman I assumed was their mother. She was hoeing in a large garden plot and the children were preparing it for planting.

"Good day, Frau Poulsen?" I asked, and curtsied. "My name is Berta Erichsen. I'm here caring for my aunt Thora." I nodded toward her house.

"Ja, ja, Christopher told me." She held the hoe in her hands and rested against it. "He said someone you know is coming on Friday?"

"That is correct." I gazed downward, ashamed to beg. "My problem is that there's no food in the house."

"I am sorry. We have helped all we can." She clicked her tongue and started hoeing again. "We have done more than our duty, and all we got in return was the authorities called on us. I'm sorry you are in the middle of all this, but we only set the firewood out so that she doesn't freeze to death. Now that you are here, all I can say is good riddance to the cantankerous old woman."

"I am sorry for your trouble. Truly." I curtsied. My ears burned with humiliation as I turned and walked back to Aunt Thora's house, worrying about what to do.

Aunt Thora had disappeared, so I went straight to my room. I had unpacked my few things, but I pulled my travel bag out from under the bed and opened it. Inside was a pocket, and inside that pocket was the money Papa had given me. My skilling could buy food, I didn't know how much, or my skilling could buy something nice for my wedding. I fingered the coins, reluctant to part with them.

Chapter 9

"When your mama was little she loved to play in the alfalfa," Aunt Thora said. "On occasion, we'd make ragdolls and hide in the barn to play, but oh how I hated those mice!"

We hadn't had a meal since last morn's oatmeal. I had stubbornly held on to my coins. Aunt Thora stubbornly refused to offer hers. My stomach growled. I'd had enough. I did not want to reminisce. We needed food in the cupboards.

"Aunt Thora, there is no food. We need to go to market." I stood and grabbed my shawl. She already wore hers. I helped snug it around her shoulders, and handed her the walking cane near the door.

She followed obediently as a small child and offered no protest. We moseyed to town, and I listened patiently as she told stories of growing up and working at the mill.

"Here." Aunt Thora pointed. "This is where I like to buy my groceries."

We went in and gathered the supplies we needed. It took longer than I expected. Aunt Thora kept telling me that anything was good, and was not at all helpful in telling me what she liked. I put the food from our basket onto the counter for the clerk to ring us up, expecting Aunt Thora to pay. I was taken aback to find her nowhere.

"Oh." I looked around. "Where did she go?" How had she disappeared in so short a time?

The clerk shook his head. "Do you not want the groceries then? We cannot extend more credit."

"Ja, ja. We still want the food." I started to leave the food to search the store for my aunt, but customers were lined up behind me. I clenched my teeth and reached in my apron pocket, having brought my wedding money with me while hoping I wouldn't need it. Aunt Thora would pay me back, I said to myself, but worry nettled my heart as I watched the coins go from my hands to those of the clerk.

He took my skilling unaware of how important they were to me, and I sickened to see a portion of my wedding money go to pay for flour, milk, cheese, fresh vegetables, and smoked herring.

"Perhaps we don't need the herring just now," I said. "And maybe not so much cheese."

"This is good, ja. You can use the rest to pay down what your aunt owes us," the man said.

"What does she owe?" My brows creased into a frown. Papa said never borrow money. "I will pay if I can."

A heavy feeling of sadness filled me as I watched the store clerk take one coin after another from my handkerchief.

"That should do," he said. "Since you are so kind to come in and offer payment, I shall give you a break and not leave you penniless."

Only a few coins remained in the pouch. The air gone from my lungs, I smiled feebly. "Good day then." I grabbed up our groceries feeling as though I'd sold my birthright for a mess of pottage, and stepped outside.

Aunt Thora sat on a chair across the street. Who had put it there for her? "Where did you go?" I hurried to her. "This money was for my wedding." I tried not to scold or sound as exasperated as I felt.

She didn't reply but merely walked away. I had upset her. With groceries in hand, I took a deep breath and rushed after. It wasn't hard to keep up.

"Aunt Thora," I persisted, trying to sound calm. "I shall like repayment for this food, and I will work hard to earn my keep."

"And I should like to repay you as well," she snapped.

Although her tone was not appreciated, she was old and her bones probably hurt. Her comment satisfied me.

We arrived home, and Aunt Thora disappeared into her bedroom while I put the food away. After this chore was finished, my aunt still had not shown herself, so I went to the service porch. To one side was a cupboard. I opened it. On the left was a pair of hedge trimmers. A long wooden handle lying on the ground was half covered by an old apron. I peeled the old cloth away. Underneath was an axe.

I hadn't found it soon enough to uncover the first eight logs, but it would help the next time I needed wood. I grabbed up the trimmers, went outside and clipped the rose bushes down so Mama would be proud of them if she were here. After finishing that, I began trimming the ivy growing on the western wall of her house. Though my aunt did not seem happy for my company or help, I would make her proud of me.

Each day ticked by slowly. I spent them working to clear Aunt Thora's yard, and I even started working toward planting a small garden. This way, we wouldn't need to purchase vegetables at the store. I tried not to think of the money, but in the late afternoons and early mornings I wondered about it. When would she pay me back? Aunt Thora behaved as though she'd forgotten about the money. Should I mention it?

In the evenings back home, I had read the Book of Mormon by Papa's fire. Since Aunt Thora hadn't joined our church and didn't own a copy, I listened as she told stories of her childhood, Uncle Eric, and any other story she thought to tell. After she grew tired, I dusted and straightened.

One evening, as I set about cleaning long ignored corners, Aunt Thora came from her room and followed me. "Berta, dear, this is unnecessary," she said.

"Don't worry, Aunt." I shook my head, bemused at her continual insistence that I leave the house a mess. "All is well and good." As I continued cleaning, I happened to glance down and saw something. A flash of light, unexpected from the wood-box, and I knelt for a closer view. My heart pounded in anticipation.

A drop of amber glistened in the lamplight. My ring! Tears welled in my eyes. I grabbed the ring and hugged it to my breast. Then I said a quick prayer of thanks and put it on my finger.

"Look, Aunt!" I held my hand out for her to see. "Look what I found in the wood-box."

"My, my," she said. "It really is meant for you to marry this Jens you talk about. God wouldn't have allowed you to find his ring if this wasn't so."

I twirled Aunt Thora and danced a few steps with her. I missed Jens. My aunt's declaration let me know that all my trial would be worth it in the end. I would help Jens begin his spiritual journey on Friday. I would help with all my heart, and I practiced what I might say to encourage his interest in the gospel. Since Jens didn't know where my aunt lived, everything depended on my being out by the road and seeing him as he and his father passed by Aunt Thora's home.

By the end of the week, I'd become quite anxious. It was Friday. Finally. This was the day Jens and his father would travel to Vejstrup. I hurried to the window. The sun had yet to rise. No one was on the road at this early hour.

I dressed and went into the kitchen hunting for something to breakfast on. The cupboards were empty. Once again, we were at the absolute end of all food in the house. "Aunt Thora, we need more food from the market."

"Ja, ja, that would be a nice thing, wouldn't it." She wiped her hands on her apron and left the room. I thought perhaps she went to get some money and her shawl. When she didn't come back, I went to investigate. She lay on the bed in her room—a partially packed suitcase lay open on her dresser.

"Aunt Thora?"

She opened her eyes, watching me, but said nothing.

"I thought you were going to the market. We need groceries."

"I am too tired. You go along without me." She closed her eyes.

"Aunt, you know today is the day Jens is coming to town. I cannot leave." How could she not remember this?

Aunt Thora remained unmoving. I looked from her to the front door, wondering what was the best course of action. "But ... can you give me some money?"

"Now that's the problem, isn't it." Her eyes remained closed. "I have no money."

I thought I saw a tear drop from her cheek and onto her pillow, and I took a step into her room. "Aunt Thora?"

She wouldn't acknowledge me further, so I backed out and went to my room. No money? She had no money at all? My fingers covered my mouth, dread overcoming me. So, this was Aunt Thora's problem. I don't think Mama and Papa understood. Not only did she need someone to help her with the cleaning and yard work, but she also needed someone to care for her financially. I heaved a sigh. This meant that she could not repay me. Ever.

Papa's remaining coins weighed in my hands as I transferred them from one hand to the other, considering the consequences of spending them. But what kind of niece would I be if I let my aging aunt go hungry when I had skilling in my possession? Finally, not knowing of any other course of action, I put them in my apron pocket.

"I'm going into town, Aunt Thora. I'll be back shortly." I

grabbed my shawl and rushed out the door. I could make it to town and back, I hoped, before Jens and his father could get here. Nonetheless, I kept a vigilant watch up and down the street as I hurried. If they came before I got home, I couldn't miss them while on the main road.

I hurried to the village, ever vigilant for Jens, and at the same time wondering if I should get employment. I didn't know anything about Vejstrup. I'd never had a job before. What was I capable of? Surely someone would help us. When I saw the bakery, I smiled and went in. I loved helping Mama cook.

"Hello?"

A large woman a hand's width taller than me came from the back room.

"Ja, ja, may I help you?" A floury white apron covered her dress, and her graying hair was braided loosely and sat atop her head like a big cinnamon bun.

"I hope so," I said curtsying.

Minutes later, I left with a sweet roll to share with Aunt Thora, and the promise of employment. I would come every afternoon, Monday through Friday and clean for Frau Thomsen. It wasn't much, but hopefully it would keep food on our table. Jens would be proud of me. I went next door and purchased a very small celebratory roast and headed back to Aunt Thora's all while wondering how to make it last the week. My heart felt light. I watched the traffic to town, hoping to see Jens. With each wagon that wasn't his, a little disappointment clouded my day. However, it was still early. He would soon take me in his arms and make me his.

I skipped around the corner to Aunt Thora's house, and skidded to a stop. Something was amiss. Aunt Thora's suitcase was on the ground near a wagon—it didn't look like the Larsens'.

"What is going on?" I rushed to the front lawn. Two officials were escorting Aunt Thora to the wagon.

My Sweet Danish Rose

"Is this kin of yours?" One of the officers asked Aunt Thora.

"Nej." Aunt Thora shook her head adamantly. "She is merely a kind girl who lives on this street."

"How could you say such things!" Tears pushed their way to my eyes and I inhaled a shuddered breath at her denial. "I've worked so hard to make you proud of me." I reached for Aunt Thora, but she avoided my grasp.

"May I speak to the little darling before we leave?" Aunt Thora's eyes were pleading, and the officer relented.

"What is happening?" I asked as Aunt Thora led me to the end of her property.

"You must forgive me and not feel harshly. I tried to contact your mama." Aunt Thora took hold of both my arms, blinking tears from her eyes. "I couldn't afford a stamp."

"I do forgive you of everything—but please tell me what is going on so I might understand." I put my arm around her and dabbed at her face with my hankie, and squeezed her affectionately.

"I haven't been able to care for myself financially since my dear Erik passed on—I should have asked your papa for help, but I was too proud." Aunt Thora peeked at me through her eyelashes like a scolded child. "I am in debt to the government. They are merely coming to collect what is rightfully theirs and to escort me to the poorhouse in Svendborg."

"Nej! Nej! It cannot be." I took her by the arms. "You cannot go to the poorhouse. It is a horrible place, and you cannot leave me here alone. I won't let you."

"All is well and good." Aunt Thora patted my hands and then held them in hers. "It will be a blessing for me—they will have fire in the winters and food on the table. I am old and have no pension. They will allow me to work for pay, and I'll sign on to help in the kitchen." She smiled in hopes to convince me, I think, but her lips quivered.

"Aunt Thora," I hissed. "You cannot do this. They house

drunks there, and the insane, and…" I grimaced at the thought of bug infestations and was unable to go on.

"It's time to leave, Widow Kjar." One of the officers came forward.

"Give me one minute more. I need to explain what's happening so that the frøken and her mama don't worry." Aunt Thora gave him a determined expression. He smiled kindly and walked a few paces away, giving us privacy.

Aunt Thora leaned toward my ear. "You are young, and I cannot have them taking you with me, so please forgive my denial—I am most proud of you, my Berta." She grinned sheepishly. "I knew they were coming today, so I placed your bag and its contents near the berry brambles. Go back to your home and marry that young man you're always talking about."

She shuffled to the waiting officer and took his arm.

I chased after, screaming, pleading, "Please don't take her from me! Please don't go!"

Chapter 10

I plodded back to Aunt Thora's home not recognizing my life, my world. Fingering Mama's locket with one hand, I clutched Catherine's handkerchief with the other, as I walked around the empty structure. I tried the doors, though it was no use. They were all locked. My insides skittered, and I slumped onto the back step. My most vivid nightmares were nothing compared to this. I was utterly alone.

And then I remembered that wasn't true.

The apple tree in Aunt Thora's backyard offered privacy. I went there and knelt, opening my heart to my Savior. Only Divine intervention could keep me from Aunt Thora's or a worse fate. Part-time employment surely couldn't keep me from the street. Moments later, eyes moist with thankfulness, I stood and wiped the earth from my knees feeling comforted, and went to the street to wait for Jens. He would come, and I would go with him regardless of my promise to Mama. I had no other home to go to.

As I waited, the sun traveled across the sky. I stood at the distant sound of each traveler, waiting, watching, anticipating, refusing to give up hope until the dust from their wheels had long settled. There were twelve travelers that day, none of them my Jens. My hope and my spirits dropped as each disappeared in the horizon. Of all the times in my life when I'd cried myself silly, those times were nothing like this. And yet no tears came. I was a hollow ghost of myself and empty of tears.

My knees ached, my skirt was damp from sitting, and the

golden sun shimmered near the horizon. Jens had not come. Did he change his plans when I hadn't sent word of my staying? Had something happened along the way? My heart skipped a beat, and I prayed that no harm had befallen him. I picked up my bag and started my trek to the village bakery. I would throw myself at the mercy of a stranger.

The cool night air had chilled my arms by the time I came to the bakery. Yet, as worn as I was, a slim smile etched my face at the light glowing from a back room. She was still there. I pressed the door open and stepped in, dropping my bag just inside the bakery door with a thud, having grown weary of carrying it. Frau Thomsen came running from the back room covered in flour. "We are closing, make it quick." Upon seeing me, she stopped abruptly, eyeing me with concern. "Ja?"

"I've found myself in need of a place to stay." My voice quavered from exhaustion and disappointment. "And I wondered if you could put me up until I earn enough money to travel back to Radstrup."

She eyed me suspiciously while her fingers drummed the service counter. "What happened to your home?"

"My parents had me helping my aunt, but she was called away just today—I didn't know anything about it." I smiled weakly. "My home is in Radstrup, and I will go there." I could not confess my true situation for fear I'd be sent to the poorhouse to meet Aunt Thora. A shudder pricked the hairs on my neck. Surely there were horrors at the poorhouse that I could not endure.

"If you work hard, I will pay your fare after one week, but you cannot stay longer."

"Ja, ja." I nodded my agreement, excited that I didn't have to sleep on the street. "I will work very hard."

"Well, turn the sign if you're to make yourself useful."

After I did as she directed, I helped her cover the few loaves of remaining bread and pastries to keep them fresh.

"I have very little waste here, but I bake some extra each day to have a sale each morn. Many of my customers like it better when they can purchase my breads for less." Reaching under the counter, she took a paper bag and walked toward the back to a tray of older breads. "On occasion, I have items older than two days. I feed them to my animals, but you can take one large or two small from here each day to eat. I don't want you to starve." She regarded me sternly.

"You are very generous but I still have the sweet roll I purchased this morn."

"Pish-posh," she said. "So you'll feast like a queen this one night."

I watched as she picked through the loaves and put one in the bag. "I also have a gift for you," I added. Reaching into my travel bag I pulled out the small bundle of butcher paper that held the roast. She received it with gladness. We walked together to the door, and I waited as she locked up.

Frau Thomsen chatted endlessly as we walked past two city streets to her house. I only caught snippets of her conversation between my thoughts of Aunt Thora, Mama, Papa, Catherine, and Jens.

"Here we are." She led me around to the back of a two story red-brick structure. "I have leased out the first floor to a pleasant couple. I keep the ground floor and basement for my own use." She opened the back door and stepped into the service porch. "You may stay here."

My heart sank a little. I longed for home, but I nodded my approval and thanked her. There was a chair and table, a shelf with a few books, and boxes stacked in a corner of the very small room.

She left me then, and although I didn't expect her to, I hoped she would bring me a slice of roast after it cooked. I took a few volumes from the bookshelf and perused them while sitting in the rickety chair. The aroma of cooking food filled my nostrils and I inhaled deeply, enjoying the sharp scent of onions, meat, and spices.

She hadn't given me permission to leave the room. So I waited. Surely she would bring me pillows or a mattress to sleep on, or some of that delicious-smelling food. Yet, it became apparent that I'd been forgotten, so I ate the cinnamon roll and thought of Aunt Thora. It wasn't filling, so, reluctantly I pulled out my loaf and picked a piece of mold off, flicking it back into the bag.

Although not fresh, it was wonderful bread with chewy wheat berries, ground oats, and caraway seeds. At first I picked bite-sized pieces and plopped them in my mouth, but soon gave up on convention and chewed large bites straight from the loaf.

After a while, the light shining from underneath the door went black. Frau Thomsen had gone to bed. I sat alone in the semi-darkness feeling somewhat like an orphaned church mouse as I continued nibbling on the bread. A row of windows let a hazy gleam of light shine across the room. Drawn to the windows like a mouse to a horn of cheese, I stood and peered at the stars and clouds mingled together.

Did my family see these same stars? Were they having a safe journey, or had their ship sunk? Were the passengers dying from measles or some other plague? A lump formed in my throat, and I dropped to my knees in prayer.

In the morn, I awakened to the clicking sound of Frau Thomsen's wooden shoes on her hardwood floor. The sun's rays hadn't yet thought of shining through the small windows. I sat up and stretched the kinks from my back. I wouldn't leave the room a mess, and packed my mattress—the Faroese blanket—and Grandmother's quilt back into my bag.

"Are you ready?" Frau Thomsen peeked through the doorway.

"Ja, ja. Thank you." I took my bag and hid it behind the chair.

Frau Thomsen waited by the back door, locked it after us, and we started on our way to the bakery. She explained my duties for the day while I watched for Jens. Perhaps I'd had the wrong day.

"You will be helping customers at the front counter, and you will tell me when I need to bring out more bread. In between customers you will sweep the floor and dust."

"I know how to cook—I could also help with the baking." I liked baking much better than cleaning.

"Nej. I am the only one who bakes. My customers know what to expect from me."

Once we got to the bakery and put the open sign in the window, customers lined up at the counter. It seemed everyone in the village loved her breads and came in two groups—one in the morning, and another in the afternoon, with a steady stream in between.

The bakery closed early on Saturday, thus in order to earn my keep, she had me help clean her home, feed her chickens and goat, and prune her rosebushes.

On Sunday, I expected no different. However, she entered my room Sunday morn wearing a nice dress.

"You may use the wash room to freshen up and then we will go to church."

"Ja, ja. That will be good." I jumped up, grabbed my travel bag and rushed into the wash room.

She had the basin filled with warm water, a wash towel beside it, and a towel for drying hung from the wall. I smiled happily and undressed.

A bar of handmade soap sat on the counter near the porcelain basin and pitcher. I splashed water against my skin, rubbed soap onto the wash towel, and scrubbed myself clean. It was enlivening. I loved the soft feel of my hair and skin after a good cleaning. After drying off and dressing, I opened the latch on the window, pushed the pane outward and poured the water onto the flowerbed below.

Frau Thomsen waited at the service porch.

"Thank you, ja. I feel much better." I curtsied.

"Well let's get on our way before we're too late." She shooed me out the door and locked up, and we were on our way.

I dared not ask about a Mormon church in the area; instead I followed along as she led the way to her church—an aging building made of whitewashed brick. I noticed the architectural similarity between this building and our old church in Radstrup. Large, knobby English Oak trees surrounded it, and their cemetery filled the lawn to the left. A few families knelt at gravesites.

We went inside and took a seat. The pastor's sermon, on living a golden life by treating others kindly, brought me a measure of comfort. Frau Thomsen tried living this very principle by taking me in for the week. My heart swelled in gratitude for her.

On this day, however, I missed my Book of Mormon most acutely and thought of that young man—Anders—with no small measure of malice. Why had he felt compelled to steal it? He had no idea what he'd taken from me, or how he'd diminished my chances of survival, for if I had it to read, I could be strong enough to withstand any trial.

So the week went. I spent each day Monday through Friday working at the bakery, keeping an eye out for Jens and his father in case they were still coming, living on old bread and pastries, all while trying to push down the growing ache in my heart for Jens.

I stayed the extra Saturday and Sunday, and the following Monday, Frau Thomsen stood in her doorway to say goodbye. I hesitated. Should I give her a hug, or not? I'd grown quite fond of her. "Thank you kindly for taking me in and for paying my fare." I gave her a quick hug.

"Nonsense," she said, and grabbed me into a full embrace. "You feel like my own daughter. That is, if I had a daughter, of course." She held me out at arm's length. "Once you're married, you bring your young man by for a visit." She wiped at her eyes with her handkerchief. "Godspeed."

With a lump lodged in my throat, I nodded, took my bag in hand and rushed to the awaiting carriage.

"Radstrup, please." I handed my bag to the driver, who helped me to my seat and set the bag by my feet. "Good morning." I nodded to the other passengers as we made our way down the road.

A light mist dampened the earth, but it couldn't dampen my spirits. I'd had a two week setback, but now I was on my way home! Jens hadn't come to Vejstrup, but I refused to entertain depressing thoughts. Jens loved me two weeks ago, he loved me now. And on this glorious day we would finally be reunited. I delighted in thinking of the surprise on his face.

Hours later, and just as we neared the small village of Ringe, one of the horses developed a limp. Knowing horses as I did, I noticed the problem nearly as soon as the driver.

"We will stop here the night. I know the men at the stable." He stepped down.

"What is the matter? Did he step on a rock?" I walked forward and rubbed the horse's nose and then stroked the underside of his neck and chin.

"Ja, ja, but it is all good. The stable is near, and the other passengers are getting off here. You will stay the night and I will take you to Radstrup on the morrow." He un-harnessed the injured horse and walked away.

I followed him, fretting. "Where will I stay?"

"There are rooms in town."

But I couldn't stay someplace that wanted money. "Can you not trade for a fresh horse?" I hurried beside him as he led the animals and carriage toward the stables.

"Nej. I will not abandon my horse. I have a very good poultice—he will be better tomorrow. You will see."

"Ja, ja. May I come with you to the stable?" Perhaps I could find the mercy of the stable owner and he would allow me to stay the night there—or perhaps I'd find a way to stay without him knowing. My heart sank; that was dishonest. "I can help." I reached for the injured horse's bridle. If I earned my way it wouldn't be wrong.

"He is injured and needs me. Ja? For his sake I will lead him." He would not let loose of his animal.

I felt like a nuisance, tagging along like a small child, but was compelled to continue. There was nowhere else for me to go—this stranger was my lifeline, my security in a strange town.

"Where will you stay the night?"

"I will stay with my horse." He frowned as though I should know this.

At the stable, he attended his horses by feeding them, brushing them, and treating and wrapping the injured horse's hoof, and at all times refusing any help from me. Indeed, the only hint he gave of remembering me was an occasional and brief frown. I walked from stall to stall glancing to see some occupied and some empty. I couldn't stay here, it wouldn't be right, and yet what other choice did I have? Sleeping out in the street could be dangerous.

I edged my way toward the stable door, studying the buildings, businesses, and anything up or down the street for better options.

A sturdy gentleman approximately Papa's age approached me. "Good afternoon." His hair, the color of pumpernickel, fell straight around his ears. "I am Herrer Jensen."

"Good afternoon." I curtsied and smiled. "Are you kin to Maren Jensen? This was my mama's name before she married."

"The daughter of Dyri and Ana?"

"Ja, ja. Those are the names of my grandparents." Maybe I had more relation in Denmark after all.

"They called your mother 'the honest miller's daughter,' ja?"

"Ja." I smiled, feeling pleased. "That is my mother."

"I knew your mother back in school." He removed his cap. "A terrible thing to have so many of her family pass from this life, ja?"

"Ja." I nodded, remembering Mama tell us of a terrible sickness taking all of her siblings before Mama was even born, all but Aunt Thora.

"Are you somehow related to Herrer Jull, or are you here for supplies?" He surveyed the area. "After all these years, I would love a chance to say hello to your mother."

"Nej, Mama and Papa are not here. Mama married Hans Erichsen. I am on my way to Radstrup, but the driver's horse went lame." He seemed nice. He knew, or used to know Mama, and I ached to tell him my situation—surely he had a family, and they could put me up. Instead, I bit my bottom lip and hung my head, too afraid to ask.

"What are you doing on the road alone? You can't be older than my Greta. She is fifteen." He eyed me, waiting for my response.

"Ja, ja." I nodded. "I am fifteen. My name is Berta Erichsen." I curtsied. "I was visiting my aunt Thora, and am returning home to Radstrup." This half-truth implied I had a home to return to, but I could not say more to a stranger.

"Do you have a place to stay the night?"

"Nej." My heart thudded at this confession. "My parents did not count on the horse becoming injured." And then I had an idea. "I could do work for a place to stay." I said this half to myself, and was ready to find the stable owner to ask him.

"Frau Jensen would be angry with me if I didn't offer you room and board." He motioned toward his horse and wagon outside. "You needn't work for your stay."

I nodded, happy for his help but cheerless for needing it. Almost before I had a chance to say a silent prayer of gratitude, Mr. Jensen had finished his business at the stable and bid me join him for what proved to be an amiable ride to his home. He stepped off the wagon, and as he did, I jumped off the other side anxious to be of service.

"Please let me brush your horses down." I saw a brush lying nearby and rushed to pick it up.

"That is a good idea. It will give me time to tell the Missus. Please come in for supper when you're finished." I watched from the doorway as he walked through their courtyard and toward the house.

"Mama, we have a guest for dinner!" He stepped into their home and disappeared behind the door.

I turned to the horse. "There, there, good boy. We're going to be sleeping partners tonight, you and I." This horse, a deep chestnut Frederiksborger, seemed to enjoy my attentions. I was glad we could be friends.

A little mouse scurried across the floor, probably searching for something to eat. Wishing I had even a crumb to offer the cute little critter, I watched it escape through a hole in the wall. After I finished brushing the horse, I stayed back, not certain about going into the house before preparing a place to stay the night.

The barn was clean. There was space for me to sleep. I took a pitchfork off the wall and arranged the hay into a nice bed in the corner.

"What are you doing?" Mr. Jensen stood in the doorway, his knuckles resting on his hips.

"I—I'm sorry. I was preparing a place to sleep. Your straw is very soft—and clean." Realizing I'd caused him displeasure, I began smoothing the straw back to its original state. I would sleep elsewhere.

"The honest miller's granddaughter shall not sleep in the barn. You are not an animal—you are our guest."

Mr. Jensen put the pitchfork away, took my elbow kindly, and with paternal authority led me into his home.

"Mama, children, this is Berta Erichsen, Maren Jensen's daughter. She was on her way to Radstrup when the driver's horse came up lame."

A lanky boy who couldn't be much older than I stepped in front of the others and extended his hand. "I am Nathan." He nodded to his right. "This little lad here is—"

"Now, now, there's no need in getting ahead of yourself," said Mr. Jensen. He stood behind Nathan, resting his hands on Nathan's shoulders.

"Ja, Father," he said, and gave me a smile.

A towheaded boy stepped forward. "I am Hans." He bowed and stepped back. "And I'm not a little lad. I am nine years old. Nathan is merely too tall." He stuck his tongue out at Nathan playfully. "He's like a giant or something."

I smiled. "Hello, Hans, it is—"

"Why you little ..." Nathan lunged forward. Hans ducked, and the chase was on.

"—a pleasure to meet you," I finished, glancing up at the Jensen parents. They watched their children's shenanigans with patience as they tore through the house.

"Don't mind those boys," said a girl of about my size with long blonde braids. "They are always acting like this, but it is all well. Their tomfoolery will allow us to know one another better. We will be like sisters, I can feel it."

"I feel it as well." And I did. They were all friendly and eager to please.

"Berta, this is our oldest daughter, Greta. She is the one I mentioned earlier who is your age." Mr. Jensen squeezed his daughter's shoulders.

"You will join us for supper," said Frau Jensen. "Boys, if you want any, it is time you settle down."

"Ja, ja, Mother." They jumped up off the floor and sat on the sofa, arms in their laps.

She was a thin woman no taller than me, but like my Mama, she knew how to get her children's attention.

"Greta, show our guest where to wash up."

"Ja, ja, Mother." Greta took my elbow and we started across the room.

"I did not get a chance to meet her." A young girl, a towheaded blonde like her brother, frowned at her papa.

"Of course, darling. And a terrible oversight it was." Mr. Jensen swept her into his arms. "Berta, this is our youngest daughter, and the baby of the family."

"Father! I am seven years old. I am not a baby."

"Of course not." He placed her back to the floor. "This beautiful young lady is Kirsten."

"I am pleased to meet you Kirsten." I curtsied.

"You get to stay in our room," she said. "You will sleep in my bed, and I get to sleep with Greta." She gave a satisfied smile and followed as Greta showed me to the washbasin.

As we sat to the supper table, which reminded me of meals at home, I was nearly overwhelmed and blinked back a feeling of homesickness.

Chapter 11

"Thank you for everything, ja." I curtsied to Mr. Jensen, but he pulled me into his arms.

"You are always welcome here," he said. "If ever you need anything."

Frau Jensen stepped forward and gave me a quick hug. "You're such a dear. I feel as though I'm saying goodbye to one of my own." She handed me a cloth bundle. "This is to tide you over until you meet your loved ones tonight."

"Thank you, kindly." Her gift of bread and cheese touched me. I felt a close connection with her. She doted after me like I was one of her daughters.

Greta and Kirsten rushed to me, almost knocking me over with their hugs. Hans and Nathan stood back, waiting to shake my hand.

It was a strange feeling I had as I stepped onto the carriage—almost like leaving home again—but different. I felt as though I should stay, but I shook the feeling away. The Jensens had offered me security for the night. Nothing more. They were pleasant and kind as my parents would have been if someone needed their help. I should not get so attached to someone I'd never see again. I smiled and waved as I took a place behind the carriage driver.

"Your horse looks much better. It seems that your poultice worked."

The driver nodded but otherwise gave no sign that he'd heard me. I think possibly he wasn't supposed to visit with the passengers.

"Good day," I greeted the others. "Are you travelling to Odense?" It was the largest city on Fyn.

Some muttered their accord; others remained busy visiting with traveling companions.

To occupy my time, I watched the gently rolling landscape bring one farm after another into view. The arms of the windmills dotting the countryside twirled lazily in the breeze as though dancing to a melody no one but they could hear.

The hours-long ride gave me plenty of time to contemplate my situation and wonder exactly what Heavenly Father required of me. I wanted to go straight to the Larsens'. Perhaps they could put me up. But when Mama's locket suddenly weighed heavy around my neck, I knew she would not approve.

I fingered the delicate amber on the ring Jens had given me. What then?

Finally, I decided. I would go into the village and ask for work—Frau Thomsen had taken me in, allowing me to work for room and board. I'd been a stranger to her.

"Take me into Radstrup, please," I told the driver.

Though I seldom went to town, I knew many of the people in Radstrup. We'd gone to the same church for years. Many of them had sons and daughters mine and Catherine's same ages. When the driver stopped, I stepped from the wagon with a full plan and high hopes.

After securing work and a place to stay, I would go to Jens. I was still nervous about finding work, however, and worried Catherine's handkerchief between my fingers. In order to gather more courage, I closed my eyes and took myself once again to that day when Jens had kissed me. It felt so long ago. Aunt Thora had assured me that God wanted Jens and me together. This would all be worth it. These hardships were nothing compared to a lifetime of happiness.

I walked along the narrow cobblestone street, absorbing myself in the sights, trying to think of what to say, and contemplating the uniqueness of village life.

Our home and many others in our part of the country were built in a U shape with the barn being built across the open part, and making a nearly enclosed courtyard in the middle. Here in town, the homes were built in long lines of small, connected and colorfully painted buildings with no property for a cow or a horse, or anything.

Yet I could tell at a glance when one home ended and another began because each resident used a different color of paint. Some were blue with white trim, others were maroon, or mustard, or tan. Almost all of them had mirrors attached to long metal arms and secured near the front window. I'd heard of this before. From the comfort of their sofa, a person could witness the goings-on of their whole neighborhood with only slight adjustments to their mirror.

Busybodies.

A shiver coursed through me as I thought of it. No one could have even the least amount of privacy living in such near proximity to their neighbors, and because of the mirrors, everyone would be talking about who visited whom.

However, I thought, it would also be an easy way to keep an eye on one's children. This helped me to feel more kindly. I did not know these people, nor did I know anything of their lives. Who was I to judge?

When I came to Mr. Petersen's store, my heart skipped with glee. There was a sign requesting help in his window.

He sold a little bit of everything, and Mama had brought us here once or twice and bought for us a piece of candy. I pushed the door open and stepped inside ready to start work that instant. A bell hanging on the door chimed a happy greeting as I walked in. Just hearing the pretty sound gave me added hope.

"Berta Erichsen." He put something on the shelf behind the

counter and turned to face me once more.

"Good day, Herrer Petersen." I curtsied. "I am here inquiring about the available position." I pulled the sign from the window and brought it to him.

He started to speak, but the door chimed again. He looked past me and I turned to see.

"Berta? Berta Erichsen?" Isaac Thompsen stood in the open doorway frowning and appearing as though he might explode with anger.

"Ja, ja. It is me." The hairs on my neck prickled, but I gulped and then forced a halfhearted smile. I hadn't planned on encountering the man who broke Catherine's heart.

"Your family has decided to stay?" He glared at the sign in my hand, took a step inside the shop and closed the door.

"Nej." I shuddered and stepped away. "My family has gone, and I am the only one." Did he still wish to court my sister after his harsh actions?

"Herrer Petersen." Isaac jerked the sign from my hand and strode to the counter. "You'd be wise not to employ liars such as this." He pointed in my direction. "The Thompsens don't deal with fools." Isaac thrust the sign onto the counter and spun on his heel. The door boomed shut as he left.

I watched Isaac disappear down the sidewalk, and then I turned to Mr. Petersen. Would he heed Isaac's warning? His face had grown pale. I took a shaking step forward.

"I've left my aunt's and returned to Radstrup. I would like to work for room and board." His expression made me nervous, but I continued. "Although I do not have a lot of experience, I worked in a bakery while staying with my aunt, and I am a hard worker and also a fast learner."

"Nej!" Mr. Petersen pounded his fist on the counter. I jumped at the sound. "I cannot, I will not be having you here." He spat the words and I shrank away. "I rely on the Thompsens for my business. You must leave this instant!"

My heart pounded in my chest, so shaken was I by his rudeness, but my parents knew him and I tried again. "I am Berta Erichsen—the daughter of Hans and Maren Erichsen."

"I know full well who you are, and I'll not be having you in my store." He slapped his hands on the counter.

Mortified, my ears and neck went hot, but his demeanor wouldn't change so thoroughly with one word from Isaac. Would it?

"You were friends with Papa," I smiled in encouragement as if such an action would pacify him. "He helped you when your son's cow was ready to calf, and you couldn't get anyone else. It was my papa who came and helped save both cow and calf."

Mr. Petersen's solid frame shook, his face and neck turning dark red. I had never before seen anyone behave like this. My heart beat furiously; I turned and ran out the door.

Finding a nearby tree, I collapsed to my knees under its shelter. Shaking and unable to stop the flow of tears, I succumbed to them for a moment and unleashed my fears and frustrations until I became aware of the townspeople walking past. No friendly faces offered help or comfort.

If only Jens could be in town. He would make everything all right. Shuddering sobs once again escaped before I could bring myself under control. At last I patted my face dry and looked for him. He wasn't in town, but surely, someone would take me in.

Yet, to my increasing alarm and dismay, shop after shop denied me. Olaf, the dressmaker, Niels the butcher, Jørn the baker—none were willing to help. Had Isaac run through the town and defamed my name? It appeared that the banker's son ruled the village. No one seemed to remember the previous kindness my parents had shown—for until their departure, they had been highly esteemed.

It wasn't as though I wanted a handout—why should Isaac

care? I was perfectly healthy and eager to work, and I wasn't asking the Thompsens to employ me. But the townspeople would not listen to my pleas.

I loved horses and tried the stables on my way out of town. Surely Mads would let me work. But it was the same.

"Out with you!"

"Please. I will work hard." I don't know why I pleaded other than pure desperation, for I knew from the day's experience he would not change his mind.

"If you have no home you must go to the poorhouse."

That would be a sorry solution. I nodded and turned back to the road. Aunt Thora would give me a piece of her mind for not being any more clever than that. And, if I wasn't, perhaps I deserved the poorhouse.

Nej. I would find a way. I would find a place to stay and work. Jens would read the Book of Mormon and join the church, and we would be married and live happily ever after. Some of Hans Christian Andersen's stories ended happily, and mine would too.

The translucent amber of my ring shone in the afternoon light like a drop of gold. I could not face Jens as a homeless, penniless waif.

Yet, I had nowhere to go.

A spring shower dampened the earth, and chilled, I wrapped my shawl tightly around my shoulders. My feet propelled me forward, anxious to be somewhere familiar. To be home.

A neighboring windmill creaked, and I considered this once friendly sight. Now, instead of the slow-moving blades offering comfort and a sense of home, they taunted me with each turn. Wiping my face dry with my apron, I trudged up the last incline to my former home, and stopped.

An evening glow rested on the thatched roof, circling it in angelic radiance. The enormity of my decision glared at me from the golden windows of the abandoned structure. It didn't appear much different—as though at any moment I might see Papa riding in from the field for supper or that Mama might walk out to water her flowers.

How I wished it could be.

Knowing it wouldn't be so, I took a couple of deep breaths to calm my aching and troubled heart. What was once my home, full of love and happiness, was now an empty shell offering nothing but loneliness and fading memories.

It was already May. The rosebushes lining our front lawn were starting to bud. In my mind I could smell their sweet fragrance. Mama had earned a special regard for her roses from everyone far and near. Although Mama cared nothing for what others thought, she loved the earth and all the beautiful things that could grow from it.

The earth, the flowers, her family—nothing could help but be beautiful when Mama was near. Mama was beautiful inside and out, and everything and everyone responded to her touch, wanting to be their best for her.

Mama and Papa had that in common.

As memories flooded my mind, I wiped at my face and wished that my family and the other Saints could have stayed in Denmark. Our family was well respected in Radstrup and the surrounding farms. The townsfolk had, I thought, accepted our conversion to what they deemed a strange religion.

If only the Larsens had felt the Holy Spirit and become converted, as we had. It would have made my life much easier—Jens and I would have married right away and gone to America together.

Now more than before, I understood the wisdom in leaving—in having all the Saints gather together in Zion. Also, everyone who converted, or mostly everyone, wanted to be near the prophet Brigham Young—a man who talked with God—and to hear his words firsthand.

I gazed up at the large, still empty nest sitting atop the chimney of my old home. The stork who lived there would return any time now and bring good luck to the home's new owners. If anyone ever came to live there. We had always felt blessed to share our lives with a stork. The fanciful bird had been a part of our family for so long that I didn't know when it had first built the nest.

I'd been foolish to think staying would be easy and I breathed deeply the comforting aroma of clean, moist earth and tried to take courage in the sight of the empty shell of my childhood home. I was not alone. My God would guide me.

Pulling Mama's locket forward from beneath my blouse, I held it while I strode purposefully through the gate. My home had become a stranger to me, and I felt like an intruder here, but I pressed forward.

At the base of the ash tree in the front lawn, I knelt to pray and opened my heart to my Lord and Savior. I needed help—someplace to stay and to work—and some way to make my dreams of a happy life come true.

Chapter 12

"Frøken. What are you doing here?"

The sound of another person startled me. I jumped up and turned to see Mr. Ilse standing near. "Herrer Ilse," I said dumbly. I hadn't planned on having him discover me. I struggled with what to say. "I—"

"Did you not go to Vejstrup to care for your aunt?" He stared at me with quizzical brows—they were bushy and unruly. It made him seem angry.

"Ja, ja." I curtsied, feeling the fear and anxiety bubble inside me. "My aunt is a very good woman." My heart thudded anxiously, and I chewed the inside of my lip, waiting for what to say. If he knew my situation, he would send me to the poorhouse for sure, or send me into the streets. I could not do the things women did in the streets to survive.

His brows furrowed, and I gasped in trepidation.

"I had to come back," I said, and then I couldn't seem to stop my talking. "I missed my home and, and Jens Larsen. We love each other, ja. And I came back to marry him. But no one will take me in, and I have nowhere to work and earn my keep. I tried everyone in the village. Isaac Thompsen has set them all against me, I think. They all yelled at me. They said I was foolish and should move to the poorhouse."

Tears fell down my face as I remembered the embarrassment of the day, but I wiped at them furiously. "I won't go to the poorhouse, and I am not foolish—well maybe I am—but it's no reason for them to be unkind. And, and I'm sorry I'm here on your property, but I needed to come someplace familiar. I miss my family, and I don't know what to do." My words choked in my throat, and I gulped.

His eyes brightened, but he was perfectly calm. "You need a place to stay? And employment?" It seemed as though a sort of half-smile crossed his face, but it immediately dissolved into an air of disinterest.

I nodded in agreement. "I'm a hard worker. I know how to sew and clean house, and I'm especially good with animals. Mama and Papa only had us four girls, and I learned at an early age how to work and keep our land profitable." I looked at him hopefully. "Do you know of anyone? I cannot go to Jens homeless."

"Indeed, I do." He scratched absently at his cheek. "However, this person needs someone who is obedient to commands and follows the household rules."

"Ja, ja. I will always do what I am told by my employer." My heart leapt at the thought that he actually knew of someone who would hire me. That his influence held more weight than Isaac Thompsen, the banker's son, was remarkable.

He tapped his chin as he thought again. "This person needs someone who is an exceptionally hard worker."

I nodded. "That is me. I work very hard." I clasped my hands together.

He took a deep breath. "You can start right away, I suppose." One eyebrow lifted.

In spite of my fear of him, I rushed forward and gave his arm a quick hug. "I will work so hard." I stepped back and curtsied. "You will never be sorry that you recommended me."

"Come. Daylight is wasting, and I don't want to miss my supper." He turned and strode to his horse, mounting it with the seamless grace of someone well acquainted with his beast.

He reached his hand out for me to join him, but I hesitated.

His horse appeared expensive, and sitting on it with him seemed too personal. I was not a woman of loose morals and did not want him to think otherwise.

A dark shadow crossed his face with his scowl. "You needn't worry about your virtue. I'm a man of honor, but should my supper get cold while waiting for you to walk to my home, I'll be sorely tempted to flog you."

Surely he wouldn't, so I ignored his remark. "Your horse. It's a Knabstrupper?" I'd never seen one in person and stepped back to admire him. The horse's legs and face were charcoal in color, and they met the white body of the animal with a splash of varied-sized spots. "He is beautiful, ja." I rubbed his velvet nose.

"Ja, ja," Mr. Ilse said with a note of pride. "I breed them." With a firm resolve, he stretched out his hand.

It wasn't proper. Nonetheless, I took my bag in hand with the hem of my skirt and made haste to his side, hoping that my new employer would be nicer than this man. He grabbed hold of my arm and helped me to the front.

"Had I known I'd be picking up a stray, I might have brought my carriage." His voice sounded pleasant, but his arm pulled tightly around my waist did not settle my nerves. "Though why would I think to do such a thing when Zeus here needed exercise?"

If he hoped for a reply, I did not know, but I had no way of commenting politely, so I remained quiet. It was an uncomfortable silence that accompanied me, and my skin crawled with worried anticipation of foul play on his part.

After a space of time, and with the setting sun at my back, I felt that I really must try to be nice to the man who had so easily offered his help. By my silence I was being rude and arrogant myself.

"Do you plan to sell the house?" If he held on to it, perhaps Jens could buy it for us to live in. I focused on the horse's mane, too nervous to enjoy the ride, as we made our way down the dirt road.

"I haven't yet decided. I may tear the old farmhouse down and use the extra space for planting."

My mind rejected the thought and my jaw clenched, yet I tried to continue in a pleasant manner. "Ja, the home is nearly two hundred years old." I pictured my beloved home as a pile of firewood and tried steadying myself.

"This distresses you." He sounded accusatory.

"Nej, nej. I have many fond memories there, of course. But it's not my home now." My heart ached at saying the words that I must in order to appear strong and remain in this man's good favor.

Not long after that, a large manor made of white plaster with a tile roof came into view. It was surrounded by trees; however, I caught glimpses of gleaming plaster, and the golden windows of dusk as we rode. Since the old church in the village was also made of white plaster with a red tile roof, it bore for me a reverential feel.

"Is this where I will stay and work?" I couldn't believe my good fortune.

"Indeed it is. You can stay here forever, if you desire." His hot breath played with the strands of hair by my ear, making my skin crawl.

"Whose home is this?" My whispered question was not immediately answered, so I spoke louder and asked again. "Who is the lord of the manor? What is his name?"

"Do you approve?"

I nodded, and added, "It's very lovely." Lovely, however, was inadequate. The sprawling multi-level home bade us approach through a tree-lined street. Mr. Ilse stopped to open the wrought-iron gate. Each bar twisted and spiraled upward. The top was crowned by an iron eagle perched and ready for flight.

Riding underneath a shroud of trees while sitting atop a charcoal Knabstrupper might have been like living in a fairytale if Jens were the rider. For a moment, I pictured myself as the little cinder-girl being carried to the home of her Prince Charming.

When the full view of the home appeared, like magic, from the shadow of trees, I gasped. Mr. Ilse stopped the horse. It pawed in the dirt, anxious, while he allowed me a moment to appreciate the view. The double front door appeared abnormally huge even from this distance. The home bore at least a ground level and a first story. The front with its white, plastered brickwork, squared and then came to a near-peak at top. It intimidated at this closer view.

Though it was much grander than any home I'd seen before, the manor's windowed depth lead me to believe this home bore the traditional U-shape, although I was certain the owner never worried about caring for his animals in the dead of winter. There would certainly be a host of servants for that. Tree-shaded grasses surrounded this home, and the bridge we waited near spanned an actual mote. A swan and her young cygnets glided across the water's surface.

The clip-clop of the horse's hooves walking steadily over the wooden bridge startled me out of my awe. Yet, instead of thrilled anticipation, a chill of dread trickled through me that I couldn't begin to explain. For a brief moment, the manor and the surrounding grounds took on a dark, menacing feel. My heart thudded its protest.

"Is this your house?" The question squeaked from my lips like a timid mouse's cry. I dreaded his response, though for some reason I knew the answer.

He stopped. "Indeed. I am your new employer. Unless, of course, you have somewhere better to go." He leaned sideways and regarded me with a stern eye.

Unable to verbalize a response, I shook my head, and we

continued. We veered to the right to a building I hadn't noticed before, far across the manicured lawn, and as large as my former home. I thought perhaps it was the living quarters for his hired help, and where I would stay.

When we neared the doors—they were the wooden doors of a barn although more decorative than any I'd seen—but instead of being a series of beams nailed to form the large wooden rectangles of a door, these doors rounded at the top, and the hardware hinging them to the barn was large and ornate.

The left side opened. Anders Jensen stopped and grinned at me like the morning sun.

His countenance had changed somehow. This was a very different person than the angry man who greeted me at my parents' old home. He was handsome in a way I hadn't remembered. My heart skipped a beat. I started to wave, and then let my hand down. Nej. Regardless of his smile, this was the man who had stolen my Book of Mormon.

He tipped his cap and walked forward. I clenched my teeth and turned my head.

"Anders, Zeus here has had double the burden this past hour; see that he gets double the oats." Before I had time to react, Mr. Ilse grabbed my waist with both hands and handed me down to this Anders—this thief.

"Good day, Berta Erichsen." He regarded me with a playful twinkle in his eye before setting me on the ground. "It seems the goose has come willingly to the fox's lair."

What did he mean by his goose and fox remark? Did he consider himself a fox? If so, I already knew to stay far away from him and his so-called lair.

I returned his remark with a sniff of indifference. But, when I saw that Mr. Ilse had already walked half-way to his house, I became confused. Was I to stay in the barn?

The smirk of self-importance on Anders's face irritated me.

"He expects you to follow him. That is unless you'd like to board in the loft, but I must warn you that's where I room." He winked.

His feign of innocence was more irritating than his smirk. I grabbed my travel bag, which had been left sitting on the ground, and marched off without another word, hoping to stay far away from Anders and his fresh remarks. Mr. Ilse stood at a side door acting impatient for my arrival so I ran the remaining distance.

"Your room is off the kitchen." Mr. Ilse led the way inside.

"Isn't that where the lead cook stays?"

"I only require one cook, and her husband works elsewhere." His mouth pinched together in annoyance. "One day I'll have him too. But for now Tovi Jensen prefers staying nights at home with her husband."

"Jensen?" Surely it wasn't the Jensens I'd stayed the night with. It was too far away.

"You have a problem with the name Jensen now?" Mr. Ilse regarded me impatiently.

"Nej. Nej, of course not." I stepped back. "Your other servants—do they also sleep in the room behind the kitchen?" Having a room to myself in this large manor terrified me.

"My other servants stay on the other side of the kitchen. There are more rooms there, and the large oven also helps to warm them in the winter. The lass who stayed here quit without so much as a word." He huffed. "I should hunt the woman down and have her flogged. My home has grown into quite the state of disarray in her absence." He glowered as he eyed me up and down.

Flogged. He'd said it again. Would he then, flog someone who dared annoy him? I chewed a nail and once more felt the tingling motion of my skin crawling.

"You won't disappoint me though. Will you?" He smiled, but not a friendly smile, and touched my elbow.

I shook my head already knowing I should not want to displease this man.

"Quit chewing your fingernails." He slapped my hand away from my mouth. "It's a disgusting habit." He glared down the tip of his nose. I tensed with the shock of his action and clasped my smarting fingers behind my back. He gave a nod and then once again started walking.

I hurried along behind him. Even so, my heart squeezed with trepidation. "Surely one of the other women in your employ will share my room." How could I sleep alone in a house with a grown man?

He turned and regarded me sternly. "As I told you before, I'm a gentleman. You needn't worry about your virtue." Glancing up and down my person, he scoffed. "You're barely more than a child. No, I'll not touch you inappropriately, and no one in my employ would dare." He turned and continued.

I started to protest his description of me but promptly closed my mouth and followed.

The kitchen had an amazing array of copper pots hanging from the ceiling—most of them bigger than anything we had at home. My fingers swept across a wooden counter made especially for chopping food, and I breathed a whiff of freshly baked bread.

The warm tangy aroma of sourdough sent me home to the last loaf Mama baked. We were in the kitchen pulling it from the oven. Catie, Mary and Ana were laughing with Papa at the dinner table. I missed a step. My memory vanished, and I held to the counter, embarrassed.

Mr. Ilse stood in an open doorway straight-faced and giving no indication he'd seen. I inched past him, wondering if he'd be true to his word or if he'd grab me and take advantage of the nearby bed. I closed my eyes and took a deep breath to calm myself. I was a stranger here, and tired. Things would be better in the morning. They had to be.

"Did your parents not teach you any manners?"

"Sir?" I stood in the bedroom and held the door as a guard in front of me.

He clenched his jaw, working something around in his mind. "There's a bowl and fresh water in the pitcher. Freshen up and meet me in the breakfast room. I'll allow you to dine with me." He started to leave.

"But, sir." My eyes, I knew, widened in fear and disbelief, but the action had come before I could stop.

"You are hungry. Don't deny it." He leaned forward in challenge. "You treat me as though I've stolen you from friends and family instead of saved you from the streets. I'll not be treated as a letch in my own home!" His neck reddened. "You said you'd be obedient to your employer, and so far you've questioned my every move and my every motive. It's tiresome, girl. I've given you no reason to fear me, and if you can't be civil, I'll be forced to call the authorities on the morrow." He crossed his arms in front of his chest and scowled. "Well?"

"I'll be out directly." I curtsied and offered what I hoped was a friendly smile.

He nodded, satisfied.

I shut the door and leaned against it, my heart fluttering like a little bird.

When I finally pulled away from the door, I went to the bed and sat there. The stucco wall was slightly rounded, and warm. The room was directly behind the large oven. I put my cheek against the wall. This would keep the occupant warm on cool evenings. Certainly I wouldn't still be here when the weather chilled.

What would become of me?

Aunt Thora had said they didn't sell stamps in Vejstrup. Now that I thought on the situation, I wondered if the town merchants wouldn't sell Aunt Thora stamps because she had no money. I'd been foolish not to ask while I had a few coins to purchase one with. Perhaps Mr. Ilse would let me walk to Jorgensens' in the near future. Trembling in the dim evening light, I saw something against the opposite wall and went to have a closer look.

It was my chest! I opened it, half expecting to see Catherine's fabrics inside. There were a few blankets and a spare set of sheets. I closed the lid reverently, stroking the top and fingering the pretty flowers Mama had painted there as well as tracing Papa's carved scrolls.

I lay my face against it, feeling the cool wood and inhaling its scent while imagining I was at home with my family.

The peaceful feeling disappeared when I heard the floor creak outside of my door. I grabbed up my shoes. Wielding one like a weapon, I tip-toed to the door.

Chapter 13

"Herrer Ilse, I do not understand."

It was a woman's voice. She sounded upset. I put my shoes on and crept toward the breakfast room.

"There is nothing to understand," said Mr. Ilse. "The place has been set for another."

I peeked around the corner. Mr. Ilse was talking to a slip of a woman with grey hair.

"Sidsel. You have been good to keep me company these past years. I'll have Tovi send something to your room."

"Is it something I have done?" She appeared near tears.

"Nej, dear." He patted her hand between his, lifted it to his mouth and laid a kiss there. "Do not worry yourself so," he said, looking up and seeing me. "Ah, there you are. Come in." Mr. Ilse motioned me into the room.

I was hesitant to join in what seemed a personal conversation.

"Come." He motioned again. "Sidsel, this is our new maid. She will have supper with me tonight. You will help her learn her duties tomorrow."

"Ja, ja. Tomorrow." She curtsied for Mr. Ilse, then she turned to me, bristling with contempt, and hurried from the room.

"Your place is right here, my dear." Mr. Ilse pulled out a chair near his.

I gulped. Then I smiled and walked meekly to his side.

"Ah, your cheeks glow with the innocence of youth." He smiled magnanimously.

"Thank you, sir." Feeling at once uncomfortable, I stared

down at my empty plate.

"Surely a nice-looking child such as yourself is accustomed to receiving compliments from gentlemen."

I shook my head. "I'm not a child. I'm fifteen." I chewed my lip, not having intended to share that information.

"Fifteen." He rested his hand on his mouth in contemplation before speaking. "No wonder you're anxious to marry Master Larsen. You're just the age for believing in fairytales."

A fairytale and not a reality—how could he insinuate such a thing? I opened my mouth and then closed it. A middle-aged round woman, her hair braided around her head, came in carrying a plate with a loaf of bread resting under a linen dinner napkin. This was the cook and not the Frau Jensen I'd stayed with. Although I hadn't expected her to be the same person, it was disappointing nonetheless.

"Sir. Dinner is ready," she said.

"That is most agreeable."

Upon his word, Frau Jensen brought out a wonderful feast. This supper was nicer than most Sunday meals at home. It consisted of warm sourdough bread with fresh butter, sugared new potatoes, and fried plaice on a bed of greens with a sweet-tart dressing. My mouth watered, and I took a bite. The fish was crispy, yet tender and flaky, and I wondered if Mama had ever had anything so delicious.

"Tell me a little about yourself." Mr. Ilse took his knife and fork, cutting his fish with exactness, and continuing to eat as though not the least interested in my reply.

Although I couldn't understand why he'd be interested, I had already questioned him too much on this day, so I contemplated what I could tell. "What is it you'd like to know?" I speared a piece of potato and put it in my mouth.

"Your likes and dislikes. It's important to know one's hired help."

"I very much like horses and helping Papa to plough the crops in summer, but I can also cook and sew." And then a memory of me and Catherine entered my mind. Before I could even think or stop myself, I uttered, "And I love to twirl in a field of hay that's just begun to flower, with little yellow butterflies flitting about my hands and waist." My eyes closed and I sighed while remembering the simple joys of my previous summer.

When I opened my eyes again, Mr. Ilse was watching me stoically.

"I miss my family." I shrugged a shoulder and wiped a tear from my eye.

"That's a poor lass." He patted my hand. "It must be terribly lonely without your family near."

By the end of supper I felt slightly more comfortable. Mr. Ilse was a shrewd businessman getting our property so cheaply, but he would be a good and empathetic employer. I hoped.

"Good night, my dear child." He scooted his chair away from the table and stood. "Tovi has gone for the night. Clear the table and wash these dishes. I'll see you first thing in the morn."

I felt too tired for work but nodded. "Ja, ja, Herrer Ilse."

He left the room as I pondered, was Frau Tovi Jensen the mother to Anders? I thought of his smoky blue eyes, and shook my head. Anders was a thief. What did I care who his mother was?

The empty room felt eerie as I stacked the plates and dishes. I jumped and turned at each noise and creak, and then I rushed to the dark kitchen. Fire from under the stove lit the room enough to reveal the nearby lantern. I lit it and then startled at the long shadows. Was someone there? Where were the other maids? I peered into the shadowed crevices but saw nothing.

Bless Frau Jensen. She left a kettle of hot water on the stove. I poured it in the sink and quickly scrubbed everything clean. I dried my hands on a towel, rushed through the opposite doorway and down the short hall.

When I got to my room, I closed the door and leaned against it, tired enough to slump to the ground and sleep right there on the floor. The handle felt old and smooth in my hand—there was no lock. Why? I opened the door and peered into the darkness. The hall was empty, or rather it appeared empty.

What if someone lurked around the corner? I closed the door, my heart thudding, and scooted my chest against it before removing my outer-garments and dressing in my nightclothes. Why couldn't I just have had one of the other maids stay in the room with me? I'd never had a room to myself before.

A noise startled me. I pushed the window curtains aside and looked into the black night. Could it have been an owl? My breathing was shallow and forced as I sat on my bed, leaning against the warm wall. With grandmother's quilt pulled up to my neck, I listened to every sound, waiting for some dreadful thing to happen.

Chapter 14

Water splashed in my face, awakening me. I sputtered and rubbed my eyes. Where was I? Mr. Ilse stood over me fuming like an angry rooster.

"I'll forgive the trunk in front of the door this once, but try to block me from my own home again and you'll rue the day you were born." He yanked me from bed.

I struggled to free myself.

"If I were the monster you believe me to be, I could have had you last night." He pulled me close and spoke into my hair, "Or now for that matter."

"Please. Don't!" I squirmed and protested. He wouldn't. Would he? His hot breath wisped against my neck.

"You're much too pretty for your own good." He pushed me hard.

I fell onto the bed. Trembling, and grateful that I'd been released from his lecherous embrace, I scampered to the corner and grabbed my quilt to cover me.

"Get dressed, you lazy waif. Your day started half-an-hour ago." He strode to the door. "You can forget about breakfast. If you don't improve before the day's end, you can forget about supper as well." He closed the door behind him, leaving me to dress.

Despite my fear that he'd return even angrier than before, I could not make myself get dressed. I sat against the wall and stayed for a time under the safety of my grandmother's quilt, shivering. Tears fell off my nose.

Would he come back? I felt for Mama's necklace and opened the locket. My parents' faces smiled at me and I kissed them. "I love you." I closed the locket in my fist, placed them to my bosom and held them there until I could face my day with a small semblance of dignity. Before I dressed, I slid to the floor and called on the Lord for strength.

This man could have harmed me in shameful ways, but for whatever reason, he hadn't. I was thankful for that. Nevertheless, I needed to keep alert, do my best to please him, and stay out of his way.

I opened the door and left my room. Where was I to go? What was I to do? How would I get around without even knowing the layout of the house? My growling stomach led me into the kitchen.

Anders stood at the side door. "Good day," he said.

"There is still plenty of morning left," I replied, still shaken.

"Either way, it's a good day, ja?" He tipped his cap and headed outside.

I'd had better days.

"Berta." Frau Jensen washed dishes at the sink. "Herrer Ilse is waiting in the parlor." She nodded toward the door.

"Is there a slice of bread or something I could have?" I asked hopefully.

"I am instructed not to give you anything for now."

"Oh." He was serious. What kind of man withheld food from his servants? I hurried from the room.

A young woman of approximately my age was in the hall dusting paintings and their elaborate wooden frames with a long feather duster.

"Good day." Noticing a bright red mark on her cheek I said, "What has happened?" I raised my hand toward the spot.

She turned away. "When you disappoint Herrer Ilse, we all suffer the consequences."

"You don't mean?" Had Mr. Ilse slapped her?

"You're trying to get me flogged now, are you?" She scowled and went back to her work.

"Has he hurt you before?"

She refused to acknowledge me further. I sucked in my breath and hurried into the parlor.

Mr. Ilse was there. "You have taken much too long," he said in an accusing tone.

My shoulders drooped. "I apologize." I curtsied. "Since I am new it takes longer to find my way," I said, though I hadn't gotten lost.

"I've put off my business for the day in order to show you your duties." He rocked on his heels impatiently.

"Thank you, ja, thank you." I curtsied. He must be very meticulous on how things were done to take time off rather than have someone else show me.

He nodded once, seeming satisfied. "First, I'll take you on a short tour of the manor." He indicated the direction from which I'd come. "Your room, of course, is situated in the nethermost corner of the right wing, behind the kitchen."

He strode through the opposite door without another word. I tagged along like a lost puppy, wary of upsetting him more.

The pantry, as large as mine and Catherine's room back home, and the laundry area—which included a large barrel for soaking soiled things, rows of wooden racks for hanging sheets and clothing to dry, a fireplace, several irons and a shelf with rows of clean and folded linens—were incredible in size and neatness.

"You're acquainted with the breakfast room, of course. This is where I eat my informal meals."

He led the way through the room, his hands clasped behind his back.

It seemed even more wonderful than I remembered and was

papered in pastel green with grey brocade print. The same girl I'd seen dusting paintings was now pouring oil into a decorative lamp that sat on a corner table. Though she didn't stop her work, she inclined her ear as Mr. Ilse began talking, telling me the history of the manor and the important people he'd entertained through the years.

Once he'd finished, he nodded once, turned and left the room.

"Sofie." Mr. Ilse greeted the woman sweeping the floor.

She curtsied and hurried through the opposite doorway.

I followed this strange man through room after room feeling increasingly inadequate in this position as maid. Would I be able to keep the wall of books in his library dusted and clean? I didn't know the first thing on the proper care of his marble-floored entryway. Could I keep the imported crystal vases clean without breaking them? And, how did one care for antique tapestries?

Wall after wall was papered in the most exquisite papers, some had a fuzzy textured print—could they be washed? Then, as I looked at the ceiling in the dining hall, I felt the total ineptness of my farm-girl status. With my hand on a mahogany dining table that I imaged was large enough to rival the king's, I peered up at a light-fixture made of delicate crystal baubles. A chandelier.

On the first floor, directly above the sitting room, was the master bedroom. "I have a desk here, too," he said, "and since I take pleasure in the view from my window, I often bring my work here."

I walked to the window and peered out. A fleeting thought entered my mind, of Anders. I shook it off, frustrated. I should not think of Anders when it was Jens I would marry. It was because Anders had my scriptures, I decided.

"It is a lovely view," I said. Mr. Ilse could see the front courtyard and down the tree-lined lane and therefore anticipate a visitor's arrival.

"Ja, ja," he said. Moving beside me he rested his hand on my shoulder. "Though it is no less than I deserve. I have worked hard and have earned my special regard." He then led me by the arm, in a too familiar way, to the other end of the room and through a door. "The cost of modernizing the toilet room is prohibitive, but one day." He smiled. "One day."

The room with a tub for bathing, tiled in small square white tiles, was nicer than anything in my home. My knees wobbled a little when I thought of the responsibility of caring for a place such as this. It was daunting. Yet I'd gladly work in a hovel if the employer would keep a respectable distance.

"Sidsel," he bellowed. He turned to me, muttering, "She keeps me waiting, and who knows what she does when no one is watching. It couldn't be work."

The same petite woman with graying hair from the previous night hurried into the room and curtsied. "Herrer Ilse."

"You remember Berta. Teach her well. She may replace you one day." He turned to me. "This is your duty, keeping my room and toilet room clean and fresh, helping Sidsel with all first floor duties, as well as other things as needed." He began walking across his room fully expecting us to follow, I was sure, but Sidsel held my arm.

"Herrer Ilse calls me what he wishes. You may call me Frau Olesen."

"Of course." I gave a polite curtsy.

I'd heard it was commonplace for wealthy landlords to call those beneath them by their first names, but had never experienced the separation of classes until today. I found it rude and disrespectful. A person was a person, and I would give the older maids their due respect. I hurried to Mr. Ilse, but he stopped too suddenly, and I bumped him. "Oh, pardon," I said.

"You have a question," he accused.

"Nej." I shook my head. "Nej question." I curtsied and kept my curiosity silent. Mama and Papa always encouraged questions. Here, I didn't dare take one step out of line. The withholding of meals, a slap of the cheek, flogging—I didn't wish to experience more of his ire.

"Get to work. Everything you need will be found in the supply room off the kitchen." He turned and left the room.

Where was Frau Olesen? Mr. Ilse had just put her in charge of me. How did I know what to do without her? I peeked out the door. From across the way, I saw Mr. Ilse and Frau Olesen sharing a personal moment. He caressed her cheek and rubbed his thumb across her lip. They were in love. I would give them privacy and headed down the stairs. I could do some things on my own. Without instruction.

The minutes ticked away as I walked and alternately ran from the first floor down to the ground floor and then to the supply room. I grabbed a broom and a duster and hurried back up to the first floor.

Sweeping took until the noon hour, and at no time did I see Frau Olesen. At no time did anyone tell me what I should be doing. I had an inkling of Frau Olesen's resentment, but why did the other wait-staff avoid me with glaring eyes?

With the grandfather clock ticking the minutes away and reminding me to work in all haste, my stomach growled also reminding me it wanted fed. I held my dusting pan full of debris in one hand taking care not to spill, the broom in the other, and marched to the kitchen hoping that Frau Jensen had reserved a morsel for me. I did not like working on an empty stomach.

"Have you cleaned the master's room yet?" Frau Jensen stood at a big wooden chopping table preparing the vegetables.

"Nej. It didn't look dirty, and smelled perfectly fresh." I sat on a stool and reached for a carrot.

She snatched it away. "Master Ilse is very particular on how his home is cleaned, and he expects his toilet room freshened first thing every morning. Making his bed daily is next. You're to change his bed sheets every week." She handed me one slice of pumpernickel bread and the crock of butter. "Did Frau Olesen not explain your duties?"

"Nej. I have not seen her." I buttered my slice. "Only when Herrer Ilse introduced us." Thankful for its thickness and density, I started to take a bite.

"I am not so surprised." Frau Jensen held my arm gently from my mouth. "However, it's been a week. You'd best get up the stairs and change those sheets.

"Now?" My shoulders sagged. I would starve before making it to his bedroom.

"Be sure to eat that before going up the stairs. Herrer Ilse should be here any minute, and he'll go straight to his room to freshen for his noon meal. There'll be hell to pay if he finds you with that, or if you're negligent."

Believing in the truth of her words, I hurried and ate it before dashing from the kitchen and hurrying up the stairs. It wasn't until I got all the way to his room and had pulled the old linens off that I realized that I'd forgotten to bring the clean linens with me. "Great, dashing egrets!" I exclaimed, then I slapped my hand over my mouth, furious with myself.

Scooping the dirty linens into my arms, I started for the door and was nearly there when I bumped into something hard. It knocked me off balance and I took several steps back in order to gain my footing.

"Herrer Ilse." I went to curtsy, but so overloaded were my arms that the linens fell from my grasp. "I'm so sorry." I lunged to the floor and grappled with my load. As soon as I grabbed up one part and set about to grab the rest, it would fall from my hands again. My face burned with shame.

He grabbed my elbow and pulled me to my feet. "I see you need more detailed instruction on carrying out your duties."

Keeping hold of my arm he escorted me to his bathing room.

"See this?" He pointed to a square door in the far corner.

"Ja, I see it." My heart thudded. I resented being treated like a child or simpleton. If this door were an important part of my duties, why hadn't Frau Olesen pointed it out?

He opened the door. It was empty. I shrugged then stepped closer and peeked inside. There was no bottom to the cupboard. It was a square hole with a dim light coming from below. I looked at Mr. Ilse, questioning.

"This is the laundry chute. Rather than traipsing through my home with large bundles of soiled laundry, use this." He scowled. "It goes straight to the laundry room." He strode to the doorway. "Sidsel!"

She came running to him, smiling and straightening her hair. "Ja, ja, Herrer Ilse. May I help you?"

"Have you not instructed Berta on the proper execution of her chores?"

"Ja, Herrer Ilse." She stared at me. "Your room and toilet room should be cleaned first. The soiled linens go into the laundry chute." She pointed to it.

"How do you explain that it is noon and she is just now getting to my room?"

"She told me she could handle it." Frau Olesen put her hands on her hips and glared at me. "I left to clean the fireplace in the formal hall." She blew at an unruly hair on her forehead.

This woman was full of lies. With each word from her mouth, I became more and more indignant. Mr. Ilse turned to me, expecting my response. My mouth opened to expose her lies—and then it closed again. I had to work with this woman. Then I saw something behind her that I hadn't noticed before.

"Where does this door lead?" I walked to the doorway and then sought their approval. Maybe I should know about it, too.

The color left Frau Olesen's face.

Mr. Ilse's eyes darkened.

My hand hovered over the doorknob. Instinctively I braced myself.

"It's none of your business where that door leads." He stormed out. Both of us followed. "This lass is even more inept than the last," he murmured. "Why do I keep hiring girls that don't know how to work an honest day?"

Frau Olesen sidled up to him. "She is too young and inexperienced, ja. She has never cared for a beautiful home like yours, but all these years I have not let you down."

While relieved that I hadn't experienced Mr. Ilse's fury, their comments were unfair. I decided to prove them wrong. Mama would expect it of me. I knew how to work hard, and although I'd never worked as a servant, nor was I familiar with the workings of a large manor such as this, I would soon learn.

Frau Olesen smirked. "Good day, Frøken. Be sure to fulfill your duties or you are the one who will be out on the street." With her nose in the air she sashayed down the hall and away from me.

"I did not come here to take over for you," I called to the irritating woman. "How do I know why Herrer Ilse said such a thing?" Then, after scooping up the dirty linens and shoving them down the chute, I ran down the stairs and to the laundry room. I stared at the basket under the chute filled with his dirty linen and peered upward through the tunnel. It was an amazing invention. After gathering the appropriate supplies, I ran up the stairs and finished his room.

The rest of my first week was no better. Only Frau Jensen was kind. Mr. Ilse loved to touch and fawn and then blame me for thinking he was being inappropriate. Frau Olesen sought out Mr. Ilse on many occasions, sharing secret glances and special moments. She loved to get me in trouble for not doing things I hadn't known I should be doing. The other servants, Frau

Claussen and Helsa, behaved as though I was leprous.

Occasionally I peered out Mr. Ilse's side window, lonely as the nightingale's song, watching Anders and thinking of his kindness toward me. It wasn't fair that he'd shown kindness by ensuring I had Grandmother's quilt since I was set to dislike him for all eternity for taking my Book of Mormon.

Chapter 15

Frau Jensen quickly became a friend and a great help. She stood over a pot of some delicious-smelling concoction as I came to the kitchen.

"You are so kind. Thank you for your direction." I curtsied. "Frau Olesen is supposed to guide me, ja, but she only scowls and tells lies to Herrer Ilse." I took the handkerchief from my apron pocket and wiped my sweating brow. We didn't have stairs at home. Chasing up and down the stairs of this large manor took some getting used to. "She does not even know me yet she pretends to dislike me." I started to mention Frau Olesen's relationship to Mr. Ilse but held my tongue. Mama didn't like gossip.

"This is why I live elsewhere." Frau Jensen smiled. "It keeps me away from such nonsense." She filled the ladle from the water barrel and handed it to me. "Inge, the young girl you replaced." Frau Jensen wiped her hair back. "The other maids thought she was after Herrer Ilse and his money. She went back to Bornholm hoping to salvage her reputation."

"This is terrible." I leaned against the cutting board. "Will they start this rumor about me as well?" People here knew my parents. I could not tarnish their good name.

"My advice is to make friends quickly, before they decide why you're here. This is especially true since Herrer Ilse has grown tired of being alone."

"It seems they have already judged me, though I am not after his money. I came back for Jens Larsen." My heart skipped a beat at the mention of his name. "We will be married soon."

"Now who's the one telling stories?" She chuckled, and grabbed a large bowl from the cupboard. "Off with you. I've got work to do and so do you."

"Ja, ja. The toilet room, his bedroom—what is next?" I put the ladle back in the water barrel. "Does he have a preference for the rest of the upstairs?"

She eyed me critically, and I knew I should have my schedule memorized by now. "Frau Olesen is supposed to help, ja, but caring for this big house is new to me, and she gives no help at all."

"Dusting. Every room, every day. You're behind schedule because that, too, should be complete before the noon hour. Start with the grand hall and sitting room."

"Will there be time for seeing Jens Larsen?" I crossed my fingers behind my back. Each night I'd fallen exhausted to my bed and slept till morn. "He does not yet know I have stayed for him."

"The son of Iver and Helga Larsen?"

"Ja, ja. Those are his parents." I was pleased she knew them.

"You are serious?" Frau Jensen frowned and clucked her tongue. "You are naïve. The Larsens live on the other side of the village proper. Life has recently been in their favor, and they are anxious to live in a more elevated style. As for you, cleaning the walls of soot and doing the laundry will keep you too busy to follow dreams such as those."

"He loves me, and I love him," I insisted. "We will be married." Why did no one believe this? Irritated, I bobbed a curtsy and ran to the supply room.

"That girl has an imagination, she does." The sound of Frau Jensen's skeptical chuckle followed me. After grabbing a feather duster and running to the grand entry hall, I began dusting with fury, hoping upon hope to finish before noon.

"Dear, dear child." Mr. Ilse stepped into the room. "Must I also instruct you on dusting?" He huffed in exasperation.

"Nej." I curtsied. "I know how to dust. I am merely behind in my duties." I started dusting faster.

"Stop." He put his hand on my arm. "You'll break a priceless vase at this rate. We must not rush through our chores."

My spirits dropped, and I looked down. The floor needed

mopping. At this rate I would be out in the streets by month's end just as Frau Olesen predicted.

"You will treat my things with great care, ja." His voice sounded uncharacteristically soft, but I heard the demand there.

Too humiliated to look him in the eye, I nodded.

"Go and retrieve a cotton dusting cloth, and I will show you a little trick I learned from my dearly departed wife, God rest her soul."

I curtsied when I left and again when I came back with the requested cloth. However, instead of merely instructing me, he stood behind me, the side of his head touching mine. The moment he touched me, I sucked in a breath and stiffened, my heart almost stopping. I took slow breaths hoping to calm myself and not anger him.

He placed his left hand gingerly on my shoulder, and with his right hand over mine, directed the cloth in a circular motion around the right side of the cherry-wood table.

Helsa came into the room and stopped upon seeing us. She curtsied, and her mouth opened and then clamped shut.

"He is helping me to dust," I said, bursting from his grasp.

Mr. Ilse straightened. "Now, see? Isn't this much better?" The corner of his lip turned up.

I nodded, upset that Helsa had seen Mr. Ilse treat me in this manner; though my legs nearly collapsed underneath me with the relief of being loose.

"Helsa?" His eyebrows lifted.

"Herrer Ilse, it is very nice, ja." She curtsied and ducked away.

The moment she left, he slid the lace doily to the right side of the table and repeated the process. His idea of gentlemanly behavior was different than mine.

"The cloth is for exquisite wooden tables, the duster for draperies, fine art, and windowsills."

His nearness gave me shivers. Once again I forced myself to remain calm. Yet, when he released me I felt my cheeks heat.

"Pardon me if I've upset you." A brief, self-satisfied smile passed across his face. "I forget you're so young, and a country girl at that."

I frowned at his condescending tone. Everyone I knew lived outside of one of Denmark's villages, with the exception of Aunt Thora. Peasants, farmers, country folk—whatever he wanted to call us. We'd all managed life well enough. And Mr. Ilse already knew I was not a child.

"The glow in your cheeks is very charming." He smiled fully and played with an errant strand of my hair before tucking it behind my ear. "I've decided to allow you to sup with me each night." He waited, brows lifted, thinking I might say something.

I didn't. Though my very being protested his touch, his familiarity, I had nowhere else to go.

"Off to work. You've got much to accomplish before supper," he demanded.

At his word, I rushed away and was glad to do so. I worked hard all afternoon and was proud of my effort by suppertime. I'd dusted the upstairs, changed the linens, freshened his toilet room, and laundered his sheets.

As I knew he wished me to, I went to my room to freshen up. To my surprise, the pitcher was full of fresh water and a clean cloth was near my wash basin. Too tired to wonder who had served me thus, I washed and smoothed my hair before going to supper.

Mr. Ilse placed an empty ale bottle on the breakfast room bureau then met me at the entry. He took my hand and placed it on his arm.

I was his servant, not a special guest, and forced back a lump in my throat as he escorted me to my seat. Had he treated Inge this way?

"You look lovely." He raised his eyebrows in expectation.

"Thank you." My mouth lifted in a smile, and I straightened my apron.

"When someone gives you a compliment, it's polite to reciprocate." He waited pointedly.

"You look—" I wasn't sure what was polite. Lovely didn't work, and handsome didn't either—he was nearly Papa's age. "You look very nice as well." Anticipating an angry response, I wrung my hands under the table, but he was smiling, amused.

"I suppose that your family never gave nice little compliments to one another for their fine appearance?"

I bit my lip and shook my head. A person's handsomeness, or their lack of it, was not important to my parents. We were expected to work hard, play nice, and keep our bodies and minds clean of filth. We were praised for a job well done and encouraged to do our best. But I'd never heard Mama or Papa give any of us a compliment on beauty.

People couldn't help their looks, and the idea of complimenting someone for something they had no control over was silly. I held back a smile.

"Does this amuse you?" His voice had grown serious.

"I am sorry. Nej." My fingernail went into my mouth, but as his hand lifted to slap mine, I jerked it out and sat on my hand.

Frau Jensen brought our meal then, and I was glad because Mr. Ilse turned his attention to her. "Tovi, you've outdone yourself with this soup."

"Thank you, sir." She nodded her appreciation and left the room.

We ate that night on beef soup with potatoes, and peas from the hothouse served with fresh, plump rolls. If it weren't for all the running up and down stairs, I might grow plump eating such fine meals every day.

"You say you're a grown woman of fifteen." Mr. Ilse watched me with an arrogant eye.

I nodded and stared at my lap.

"Would you care to put away your milk then and join me in a glass of wine?" He took a nearby goblet and lifted his bottle to fill it.

Although nervous to object, I shook my head. "I much prefer the milk, thank you."

"Who would waste fine wine on someone who doesn't appreciate it?" He lifted his glass. "*Skol*," he said, and drank it down. He gave a satisfied smile. "Does this have anything to do with that strange religion your parents joined?" He followed his question by drinking straight from the bottle.

"It is true that as Mormons we do not drink any type of alcoholic beverage," I said, wondering if he would drink the whole bottle in one breath. "However, my family didn't drink alcohol even before we converted."

He set the bottle down. "Why ever not?" He appeared incredulous. "A good shot of hard liquor is a necessary escape now and then."

I slipped my thumbnail between my teeth, observing the pattern on the wallpaper as I thought. My response would anger him.

"Answer me, girl."

"My parents both believe that only fools give themselves away in such a manner." I looked him in the eye, my heart thumping. "That even wise people do foolish things under the influence of alcohol."

"I understand their views," he said, unshaken, "but apparently they don't understand. The whole point of drinking is that most folk enjoy being able to cut loose and do that foolish thing once in a while." He picked up the bottle and drank until it was empty. "Nonetheless, I hope you aren't so boorishly candid with the Larsens, since they enjoy a good drink with friends, as do I, and since I've invited them over to sup with us this Sunday."

I jumped up. "Jens is coming for Sunday dinner?"

"Iver and Helga do have a son named Jens. Do you know him?" The corner of his lip lifted as though he teased me.

"Know him? I plan to marry him!" Before I knew it, I'd reached over and hugged him tight around the neck. "Thank you, ja, thank you."

"How about a small token right here?" He pointed to his cheek.

I hesitated only a brief moment then rewarded his kindness with a peck. My neck and ears heated from the awkwardness of it.

Chapter 16

"Herrer Ilse." I shook him. He responded with a snort. "Herrer Ilse, wake up." I shook him again. The wine had gotten to him quicker than I would have imagined.

I hurried down the corridor to Frau Olesen's room and banged on the door.

Her face peeked through the crack. "What do you want?" she growled.

"Herrer Ilse. He's passed out in the breakfast room. I need help getting him up and to his room."

"He got himself in that condition. He can get himself out of it. Let him sleep where he is." She closed the door.

I banged on Frau Claussen's door. "Help me get Herrer Ilse to his room. He had too much to drink."

"You're one to be bossing me around. Get yourself to it." She closed the door as well.

"Helga, come help me, please." I banged on her door.

"I'm in my night dress," she shouted from the other side of the door. "I'm not helping anyone, least of all you."

Would no one help? I went back to the breakfast room, tsk-tsking at their unwillingness, and watched Mr. Ilse snoring from the doorway. Would he flog me for leaving him there all night? It was summer so he wouldn't be too chilled, but he would sleep much better in the comfort of his bed.

Mr. Ilse's hand was in his soup bowl. I lifted his hand and removed the bowl. Then, taking his napkin, I wiped the remnants of soup from his fingers. He snorted but otherwise didn't stir, so I cleared the table, put the food away, and took the dishes to the kitchen. It would be a long night by the time the dishes were done and the kitchen clean. Nevertheless, I left the kitchen in disarray and went to the stable. Mr. Ilse needed help. My parents would not be proud if I left him there all night.

"Anders," I called toward the loft. "Anders." How I hated having to ask his help. He came down the steps in a ridiculous nightshirt and cap. I held back a smile.

"What do you want?" His brows furrowed with suspicion.

"Herrer Ilse has had too much to drink. He is passed out in the breakfast room and I cannot get him up the stairs and to his own room by myself." I put my hands on my hips. "Will you help me to do it?"

"Of course." He turned away, and I thought he was mocking me, but he continued, "Only let me put my pants on."

He came out a moment later. "The other women would have left him there till morn. What does it matter to you?" He walked to the stable door.

"Do you not want to help then?" I hurried to keep up.

"I am glad to help." Anders stood at the door, waiting for me to pass through, and closed it behind us. "I wouldn't want to be a woman in his employ, but as far as I'm concerned, he's a good employer. He drinks too much because he is lonely since his wife passed on."

"Has it been long?"

Anders opened the side door and we went into the manor. "She passed shortly after I started working here. It's been nigh on three years."

We went into the breakfast room where Mr. Ilse was still sleeping at the table.

"Master Ilse." Anders shook him.

"Mmph," he responded.

"We're going to help you to your room." Anders put Mr. Ilse's arm around his shoulder. "Get on his other side," he said. "Get under his arm. It'll be easier."

I did as Anders said, and together we lifted Mr. Ilse to his feet.

"Come now," said Anders. "Let's get you up those stairs."

"Ja, ja," Mr. Ilse mumbled, taking an awkward step.

Although he was too intoxicated to walk on his own, through our help and encouragement, we were able to get him to his room. When we lowered him onto his bed, and as I was maneuvering myself out from under his arm, he took me into his embrace, rolling backward and onto his side.

"Dorte. My sweet Dorte. You have come back to me at long last," he muttered into my ear. "I have missed you so."

"Nej!" I pushed against him, startled nearly beyond my capability to function. I pushed against him again. "Nej. It is me, Berta Erichsen."

Anders also tried prying him loose, but Mr. Ilse was very strong.

"Please," I begged.

"*Min lille kære*," Mr. Ilse, said and went limp.

I scrambled to my feet, shaking, and lost my balance. Anders steadied me. My heart beat furiously from the short-lived ordeal. "Oh, I was so worried," I said, finding respite in his arms. "If I'd had to stay there on the bed with him till he awoke ... oh—" I grasped my hands to my chest. "What will become of me?"

"It is all well and good now," said Anders. "And Master Ilse will not have memory of it on the morrow."

"That is a relief," I said, inhaling Anders's earthen scent. "How could I remain here if he remembered calling me his little dear?"

"Let us remove his shoes and stockings, and cover him with a quilt." Anders guided me to stand on my own, away from him.

"Oh, of course." My face heated with the realization that I'd been clinging to him. "My apologies."

We did as Anders suggested, with Anders's comfortable manner eventually putting me at ease.

"It is well now and he will rest comfortably," said Anders as we left the room and started down the stairs. "You may go to your room now happy in the knowledge that Master Ilse is cared for."

"When I get to my room." I nodded. "I've an hour's worth of work in the kitchen before that is possible."

"Why is that?"

My arm rested on the banister, and I stopped. "It is as you said. It is difficult being a woman in his employ. Herrer Ilse is a lonely man. He requires that I have suppers with him in the breakfast room." A look of judgment passed over Anders's face, so I continued. "It is not a scheme of mine to earn his household. Nor is it by my design. Herrer Ilse requires it of me as a condition of my working here."

"Ja, ja. What has this to do with the kitchen?"

"Frau Jensen prepares supper and returns home to her own family. It is my duty to clean up after supper." I walked toward the kitchen. "Is Frau Jensen not your mother?"

"Nej. Not Herrer Ilse's Frau Jensen." He turned the knob on the lantern, lighting the kitchen with its glow. "And, perhaps none of the other Frau Jensens in all of Denmark."

He pushed past me. "Now, my little dear." He grinned broadly. "Nej, my Danish rose. Let us clean this kitchen."

I opened my mouth, dumbfounded with his cheekiness. "I am not ..." I trailed off not feeling nearly as offended as I should be.

"Let me help, and you can explain to me why you are here in Denmark without any family. Is it a practice among Mormons to leave their family?"

"Nej. Not at all," I said, feeling defensive of my religion.

As I reheated the water and began cleaning the kitchen, I explained to Anders about my religion and how we highly esteemed families. Always, in the back of my mind I retained the memory that he had my Book of Mormon, but for whatever reason I did not feel inclined to accuse. Instead, I poured out of my heart the testimony that I had hoped to share with Jens. It felt comfortable doing so, and Anders, as he helped with the dishes, encouraged me with honest questions.

"What I don't understand—since you love your family so— why did you not follow with them to America?" Anders leaned against the frame of the manor's side entry, preparing to leave.

The honest answer to this question had only won me ridicule. I chewed on my lip.

"Why do you hesitate?" Anders quirked a half smile. "Is it something bad? I cannot imagine."

I heaved a sigh, and began. "If you must know, I stayed because I love a man named Jens Larsen. He proposed by saying that if I stayed he would bring me home to live with him."

"That does not sound like a proposal."

"But it was. Look," I said, showing him the amber ring on my pinkie finger. "He gave me this ring."

Anders studied it. "It is a very pretty ring," he said. "Why do you not wear it on your finger meant for engagement?" He lifted my right hand, stroking my fingers. It sent a thrill up my neck. I shook the feeling away.

"He knew it was too small, and this is the finger he put it on when he said he loved me." I thought back, frustrated. He had implied his love, implied his intentions. "He loves me," I said, my voice raised. "I love him too. We will be married. We will."

"Ja, ja," Anders readily agreed. "I only hope when I find love, that I should make my thoughts and intentions more clear."

"His intentions were very clear at the time." I blinked back the rising panic that Anders's comments stirred. "I must bid you a good night," I said, a catch in my throat. "Thank you for your help and your company." I curtsied. "I am very tired."

"It will be a long day tomorrow," he agreed, and shut the door behind him.

I stared at the door as though it could reveal needed answers to me. I needed to see Jens. I needed to hear his voice, to hear that he loved me.

Chapter 17

Anders came through the side door and entered the kitchen. I'd already placed the pitcher of cream near my bowl of porridge on the small table in the corner. All the servants ate their meals there, as did Anders, though he'd usually eaten at a different time than I did.

"Good morning," he said.

"Good morning," I replied. His hair was combed and he wore a clean shirt and trousers, fit for the Sabbath day. "There is fresh porridge on the stove." The others, apparently, had made enough only for themselves. Their evidence lay in the sink, still dirty.

"There is only a little. Have you eaten?" He asked.

"Mine is here at the table, ja." I sat and poured some cream into my bowl.

Anders joined me, sitting on the opposite side. "Tell me something about this living prophet of yours. This Joseph Smith." He poured cream into his bowl and stirred the mixture with his spoon.

I had just begun explaining about Joseph Smith's martyrdom, and that we now had a new prophet whose name was Brigham Young when Mr. Ilse came to the door.

"Today is the Sabbath. Why are you not ready?" he asked, his hands on his hips.

"The others have left without me." I had asked everyone if they knew of a Mormon church in the area. If they knew, they would not say. Yet, because of this, they had begrudgingly let me attend services with them on the previous two Sundays. On this day, I was met with an empty porridge pot and a dirty kitchen.

"You will ride with me."

"I cannot," I said. My eyes, I know, were large with shock of his implication.

"I am the master of this establishment, and, regardless of your newfangled religion, you will do as I say." Mr. Ilse thrust out his arm, pointing his finger toward my room. "Now get dressed." His hand went to his forehead, and he groaned.

"I—I cannot go with you alone," I said, voice trembling.

"Alone?" Mr. Ilse jerked his head back and winced. "Heaven forbid. Anders here accompanies me each week. You will go with us. The others have gone on ahead, even that silly Helsa. Like a little mouse, that one. Skittering from room to room." He frowned. "You will see them there."

It was not that I cared to sit with them, but I did not like sitting alone. I looked from Mr. Ilse to Anders. He nodded, and so I curtsied. "Herrer Ilse, it will take only a moment." I curtsied again and ran to my room.

Perhaps if I came to services with Mr. Ilse, the townsfolk would be friendlier. Many of the folks at church were the very ones who'd treated me so spitefully when I'd first come back. Either way, I was anxious to worship in any way I could and glad for another opportunity to visit my grandparents who were buried in the churchyard cemetery there.

Last year's Sunday dress, worn but usable, was the best thing I owned. I put it on, grateful that I had it. Although I'd just fixed my hair, I took my work scarf off, took the braids out, and ran a quick brush through it before re-braiding my hair and donning my bonnet.

Though I didn't have a mirror, I pinched my cheeks and left the room. Mr. Ilse and Anders were no longer in the kitchen. I put the cream in the icebox and the bowls in the sink with the others.

I went out the side door and found them waiting in Mr. Ilse's cabriolet. He was sitting on the bench under the canopy still appearing miserable from the aftereffects of the night before. Anders sat in the front, reins in hand.

When I approached, Anders secured the reins in front of him, leapt out of the cabriolet and offered his hand as I stepped up to the front bench to sit beside him.

"Thank you," I said, pleased with his gentlemanly behavior. He'd been so pleasant these past weeks.

"It is all well and good," he replied. With reins in hand, he gave them a little shake as he clicked his tongue. The horses started their walk down the lane.

We hadn't made it to the gate when Mr. Ilse called out, "Must you drive over every rock and pothole in the lane?"

"I am trying to be careful," said Anders. He stepped down and opened the gate, leaving it open until our return.

While I had little sympathy for Mr. Ilse's current condition, I did sympathize with his broken heart and loneliness. Frau Jensen was correct. I should try harder to please him.

"Do you believe you will be thrust down to hell for worshiping with us instead of with the Mormons?" Anders kept his eyes on the road as he spoke.

While his comment held a twinge of accusation, it felt good to be outside, and I did not rise to his challenge. "How can worshiping the true and living God send anyone to hell?" I asked.

"You have a point." Anders smiled, his blue eyes sparkling. "The things I thought I knew about you Mormons …" he shook his head. "Well, I do not see any horns, but you are wearing a bonnet." The corner of his lip lifted.

"Horns?" I laughed. "You thought we had horns?" I untied my bonnet and turned so he could see the back of my head. "Do you see any?"

"Well, there is the beginnings of something right here." I felt his touch, and then he chuckled.

"You are such a tease," I said as I put my bonnet back on.

Anders was not the hateful, morally barren person that I'd secretly accused him of being. He was nice. I kept hold of the notion that he had my Book of Mormon. Yet, again, I felt prompted to not mention it to him, nor to ask for it back. We chatted and had easy conversation until we pulled onto the chapel road.

Mr. Ilse sat forward. "What took so long—are we late?"

"Nej," said Anders. "You have plenty of time."

We were quite on time for our worship services. Members of the congregation approached the church from every direction, some walking as families while others, like us, approached by carriage. The pastor and his wife were near the door, greeting people as they came.

Before converting to Mormonism, this church, with its white plaster and reddish tile roof had been the spiritual home and keeper of my family's faith for over a hundred years. It was nestled in the center of the cemetery, and the grounds were therefore immaculate. Grandmother and Grandfather Erichsen both lay within the tidily kept grounds just inside the gate.

"Let's get on with it," Mr. Ilse grumbled.

Anders pulled the horses to a stop. "Ja, ja." He stepped out of the cabriolet, tied the horses down and lent Mr. Ilse a hand. He climbed down and hurried toward the pastor.

"What has him so keyed up?" I asked.

"He likes to have time before services to visit with the pastor." Anders gave me a conspiratorial smile. "Truth is he likes to stand beside him and greet worshipers as they walk in. I think he might like to become a candidate."

"What?"

"I think he's interested in becoming a member of the Parish Council."

"Can he do that?"

"You know Mr. Ilse." Anders started toward the church. "He usually gets anything he puts his mind to."

As we walked into the churchyard, I left the main path and meandered in-between vines and headstones, and reading those along the path. "How are you, Absolon Jensen, born 1702; died 1753? And you, Nona Simonsen, born 1795. Died 1822. I hope you are resting well."

"What are you doing?" Anders followed behind me.

"Because I don't know them does not mean they don't enjoy a friendly hello." I smiled and nodded toward my grandparents' graves. "My grandparents are buried over here," I said softly. My heart swelled at the thought of revisiting their graves. I began walking again. It hadn't been so long, and I knew right where they were.

I smoothed the side of Grandmother's headstone. "I miss you Grandmother." I pulled an errant weed and put it in my pocket to dispose of later. "Are you happy? Have you found the gospel?"

Grandfather Erichsen rested beside her. I hadn't known him well and barely held on to one memory of helping him harvest when I was a child. Grandmother had lived on for seven years after his passing.

"Grandfather, Grandmother, do you remember me? You called me your *'meget lille* Berta.'" I wished them to remember me, to have family near who loved me, even though they had long ago left this earth. As I sat there, I felt at peace. It came as a whisper of wind through the ivy and rested around me, comforting me. My grandparents knew me and loved me, and I would see them again. I leaned my forehead against Grandfather's headstone. "I can't wait to know you better," I whispered.

"These are your grandparents?" Anders knelt beside me. "Will you introduce me?"

I wiped at my eyes. "Grandmother Erichsen, this is Anders. He is a good friend, ja, and a good person." I met his gaze and smiled. "Anders, these are my father's parents. Grandfather played the harmonica." I hadn't remembered until then. "Catherine and I used to dance to his music in the evenings." I touched

Grandfather's headstone feeling closer to him. "Grandmother made the best breads, and she taught Mama about roses."

"I am pleased to meet them." Anders stood and brushed at bits of moist earth on his trousers. "I will be right back, ja?"

I watched him walk to the other end of the churchyard and then returned my focus to my grandparents, arranging the ivy around their headstones and picking another weed or two.

"For your grandmother." Anders knelt beside me, handing me a beautiful pink rose.

"It is so lovely, Anders. Thank you." I inhaled the sweet scent and then intertwined the rose with the vine climbing up the side of her headstone. "It is time for services." I stood and brushed my dress. "If we don't go in …"

"Herrer Ilse." Anders nodded. "Things have to be done his way."

We walked together toward the old church. For me, it felt familiar and strange at the same time, having been years since our family had joined the Mormon Church. Pastor Østergaard, a tall slender man, waited at the door for us and several others. His wife and Mr. Ilse waited beside him. They had been out of town the past two Sundays helping his ill mother.

"Berta Erichsen. It is so good to see you." The pastor shook my hand with both of his.

Mrs. Østergaard met me with a long hug. "It has been too long, dear. We're glad to have you back."

"Ja, ja." I smiled. Grateful for their warm welcome, I stepped over the threshold and into the church.

"She works for me now." I overheard Mr. Ilse say. "The poor girl had nowhere else to go. Townsfolk can be so cruel sometimes."

Once we entered, the building was familiar with its high-backed wooden pews and religious symbols painted on the ends, but I knew this was no longer my church. Frau Olesen, Helsa, Frau Claussen and her husband, Nels, were sitting in a pew midway up the aisle but I did not wish to sit with them.

Frau Jensen was sitting with her husband, a rotund man with a graying beard. He looked like *Julenissen*—all he needed was a red stocking hat. I slipped in beside them, and patted the wooden bench for Anders to sit beside me.

Pastor Østergaard shut the door. He was dressed in the traditional black robe and white chasuble. It swished as he walked up the aisle.

I did not mean to ignore the pastor, but as soon as he stood at the front and began his sermon, my mind wandered to past lessons the missionaries had given and our final testimony meeting held before the emigration.

In the Book of Mormon, Nephi sailed to America with his family. He had trusted his life to the Lord as I had not. Had I made a mistake in staying? Nothing yet had gone as I'd expected. If only I had my Book of Mormon. It could be my rock. I needed something desperately, some way to keep my faith foremost in my mind. I needed the strength of my holy scriptures, the assurance of the gospel.

When I glanced up, Anders was watching me. I smiled, wondering. Had he read my thoughts? Though I wanted to ask about my book of scripture, the Spirit whispered, be patient. When had Anders's eyes turned so blue—his jaw straight and masculine? Had he always been this handsome?

"Berta?"

I startled in my seat and turned toward the voice of Frau Jensen. "Ja?" I felt heat creep up my neck and ears, though I couldn't begin to explain why.

"Services are over now. I'd like you and Anders to meet my husband." She put her arm around him. "Dear, this is Berta Erichsen and Anders Jensen. They also work with Herrer Ilse."

Mr. Jensen put his hand out and shook mine vigorously. "Alger Jensen. Pleased to make your acquaintance." He let loose of my hand and shook Anders's.

On our way back to the manor, I fell silent, thinking of my

grandparents and of Anders's kindness. Anders himself seemed quiet, though Mr. Ilse chatted endlessly.

Finally, I took a deep breath, determined to try harder to make conversation. "These fields are well kept. Are they yours?"

"Indeed. I own or lease the copyholdings surrounding my home farther than you can see in any direction."

"It is so much, and I have never seen you working in the field." Papa would be busy around the clock maintaining such largeholdings.

"I employ others to work the land." Mr. Ilse regarded me sternly as though I should know this. "It is my job to acquire other properties—largeholdings like your parents'."

I nodded, and fell silent again as I thought of my family.

Chapter 18

"Be sure the manor is extra clean. You know the Larsens are coming for dinner." Mr. Ilse stepped out of the cabriolet and went into the manor. I held back.

"May I help brush the horses down?" We'd had a nice morning, and I hated for it to end.

"Only if you will allow me to help clean the breakfast dishes." Anders quirked a grin.

"That is a good trade," I agreed, and hurried to keep up as he walked the horses into the barn with the carriages and tack.

Anders unhooked the horses, Zeus and Apollo. I held their reins while he took the cabriolet to its proper place.

"Will you start going to your Mormon church again?" Anders started unharnessing Zeus.

"I do not know if there are any more Mormons here," I confessed. "Everyone I knew who had converted went with Mama and Papa. Though if there were a church nearby, I'm not sure Herrer Ilse would allow such a thing as long as I remain in his employ."

"You do not plan to stay here until you grow old?" Anders took the harness and hung it on the wall.

"Nej. I cannot imagine such a thing." I rubbed Apollo's nose. "I've never been around Knabstruppers before," I said, desiring to talk of something else. "They're beautiful animals."

"About the emigrants," Anders said. "Were there others from other regions of Denmark who left at the same time?"

His interest sounded more than casual, but I couldn't imagine why. "I'm sure there were," I said. "Though I don't know for certain. Mama and Papa left from our home, and I waited there for the carriage to take me to my aunt's." Those were not fond memories.

He handed me Zeus's reins. "You hold him while I brush him down. I wouldn't want you to spoil your dress."

"Ja, ja," I agreed. "Jens Larsen is coming tonight for supper." I couldn't hide my excitement. "This is our first time together since my family left."

If Anders returned my Book of Mormon, I could give it to Jens this very night. Tapping my finger to my chin, I watched Anders while trying to convince myself to ask.

"It's a wonder you have time to spend in the barn. Perhaps you should get into the manor. Herrer Ilse expects it spotless."

His tone had changed. What did that mean? "Ja. Herrer Ilse does expect a spotless manor." I took the brush from him, smiling. "However, we made an agreement. I can't let you off that easily. Besides, I enjoy being around the horses. It reminds me of home."

Anders seemed to relax, and once again we enjoyed easy company as I helped him care for the horses.

"It is now my turn to help you." He put the brushes away and then we walked together out of the barn.

I curtsied, pleased with his manners when he held the stable door for me and then again as we went into the manor.

"Frau Jensen will be here soon to begin preparing this evening's meal." I shook my head at the mess. "We need to get busy." The breakfast porridge had hardened on the bowls and the cooking pots. It would take forever to clean them.

"Here is a trick I learned from my mother." Anders lit the flame under a pot of water. "We will heat the water and soak the dishes while we clean the rest of the kitchen. It will only take a minute to soften the oatmeal."

"This is a good idea." Though Mama seldom let food harden on the pans, I remembered occasions when she did this as well. "Perhaps we should trade places, ja. You can be Herrer Ilse's upstairs maid. I will work with the horses." I took a wet cloth and went to the table.

"Thank you. Nej," he said as he cleaned the wooden chopping table. "I much prefer the stables."

And then we were together at the sink. It seemed the air was charged with energy. My excitement for Jens's arrival must have been the cause. I touched my finger to the water, and pulled it right out. "It's still hot."

"Ja, but the oatmeal." He pointed to the bowl, smiling and satisfied. "All we have to do is wipe them clean. He stepped in front of the sink and pulled a bowl from the hot soapy water, cleaned it with the dishcloth, and handed it to me. I rinsed it in clean water and set it on a towel to dry.

Anders was in a good mood. He talked about the horses and how he loved caring for them. "I've been saving my money. With a little luck and a lot of hard work, I'll own land one day."

"That is a noble aspiration, and I can appreciate it," I said. "Do you wish to be like Herrer Ilse, or will you work the land yourself?"

Anders looked around to see if anyone was nearby, and murmured, "I will never be like Master Ilse, and I will work the land I own."

He chatted on about his aspirations. Though I enjoyed our conversation, I grew increasingly impatient. I wanted him to mention my religion. When he did, I would ask for my Book of Mormon. He was in a good mood, and he would return it. I thought of my prompting at the church but shook it away. I wanted my scriptures back.

He didn't mention my religion again. The kitchen was clean.

The dishes clean. Anders smiled. "It is time I left." He nodded and turned to the door.

"Only one more thing," I said, standing beside him. "I would like my Book of Mormon. Jens Larsen is coming tonight. I want to give it to him. He will read it and join our Church. Then we can be married." I smiled, eagerly anticipating the return of my book.

"You are naïve like a little girl." Ander's jaw clenched. "All signs point against you, and yet you continue believing your problems are solved by the reading of a book." He opened the door. "Life does not always end up how you want." He turned and stormed from the house.

"Just give me my book," I shouted at him. "He loves me, and he will read it. You will see."

He turned and glared at me. "I have seen many things, but that will not be one of them," he shouted back.

I watched, puzzled, as he went into the barn.

Anticipating. Nervous. I was unable to hold still and inspected my dress with a sniff here and there. It was still fresh. I glanced out the window. No one was there, of course. The Larsens weren't expected for hours yet.

I'd had such a good time with Anders. Why wouldn't he just admit he took my Book of Mormon and return it? I shook my head in dismay and walked down the corridor to the next room to answer Frau Olesen's call.

"You asked for me?"

"A spoiled child needs to clean the convenience room five times a day." She folded her arms across her chest.

"I beg your pardon?" Why would she say this? I had done nothing to deserve her ire.

"Take to the master's room. It can never be clean enough." She turned and left.

I contemplated changing into my work clothing, but it was my family's habit to honor the Sabbath by wearing our special clothing for the full day. This way we weren't tempted to do things that weren't Sabbath appropriate. I would make a light job of it so as not to spoil my dress.

On my way to the supply room I met Helga in the hallway. Her hair, a rich reddish brown, was braided and wrapped around her head. A scarf of muslin lay loosely over the top. It kept stray hairs from her face and kept the moisture off an overworked brow. Why she wore it on the Sabbath, I did not know.

"It is a fine morning," I greeted.

"You think you are Mistress of the Manor, but you are nothing." She stuck her nose up, and continued toward the front of the manor.

Mistress of the Manor? I was a servant like she was. I opened my mouth to speak but remembered her seeing Mr. Ilse instruct me on how to dust and kept back my unkind words. Instead, I watched as she rounded the corner before I went to the supply room.

It was wrong for her to judge me thus, but she had never been friendly.

I took the mop and bucket of water, and lugged them up the stairs while trying not to spill any on my dress. Why Frau Olesen insisted the convenience room be cleaned on the Sabbath was beyond my knowledge, but I washed the tile flooring and then the toilet. The floors in Mr. Ilse's room didn't need mopping, I'd just done it on the previous day.

Mr. Ilse's office was a mess. Had he been here? The cushions were all a-jumble. I rushed to each sofa and plumped the pillows, smoothing the fabric of each cushion while there.

With hands to my hips, I examined the room. There were

soot smudges on the gold frame above the fireplace. How did they get there? If Mr. Ilse saw this, there would be trouble. I took the handkerchief from my apron and wiped the frame with fury.

"Come away from there before you break something." Mr. Ilse stood in the doorway. He motioned to me. "Come."

Chapter 19

"Thank you for inviting the Larsens to supper. I am thrilled for their arrival!" I hurried along beside Mr. Ilse, trying to keep up with his long strides and almost tripping in the process. "Jens will be so surprised. I've dreamt of this moment since my parents left for America, and I wish he could have known sooner that I've stayed behind for him. Will Jens think I'm different?" I turned to him, worried. "Am I different?"

"Take a deep breath child. You're going to make yourself sick with all this nonsense."

We walked from the house and across the lawn—well, Mr. Ilse effectively pulled me—and then we were at the stables.

"I assume you know how to ride."

Anders, the liar and thief, met Mr. Ilse and bowed. He behaved as though I weren't there. I returned the gesture.

"Ja, ja. I can ride." I stopped, my arm sliding from Mr. Ilse's grasp. "But riding will soil my clothing." I frowned. Doing inside chores was one thing, but as much as I loved horses, riding one would make my dress smell.

"Since you're a country girl, I also assume you don't require a sidesaddle." He lifted an eyebrow.

"Nej. I've never used a sidesaddle." I'd only heard of them.

"Saddle up the roan for the girl, and saddle my horse as well."

Anders bowed and disappeared into the stable.

"But, sir." I loved horses, truly, but I did not want to meet Jens and his family smelling of horse. I took a step away, which was a mistake. Mr. Ilse took my arm and forced me beside him. His grip hurt.

"Must you argue and whine continually?" He shook my arm. "Nej. I'm the master of this house and you will do as I say."

"I'm sorry, sir." I curtsied, and remained still.

"The Larsens are important in this community, and I can't have you chattering like an excited two-year-old." He paced in front of me. "I really should have schooled you in your manners before inviting someone over, but what is done is done."

Anders led Zeus by the reins. I appreciated the horse's firm lines, long legs, and the plentiful spots across his back. Knabstruppers were fine animals, and expensive. He handed the reins to Mr. Ilse and came back with an aging roan. It was several hands taller than Caja, my Faroese. Anders tried to help me up, but I didn't want his help. Nor would I admit that I'd ridden mostly bareback.

Taking hold of the saddle horn, I tried putting my left foot in the stirrup but didn't quite make it.

"Here, let me help." Anders grabbed me by the waist and started to propel me upward.

Thinking he would throw me clear over, I wrangled from his grasp. "Unhand me, thief." My accusation shamed me as I saw him wince back.

Nevertheless, with my hands on the saddle horn, I made to complete the forward motion he'd started. Instead of flying over the horse, I didn't even make it up, and landed on the side of the saddle with a thud. The horse stepped nervously.

"Ow," I moaned.

"You're worrying the horse. Now let Anders help you up." Mr. Ilse frowned, impatient.

I knew not to argue and gritted my teeth while Anders took hold of my waist and set me on the saddle.

"Stubborn girl," Anders muttered under his breath. He

handed me the reins and walked to Mr. Ilse's side. "Do you need anything more, sir?"

"We'll only be gone a short time. She needs the exercise." He nodded toward me. Anders gave a smirk of agreement.

My face heated with embarrassment, and I turned away.

Unaccustomed to riding with wooden clogs, I let them fall from my feet and kicked the roan. She raced forward. Mr. Ilse had already made it halfway across the lawn.

I had to admire Mr. Ilse's riding ability. He handled his stallion with precision, and I had a hard time catching up.

We galloped across the moat and through one of his fields of hay. He stopped at a small pond and allowed his horse to drink.

"That was quite a ride." I pulled up beside him and the roan began quenching her thirst as well. "You are an excellent horseman."

"You do know how to give a compliment." He gave an easy smile and dismounted. "Come." He motioned for me to join him.

I slipped off the horse, surprised at the distance. With the reins in hand, we began walking around the pond.

"This was my Dorte's favorite activity on a Sunday afternoon."

"Riding horses is very agreeable." We seldom rode for pleasure at home. It was exhilarating.

"Sidsel is afraid of horses," he said. "She believes they are dangerous animals."

"Pardon? Oh, Frau Olesen." I'd forgotten her given name. "Perhaps she needs to start on a shorter horse, like a Faroese. They are gentle and very good companions." I missed my Caja and wondered what had happened to her.

"This is a good idea." He walked in silence for a time and paused near an ornamental ironwork bench and a small patch of flowers. "My Dorte loved this pond, and she loved flowers. I planted this after her passing." He gave a huff and plopped onto the bench. "I should have planted it while she yet lived. She had made her desires for beautifying the area known. I was too busy."

"It is very nice."

"Do you mind?" He gestured toward the bench, indicating his desire for me to sit with him.

"Thank you, ja," I said as I sat. If Jens were here, this would have been the perfect place for a romantic Sunday meeting. The flowers were in bloom, and a swan glided across the water.

Mr. Ilse pointed to a tree not too far distant. "We had picnics there."

"This is all very lovely," I said. "You must miss her very much."

He didn't respond right away and I began wondering his purpose in bringing me here. I glanced around nervously. We were completely alone.

He exhaled deeply. "It is time we get back."

"Ja, ja, suppertime is nearing." I squealed and jumped up. I hurried away and tried to mount the horse, but she was too tall. "May I?" I pulled her to the bench, hoping to use it as a stool.

"Allow me." He strode forward and had his hands around my waist before I could form an objection. "It is my every pleasure to be of service," he murmured into my ear.

My heart thudded, and I felt my face heat. "Ja, ja. Thank you, ja," I said nervously.

He gave a pleased smile as he lifted me into the saddle. "There you go," he said. He turned and mounted Zeus. "Let's see if you can keep up on the way back." With reins held high, he guided his horse from the water and began a full run toward his home. Once again I raced to keep up.

I don't know if Anders kept watch on us from a crack in the stable wall or if he merely heard us approach, but upon our return, he was outside waiting.

"You've bested me again." I pulled up beside Mr. Ilse and dismounted. The speed of our ride left me breathless. The last time I had ridden was to see Jens. My heart flip-flopped at that thought.

"As well I should," said Mr. Ilse. "I've had much more experience." He scratched his horse affectionately under the ears and rubbed its nose before handing the reins over to Anders. I hurried along behind Mr. Ilse as he walked to the manor.

"You'll need to freshen up, of course. I can't have you greeting my guests appearing as you do. Your hair is frightful. And whatever you do, try not to say anything if you can help it. I'll give you lessons on manners at some future date." He walked in the front door and closed it.

I stood on the step outside, humiliated at this treatment. One glance toward the stables showed Anders watching. He shook his head and went into the stable. I rushed around to the service entry.

What did it matter if Mr. Ilse didn't let me enter his home through the front door? I was his servant, after all. Despite that, he had requested the Larsens for supper. That in itself made up for his rough exterior. This is what I tried convincing myself when my mind turned to the red mark on Helsa's cheek, and the time he'd thrown water in my face.

Something in my room smelled. I sniffed my bed and the dresser. It was me. My blue dress and my nice white apron smelled of horse sweat. They needed a good washing but there was no time. There was only time for freshening up and changing into my other muslin working clothes.

The doorknocker echoed through the manor. My nerves tingled. Jens was here. I jumped up and rushed toward the entry hall while straightening my apron.

"Do you not have anything nicer to wear as you greet my

guests?" Mr. Ilse stood at the dining parlor entry. He wore a suit and tie and fancy black leather shoes.

I considered my plain clothes and bit back the disappointment of not being able to wear my blue dress. My drab yet sturdy working clothes contrasted hideously against my elegant surroundings.

The doorknocker pounded again. "I can't wait to see Jens," I said, clapping my hands and bouncing up and down.

"Remember." His bushy eyebrows pinched together and he stood over me like an angry schoolmaster. "Good help is silent help."

"But, I thought …" My heart sank. Hadn't he brought Jens here as a favor to me?

He scoffed. "Nej. I know what you thought. 'Tis not so." He smiled coolly. "I invited them weeks ago." He grabbed my arm firmly. "This is not your social hour. You will do your duties or regret it sorely." He pushed me forward. "Well, answer it. That's what servants do, you know."

Indeed I hadn't known that's what servants did. Nor had I understood that I'd be working during supper, having thought he'd invited the Larsens over to visit with me. At least I would see Jens and dine with him.

I walked at first quickly and then slower, wondering at the greeting I'd receive. Would Jens be glad to see me? Most importantly, would he be interested in me with no chest, no fabrics, no money, no family, and working as a maid?

The large door dwarfed me as I grabbed the knob and pulled it open, the weight of my world on its hinges.

"Welcome to Ilse Manor." I curtsied. Staring past Mr. and Mrs. Larsen, I watched Jens's expression as he saw and then recognized me. I stood paralyzed, witnessing the myriad of feelings pass through those blue eyes—confusion, hopefully love, longing, hurt. I wanted to rush into his arms—to have him kiss me as he had—to reassure him of my love and to seek reassurance of his.

"Please come in." I curtsied with my gaze never leaving Jens. "Mr. Ilse is waiting in the grand dining parlor." I turned and led the way, my knees threatening to abandon me with each step. When I reached the doorway, I stopped, and standing just inside, I clung to the wall behind me.

"Iver, Helga. Jens." Mr. Ilse smiled politely. "I am glad you could come. Please do sit down and make yourselves comfortable."

I followed behind Jens, reaching toward his hand yet hesitant to touch him. They sat, and Jens's parents began visiting with Mr. Ilse. Jens did not even glance at me, but stared forward, not joining in their conversation. I stood beside him looking from Mr. Ilse to the table. There wasn't a place set for me. Should I sit? I waited to be included.

Every eve Mr. Ilse insisted I dine with him though it made the others think ill of me. Surely I would dine with him on this occasion as well. I wanted to sit with our guests—with Jens. Mr. Ilse knew how important this was to me. Wouldn't he invite me to join them?

Mr. Ilse's eyebrow went up. "Take our guests' coats and return to your duties in the kitchen."

My face heated. Duties in the kitchen? I curtsied, my teeth clenched.

Jens handed over his coat as though he were bored and otherwise ignored me. Mrs. Larsen and her husband, behaved in a similar manner. Their coats should have been taken at the door. I'd done it wrong. Was this why he hadn't included me? Was he angry with me?

As Mr. Ilse began speaking, I turned on my heel and strode toward the doorway with coats in hand.

"I'm not sure if you knew the Erichsens." He said our name like a scandalous word. "That scrawny waif is

Hans Erichsen's daughter."

I put my hands over my ears too humiliated to hear more but did not escape his booming voice.

"The poor girl came to me homeless and destitute, and, although she has no training, I was forced out of the kindness of my heart to take her in and teach her a trade."

Why did he have to tell them this? His accusation horrified me. Couldn't I just disappear? I ran down the hall and put the coats on hooks, rushed around the corner, and didn't stop until I reached the kitchen. Frau Jensen eyed me sternly.

"Did you expect that he'd treat you as his mistress with company?" She shook her head.

"His mistress? Nej." I shuddered, repulsed. "But he said I'd have supper with him each night." I wiped furiously at my face with my apron. "He knows I plan to marry Jens, and I thought he invited the Larsens here for that purpose."

"Now that would be something, wouldn't it?" Her lip curled up as though I'd told a joke. "The master of the manor setting appointments for a penniless child of no significance." She wiped the sweat from her brow. "He's an important man, and you'd do well not to cross him." With two thick towels, she pulled a pan of her delicious rolls from the oven.

I groaned at my foolishness. Frau Jensen was right, of course. Why had I expected to dine with him when he had company? It was absurd.

"I need your help tonight. Can you do it without falling apart?" She opened the oven again and placed in it a pan of breaded fish.

"Ja, ja. I will help you gladly." I wiped my eyes with my sleeve. Jens knew I was here, that was the good thing. So I would serve him and not dine with him, what did it matter?

Frau Jensen took a bowl, separated the hot rolls into it, and handed it to me. "Serve these to Master Ilse first, to Master

Larsen next, his son, and then to Frau Larsen." She draped the rolls with a linen cloth and sent me on my way.

When I got to the dining room, Mr. Ilse and the Larsens were engrossed in conversation.

"...And as you know, her parents are prominent in the community," said Frau Larsen.

I stood just outside the doorway. Who were they talking about, and why? I took a deep breath and then pressed forward. I could do this. I had to do this. Otherwise what would happen? There was nowhere else for me to go.

"She is also easy on the eye. Isn't that right, Jens?" Mr. Ilse chuckled.

I pasted a smile on my face as I served the rolls, but no one cared. No one gave any indication they knew I was in the room. Jens's jaw clenched, but he otherwise continued behaving as though I wasn't there. His parents treated me as a stranger. Why?

Frau Larsen had helped me with my sewing, treated me as one of her own. I gritted my teeth to keep from saying something to Jens and kept my head down as expected. It was pure torture to stand beside him offering rolls, salad, vegetables and fish.

"The food is delicious," Frau Larsen said, complimenting Mr. Ilse as though he'd prepared it with his own hands.

"Ja, ja. Tovi is the best cook in the region." He patted his stomach.

I took their empty plates, and when I accidentally brushed against Jens, a thrill shot through me. I hurried through the room with goose-prickles making their way up my arms. I returned soon after with their desserts—white cake filled with fruits and whipped cream under a thin layer of frosting.

"There are only a few peasants left who have chosen not to join with the People's Church," said Mr. Larsen. "We shall try harder in the coming months to encourage them to join with us."

I glanced at Jens. He shot a casual look my way and immediately turned to his dessert, eating his last bite.

Why had Mr. Ilse deceived me into thinking I'd dine with the Larsens? Well, he hadn't actually said I'd be dining with them, but I had dined with Mr. Ilse since the first night.

Why had he taken me riding to calm my nerves when he didn't intend to invite me to dinner? Why had he brought Jens only to have him see me working as a servant?

When dinner was finished, they retired to the parlor for conversation. I gathered their empty coffee cups onto a tray, and peeked one last time at Jens through the doorway.

"Between you and me, it seems like the perfect arrangement," I overheard Mr. Ilse say. "You couldn't have chosen better."

Jens looked my way, and my heart leapt with hope. He crossed his legs and turned his attention to Mr. Ilse, saying something I could not decipher. They chuckled. Disappointed, I nodded and went to the kitchen.

The perfect arrangement? He couldn't have chosen better? Whoever or whatever they were talking about, it was not about me.

When the dishes were done I went to my room not having eaten any supper myself and not having desired any. I lay on my bed fully clothed and wishing for a torrent of tears to come. I usually felt better after a good cry. But none came.

Jens had looked at me with indifference. He had plans for his future that didn't seem to have anything to do with me. Why couldn't I cry? I lay on my bed until the crickets' song aroused me. I needed to be as the crickets, breathing the fresh night air and enjoying the stars.

I grabbed my shawl and tiptoed from my room, through the kitchen and out the delivery door. After closing the door behind me, I stood on the step and gazed at the crescent moon. I thought of my family so far away and wished I was with them. I had prayed about immigrating to America and felt good about it. In the midst of Catherine's upset, I'd allowed myself to be deceived.

In the night's stillness, the crunch of the gravel under my feet sounded loud as I hurried toward the stable. I needed to apologize to Anders. The lonely cry of a nighthawk and another's distant reply filled me with longing. The crickets chirped in chorus, and the stable's side door creaked as I opened it, adding to the night symphony.

"Anders," I called. With the door ajar I lit the lantern. The horses whinnied softly, complaining at my disturbance. A barn owl flew over my head and into the sky, startling me as I stepped into the stable.

"Berta."

I whirled around, confused at the sound of Jens's voice. He'd gone hours ago with his parents. "Jens?" Quickly I lowered the wick and blew out the flame, and hurried out of the stable hoping I hadn't disturbed Anders.

He strode across the lawn and took my hand. "Why didn't you tell me you'd stayed?" His voice was a mixture of scolding and pain.

He did love me. This truth resonated with the ache in my heart. With that assurance, I stepped closer and rested my head on his chest. "I've longed for this moment since the day we last met." My voice quavered with emotion.

Jens stroked my shoulders. He then stepped back, taking me in. "Have you been here the whole time?"

I shook my head. "I went to Aunt Thora's in place of Catherine."

"But you're here now. What happened?"

"The story is too long to tell." Longing for the comfort that only he could give, I stepped into his arms again. He held me, and I felt content enough to stay there breathing his scent and enjoying the warmth of his contact until I grew old. "I thought you were coming to Vejstrup," I murmured.

"If I'd known you'd be there, I certainly would have." Jens stroked my hair. "Tell me, Berta. Has it been hard?"

Tears burned my eyes as he took my hand and kissed it. "You wear my ring," he said, and then he led me away from the stable.

We walked in silence—with me feeling whole and safe for the first time since my family left. He took me to Mr. Ilse's garden. It was a small maze of well-manicured shrubberies with occasional benches for sitting and with a centerpiece of flowers planted by his gardener.

It was here with the bewitching blue-grays of the midnight hour that I rehearsed to him my trials of the past six weeks. He sealed my confession with first one kiss and then another. I pressed myself against him, eager, accepting, and hungry for his love.

Easily he pulled me onto his lap and we kissed again, each kiss longer and more passionate than the previous. I felt his heart thudding, and a part of me enjoyed this response. I shivered with excitement as he wound his hands through my un-plaited hair.

"Come." His voice was ragged and he pulled me to lie with him on the bench as he kissed me again.

Chapter 20

Mama was right in comparing Jens to a wolf. He was wolfishly hungry in his passion. Days later and his musky smell still lingered on my frock. How would she know?

I put my sleeve to my nose, inhaling and remembering. He loved me. He wanted to be with me. But the sound of his angry frustration as I ran away from him haunted me. I knew so little of men and their emotions. Yet had I stayed, I would never have left his side. That would have dishonored my family.

I needed to convert him first and then marry him before we gave in to our passion. Would he come back? I smiled at the thought of his warm embrace. He would be back—but what plans had he been discussing with Mr. Ilse? Would he join our church as I had promised Mama, or did his parents have a greater hold on him than I'd realized? There were too many questions.

Having not eaten the previous night, my stomach roared with anticipation. I stepped into the kitchen hoping for more than a slice of bread to break my nightly fast.

"Master Ilse is in a foul mood this day. Make sure you don't displease him." Frau Jensen handed me a bowl of oatmeal and then left the manor. The pitcher of cream was on the servant's table—right in front of Anders, Helga, Frau Olesen, and Frau Claussen.

"Ja, ja," I said to no one in particular. When was Mr. Ilse not in a foul mood? I placed the porridge on the table, my stomach growling, and sat beside Anders in the only available seat. No sooner had I poured my cream than Frau Olesen, Frau Claussen, and Helga stood.

"Some of us have to work for our wages," Frau Olesen said. She snubbed her nose at me. "Come on ladies."

Frau Jensen came in the side door with a basket of vegetables from the garden and set them at the sink.

Anders stood. "You make friends easily," he said. "I'd best be getting to work as well. One of the mares is ready to foal any day." He took his bowl to the sink and washed it before leaving.

"What's going on between the two of you?" asked Frau Jensen.

"He has something of mine, and I want it back." I could not call him a thief as I'd done before.

"This does not sound like Anders." Frau Jensen poured water into the sink and started washing the mud off the vegetables. "He has been perfectly honest and forthright the three years I've known him. Couldn't find a better lad. Neither could Master Ilse. He had a long succession of horsemen before Anders. None of them could compare." She shook the water from the vegetables and placed them on a towel, patting them dry. "You are either mistaking, or Anders has a perfect explanation."

"Perhaps," I agreed, not wanting to press the issue.

When I set out to do my work, once again I noticed things amiss, soot in the tub, of all things. It took extra time getting that mess out of the white porcelain. Afterward, I worked at a frantic pace all morning to catch up, while hoping not to warrant the attention of Mr. Ilse.

As I completed my tasks, I turned each scenario, Jens's touch, and his every word over repeatedly in my mind. Would he come back? I smiled. He would—I knew it.

While I dusted the furniture in the bedroom that afternoon, I noticed a movement out of the corner of my eye. Mr. Ilse. He scowled at me from the doorway. His business that morning had not softened his mood.

"Good afternoon." I curtsied, wishing that I'd been down in the laundry room or anywhere out of sight when he came home. Had I not had the delay of the soot in the tub, it's where I would have been. But there I was, an easy target for his quick temper.

I tensed as he strode forward. He didn't yell, but still I held my breath, waiting. He stood over me, watching me like a great bird over his prey. My hands shook, and unwilling to annoy, I struggled to steady them. Jens had come, and Mr. Ilse had made that happen. Regardless of his angry temper, he could help my dream come true.

"You must practice doing it the way I show you if you are ever to get it right," he grumbled.

"Ja, ja. I will practice every day." I curtsied and smiled.

"Then perhaps I'll be here instructing you every day until I'm satisfied." He grabbed my hand and moved it across the smooth surface of the table over and over again. Without a word, he turned and left the room.

Determined to do it right, I worked for several more hours before resting against a table near the grand hall, sighing with relief at a job well done. With my duties accomplished for the afternoon, and desiring to stay out of Mr. Ilse's sight, I slipped out of the house.

When Jens came back, I needed to be ready with my Book of Mormon. The stables were a likely place to search. Why did Anders insist on making things so difficult? The large rock building stood before me, and I marveled that Mr. Ilse's stables were large enough to fit our entire house inside.

The side door, a massive rectangle, dwarfed me with its ornate iron-workings and straight wooden planks and never offered a sound as I opened it. A mouse raced past me and out the door. I stepped out of the way just as a large yellow tomcat came from the shadows and jumped on it. Once he had it in his mouth, the cat walked to the shade of a tree and began tormenting his prize.

Intent on the cat and mouse, I sucked in a breath, startled, when I heard a movement beside me.

"May I help you?" asked Anders.

I put my hand to my heart. "Oh, you surprised me."

He glared and shrugged his shoulders. "I am hired to care for the horses. Where did you expect me to be?"

I was tired of anger. I'd never experienced so much of it in my life. Frau Jensen said he was exceptional, so, ignoring his tone, I decided to start anew.

"You say a mare is ready to foal?" I offered a timid smile, unsure of how I'd be received. "I love horses. I helped Papa with them at home." I twisted at the handkerchief inside my apron pocket. "Perhaps I can see her?"

"Master Ilse's horses are expensive. He doesn't allow anyone in his stables unaccompanied. If you know horses as you say you do, you know she won't want strangers upsetting her."

Discouraged, I shrugged, and started to leave. If we couldn't be friends, I had no hope of ever seeing my Book of Mormon again.

He touched my arm. "I can show you around. Ja?"

"Thank you." I curtsied to show my appreciation.

He scoffed and turned away, shaking his head and mumbling something about my pretty little manners and something about Jens Larsen.

"What did you say?" Certainly he hadn't seen me in the garden with Jens. I fought against the rising heat in my cheeks.

"I said," he raised his eyebrows, "Master Ilse takes great pride in his horses. They are Knabstruppers—all except the roan you rode. He raises them and sells them at great profit."

We walked slowly down the center of the stable. The stalls were each made of polished wood with scrolled ironwork decorating the top edges, and each horse's name was engraved on a plaque on the back of its stall. None of our horses had names, except my Caja.

"Why does he keep the roan if it's not purebred?" I'd never ridden a pedigreed horse, so it didn't matter that Mr. Ilse had chosen one of lesser breeding for me to ride.

"It was his late wife's. She's a gentle ride and also pulls the wagon when Frau Jensen goes to town for supplies."

A soft spot entered my heart for my employer's suffering as I thought of his caring enough to keep his late wife's horse after her passing. I should repay his bad temper with kindness.

We stopped in front of a stall with the heading, Aphrodite. Her stall was filled with clean straw. A large and very beautiful mare stepped forward, whinnying.

"The stables are stunning." I rubbed her velvety nose. "And they are so clean. I can see the special care you are taking of Aphrodite."

"Ja, she is a good horse, and mine is the best job in the world."

I started to move away, but Aphrodite nudged me and so I rubbed between her ears. "She likes me." I tickled her chin.

"See, you can make friends."

He teased, but I did not like his teasing and moved away. The whole stable smelled like fresh straw, which was quite a feat considering it housed fourteen horses.

"We have another mare that will foal in two weeks." Anders walked beside me. "Would you like to see her?"

"Thank you, ja," I said.

"Besides Aphrodite, we have Athena, and Hera, and Nyx that will each produce foals within the month. Master Ilse already has buyers for each of them." As we walked past, Anders explained to me the temperaments of each animal and how he handled them. I found it interesting and listened attentively.

"This is Hestia. She is the one who will foal in two weeks." He walked down the aisle. "These three mares were too immature last season and have not yet taken this season. If they don't take by August, Master Ilse will sell them." He stopped. "Gaia and Rhea have recently taken and will foal next spring." He rubbed their noses.

It impressed me that he treated each as a friend and attended to their needs accordingly. I loved horses, but ours were work animals and treated as such.

"Our stallions and the roan are kept away from the mares." He closed a metal gate behind us.

"I have never seen anyone care for horses as you do." I rubbed behind the ears of Rhea, a mare with russet markings. "They are lucky to have you here."

Anders nodded his acceptance of my compliment. "Thank you, ja. It means a lot coming from someone who also loves horses."

I smiled. It felt good to not be at war with him.

We were back at the side entry of the stable.

"You've ridden in Master Ilse's cabriolet. Would you care to see the tack room and the rest of his carriages?" Anders indicated the way.

"Ja, ja. I'm sure they are also very nice."

Mr. Ilse had large carriages and small buggies. Some were fancy and made of black-polished leather; others were simple with no top at all. The tack room was almost unbelievable—a whole room of saddles, bridles, and gear. At our home, we had one wall for our tack and it was mostly empty. We never had a cabriolet or any type of carriage, only a wagon.

"This is amazing." I shook my head. "How do you keep it all straight?" That anyone should have so much money to spend on tack and grooming aids for horses was nearly unbelievable. The royal family, perhaps, but as far as I knew, Mr. Ilse had no title. However, the king often bestowed gifts of land upon those who found his favor. Could this be how Mr. Ilse had gained his initial properties?

"It keeps me busy." Anders led me to the stable door.

The sun had begun to set, casting an orange glow on the trees. We'd had a good visit, yet I hadn't fully accomplished my reason for coming. Since his mood seemed good, I would ask.

"I would like my Book of Mormon back. Ja?" I toyed with a leather strap. "I will not tell Herrer Ilse you gave it to me, nor will I mention that you took it. I will only be thankful."

"You won't tell Mr. Ilse regardless." Anders scowled. "He doesn't care about your book. It angers me that you want to give such a treasure to a man who abuses you so." He turned without another word and disappeared into the stable.

But wait. I wasn't giving it to Mr. Ilse. Anders knew that.

I waited for a moment, hoping he'd return with my book. I did not understand his refusal. Since my coming to Ilse Manor, Anders had almost seemed interested in my religion. Why then would he keep my scriptures from me? Frustrated that he didn't come back, I finally returned to the manor.

The scene startled me as I walked into the kitchen. Frau Jensen was leaning backward against one of the cutting tables. Mr. Ilse glared over her. She seemed both relieved and apologetic as he turned his anger to me.

"Did I not tell you explicitly that I'd flog you should you delay my supper?"

I stepped backward, thinking of what to say to appease him. "I—I am truly sorry, sir. I didn't realize. You … I thought … You didn't."

"Quit your sniveling! How am I to teach you proper manners when you disappear at suppertime?" He stepped forward. "Since you seem confused, I'll not flog you this time. Hold out your hands."

"Sir?"

His neck turned red and I thrust my hands forward. He grabbed a nearby wooden spoon and slapped it hard against my knuckles.

I gasped aloud, having not expected this punishment, and clenched my jaws together to keep from crying out. Water filled my eyes nonetheless.

The schoolmaster had only treated me thus on one occasion. Mama's scolding had insured he never did it again.

Mr. Ilse grabbed my still throbbing hand and placed it on his arm. Then, stiff with rage, he led me into the small breakfast room where two places had been set.

"Young master Larsen is a gentleman of proper breeding and requires a dame of etiquette." His tone softened, and he pulled the chair for me as though nothing had happened, and I sat. "Ridding you of your country manners will be quite a challenge."

He studied me with a thoughtful expression.

Was there a different set of manners, then, for the wealthy?

Frau Jensen brought bread first and then salad. Mr. Ilse instructed me on how to take each bite. Butter the roll just so—the way to eat it is determined by how the host eats his—only allow a small amount of salad on the fork at a time, and never stab the food.

When she brought the main course, I learned a new set of rules. Don't sop gravy with pieces of roll—don't use a spoon as a knife—and never use a spoon and knife together. My head ached from his constant censure, and my insides shivered.

"That wasn't too terribly painful." He pulled my chair away from the table when we were through. "Let us go into the library." He guided me forward, his foul mood apparently forgotten.

However, I wasn't used to having someone judge every bite I took at supper—and I felt every bit like the 'skittering mouse' Mr. Ilse had described as Helsa. My nerves jumped and twitched with each step I took. Was it proper for me to spend more time with him alone? My nails automatically went into my mouth, and I chewed them—thinking, worrying.

Mr. Ilse slapped my hand, and it bumped against my face. "Dear child, what animal in the whole world eats its own fingernails?" He guided my hand down to my side. "It is disgusting and I must insist that you stop this terrible habit."

"Ja, ja." My eyes blinked as I spoke. "I will try to remember."

"Nej. You will remember." Mr. Ilse regarded me in his stern way.

"I will. Ja, of course." I curtsied. "I'll never chew my nails again." I clasped my hands behind me, hoping this was true.

He pressed lightly against my back and led me into the library. My skin crawled but I dared not resist.

The wall of books intrigued me, and I stepped away from him, admiring them.

"I enjoy a good book in the evenings." He took a volume from an end table, and sat on the nearby sofa. "Can I interest you in a book by Hans Christian Andersen?" He picked up a small book from the table that I hadn't noticed, reached behind the sofa and handed it to me. "It is one of his travel books called, 'I Sverrig.' It's yours to read and enjoy if you wish."

"Thank you, Herrer Ilse." I slipped the book from his hands and curtsied. Taking another casual step away, I pretended to need the lamplight for reading and looked it over with my heart still thumping nervously.

"A proper thank you would be nice. How about a little something right here?" He leaned his cheek toward me.

He wanted me to kiss him! I took a big gulp of breath and stepped forward, kissing him quick before I changed my mind and ran from the room instead.

"Ah, that's a good girl." He beamed with pleasure. "Your cheeks have turned a nice rosy color."

"The book is lovely, and you are very thoughtful. Thank you, ja." Mama and Papa owned a copy of Hans Christian Andersen's, *Eventyr, fortalte for Born,* and Mama often read the stories to us. If only I'd gone with them I wouldn't be subjected to Mr. Ilse's cruelty. I blinked back the moisture that made it suddenly impossible to read, and I walked to the doorway intending to relieve myself of his company.

"There's no need to hide in your room." Mr. Ilse set his book on his lap and motioned for me to return. "The furniture here is much more comfortable."

"Sir, if you do not mind, I am very tired." I curtsied and held the book to my chest, wishing to leave his company, and awaiting his permission. "Perhaps tomorrow?"

His jaw clenched. "Am I a leper that you cannot keep my company for a short while?"

Upon remembering his deceased wife, I said, "I meant no disrespect," and sat in the chair beside him, my heart thumping in protest.

"This is much better." He nodded, satisfied, and returned to his own reading.

My knuckles throbbed, and when he'd slapped my hand against my face, it had cut my lip. I felt the sting, and rubbed my tongue across it while pretending to read and praying Jens would soon propose.

After a half hour or so, he closed his book and put it on the end table. "I have a lot of business to attend to tomorrow. It's time you get yourself off to bed so that I can do the same."

"Will I see you in the morn?" The days passed more tolerably for everyone on the days he left early.

"I will most likely be gone till supper. Now, be off. I hate to interrupt your slumber."

"Ja, ja, and many thanks for your kind generosity." I curtsied yet again. With the book in hand I started to leave hoping I would calm down enough to enjoy a few pages before falling asleep.

"I prefer you keep the book here in the library. It will be here any time you care to read it."

"Of course." I set the book on the end table near his and hurried away.

When I got to kitchen, I dipped my swollen and throbbing hands into the water barrel for just a moment till they felt better. Then I went to my room and bent over the top of my chest, embracing it. "Oh, Mama, Papa," I murmured. "Will I ever again have a home or a place where I feel safe?"

Chapter 21

Anders scowled as I came in to have breakfast. Why did he have to be there? Life was simpler without his interference. I scooped up a bowl of porridge but then didn't know where to sit. As before, the only space available was next to Anders. I hesitated and then sat beside him. He wouldn't bite me, after all. There was no need to be afraid.

"Good morning," I said.

"I've noticed that you're not getting the hall dusted well enough," said Frau Olesen. "See that you don't leave smears of dirt on everything." She grabbed up her bowl and went to the sink.

Anders shook his head and followed her, and in unison Helsa and Frau Claussen stood and went to the sink.

I hadn't been late, but they left me sitting there as though I had.

Frau Jensen breezed into the kitchen. "Berta, you will help me at the market today." She removed her apron and took it to the laundry room.

"Ja, ja." I agreed as was expected, but my heart screamed, No! I could not go to town! I hadn't been back since coming to Ilse Manor, since they'd treated me so hatefully. Some of the merchants had been at church and hadn't bothered me. Nevertheless, a shiver wormed its way from my chest to my stomach and then to my knees. What if Isaac Thompsen was there? I held onto the table for support.

But I had to go. This was not my choice. I was expected to be strictly obedient, though my feet felt strangely rooted. I tried thinking good thoughts to encourage my legs to take me to the carriage. Time away from the manor would be nice. Perhaps I would see Jens there. These thoughts should give me hope, bring me joy. But instead of moving, I frowned and chewed my lip.

While attending worship services each week, I had kept myself scarce, stayed out of view. Besides, seeing the shop owners at church services was one thing. Having to be in their stores was another. Would they remember how cruel they'd been? Would they be cruel again?

"It is time to go. Ja? Why are you waiting?" Frau Jensen came through the door and walked past me and toward the service exit. I followed our cook out the door and toward the wagon awaiting us.

If the village folk were still angry, what did it matter? Mr. Ilse cared nothing for their opinions. Neither would I. Yet my nerves protested, and my heart declared this thought a lie.

Anders held the reins, working his jaw. I paused, disheartened. Then I avoided him by walking around the back of the wagon to take my place beside Frau Jensen. I felt Anders's eyes bore into me as he watched my every move. Once seated, I stared toward the stable, missing home and family. I pulled my shawl around my shoulders, guarding against the crisp morning air.

I'd enjoyed such ease of conversation with Anders. Would I have no friends in this life—all because I wanted my scriptures back? I peered at him from over my shoulder.

"Thank you, good lad," Frau Jensen said as she took the reins.

The horse's hooves crunched on the moist gravel as they led us toward the wrought iron gate. The tree-lined lane held no magic on this day but only made me feel more alone, foreign amongst familiar surroundings.

A pheasant in the field flew up when we approached—Papa used to bring them home and Mama cooked them in rich gravy. The field of planted hay peeking through the earth—Catherine and I worked alongside Papa and others to prepare our fields. The sky with the fluffy clouds—my sisters and I danced under them until they misted the earth with rain. These things combined as painful reminders that I had no one.

"Something is troubling you. Ja?" Frau Jensen broke through my thoughts, and she regarded me with lifted brows.

I shrugged my shoulders and looked over the countryside.

We traveled for a moment in this manner, me brooding, with Frau Jensen also silent. It was well and good because what did I need to talk for? Would talking bring my family back or take me to them? No.

"No one knows when the fox is near if the goose stays silent." She patted my knee.

This of course was Frau Jensen's way of saying there was no way to solve my problems without talking about them.

"You are the only one here who is nice." Though I'd gained a fond regard for Frau Jensen, I did not feel that my problems could be fixed with talk. I said the words merely to be polite.

She paused before responding and her silence made me nervous. Had I offended her?

"You'd do well to make friends with the other servants." Frau Jensen glanced at me and continued guiding the horse down the road. "Helga is your age. Anders is a nice lad."

"I have tried being friends." I frowned. Being friends would be easier if the other women of the manor quit hating me, and if Anders returned my Book of Mormon. "I was talking with Anders the other evening, making me only a few minutes late for supper. This is when Mr. Ilse so cruelly slapped my hands with the spoon." I folded my arms and bit my lip, chewing on the memory.

"Did I not warn you he was in a foul mood?" She regarded me with a frown. "Did he not warn you that he likes his meals on time?"

I nodded. I had been warned, but how did I know he waited? He hadn't wanted me at supper when the Larsens were there. I had also tried very hard that day to please him. He had still not been happy. Mama and Papa encouraged and praised my every effort. Here, although I worked twice as hard, it seemed

I could please no one.

"Mr. Ilse expects strict obedience." Frau Jensen watched the road as she talked. "If you give him that and an honest day's work you'll find he's as pleasant to work for as any other master."

"I have tried so hard, and still he complains." I sighed and rubbed my hands. Pleasant was not a word I'd use to describe Mr. Ilse.

"You are a lucky girl coming here when you should be out on the street. You are young and inexperienced, and you'd be wise to give it a better effort."

I nodded. She was right. Living as Mr. Ilse's maid was better than living at the poorhouse, and certainly better than living on the street.

"You should be grateful—think of the grand estate you live on. You live in luxury." She clicked her tongue, and the horse hurried down the road. "We shall have a good day today. The sun is shining."

Road traffic increased as we neared the village. The handkerchief in my hands folded and unfolded as I thought of Catherine and worked out my nerves. Would I see Isaac? Riders approached. My pulse quickened as I looked, hoping they were strangers. They were, and I breathed a sigh of relief.

My hands went to my head to straighten my scarf. My scarf! I hadn't worn my bonnet. I smoothed the apron over my plain, sturdy work clothes and realized I resembled the lowliest of servants. I was. What if Jens saw me? Or worse, what if his parents saw me? How could I have left the manor like this? They'd never let me marry Jens if the town found out I was a penniless servant. On the other hand, Mr. Ilse had informed them of my indigent circumstances, and yet he indicated Jens was still interested in gaining my hand. This gave me a measure of hope.

We stopped near the soap-maker's shop at the edge of town. I hesitated, wishing to stay in the carriage. However, when Frau Jensen frowned, I hastened to her. She walked from store to store. My duty was to follow and to carry the things she bought for the manor. The village streets were busy, and I kept watch for Isaac, preparing to hide each time I saw someone who appeared similar.

"You bob around like an egret after a fish." Frau Jensen crossed her arms and studied me. "What is the matter?"

"There is nothing the matter." I would not talk of how Catherine's old beau had ruined my chances of work. I straightened and continued walking.

The shops on each side of the street sold clothing, dinnerware, cleaning supplies, hardware, and one even sold furniture. People with carts on the sides of the street sold fresh fruits and vegetables, herbs, spices, milk and cheese. Some sold plants and flowers.

We went into the soap-maker's shop and purchased soaps for the manor, after which, I hurried them to our wagon and returned to Frau Jensen. It was then that we went inside Mr. Petersen's store for household items—the very man whose face had reddened as he shouted for me to leave mere weeks ago. I used to love this store. Mama had purchased a sugar candy for us here once, and the Petersens had purchased our eggs. On this day, I stepped behind an aisle, hiding so Mr. Petersen didn't see me as we entered.

Frau Jensen bustled around the store, hurrying to finish her shopping so she could get back and prepare Mr. Ilse's evening meal before going home to fix supper for her husband. I followed behind, helping by carrying the items to the counter, and was grateful it wasn't Mr. Petersen there. Frau Jensen paid, and I held out my arms as she filled them with the heavy load. My arms ached from the weight of several packages. It seemed she was out of everything for the kitchen, and she bought added cleaning supplies that we couldn't get anywhere else.

Mr. Petersen came from the back room. "Frau Jensen," he said. "Welcome. Is there anything else we can help you with?"

I ducked behind my armful of packages. "May I take these to the wagon?" I asked.

"If it pleases you," Frau Jensen said, turning her attention to

Mr. Petersen. "I didn't see any bags of lavender. Did you move them? Herrer Ilse loves the smell of lavender in his dresser drawers."

I struggled to open the door, anxious to get away before he said something to me. A man coming in opened it and let me pass. "Thank you." I smiled and walked over the threshold. After I'd emptied the groceries into the wagon, Frau Jensen came out.

"Why did you leave in such a hurry?" she asked.

"My arms were getting tired."

She handed me a small, fragrant bag. Inside were several sachets of lavender. "We need to stop for some fish, and then we're done for the week." She led me down the street. I stopped once to smell a bouquet of beautiful pink roses and then hurried up to her.

After purchasing the needed fish, I sat back in the wagon and felt much relieved on our ride home, having not seen Isaac, and having avoided any confrontations with the merchants who'd been so spiteful before. "It's a lovely day," I said. "Can you believe there is not one cloud?"

"Some days we make our own rain even when the sky is otherwise clear." She jerked the reins.

"What do you mean?" It seemed she liked to talk in riddles.

"Don't be coy with me. I know why you were nervous to go to town. They'd rejected you before when you thought they'd open their arms. I've talked with Master Ilse, and he's agreed that part of your duties will include helping me in the kitchen and with suppers." She patted my knee. "That means there will be more trips to town." She gave me a stern look. "You came this time and saw that your world didn't crumble. I'll expect that next time you'll hold your head high and not be hiding behind corners like a frightened mouse."

"Ja, ja," I said. "I am happy to be your helper. I love working in the kitchen, and I will work hard." The prospects for my life seemed a little brighter on the way home.

Chapter 22

As we pulled onto the tree-lined lane, I glimpsed Mr. Ilse's regal white manor shining between trunks and branches. It was beautiful, and I thanked my God in Heaven for the opportunity to live here. He was keeping me safe and off the street, and my love for Him swelled.

The gravel crunched when we neared the servant's entrance, and Anders ran from the stable to greet us.

"Let me help. Ja? These things look heavy." He pulled the packages of lye soap from my hands while the protest was still on my tongue and strode toward the manor.

I looked at him, feeling puzzled. He had overcome his surly mood easily enough.

Frau Jensen winked at me. "He's a good one, that Anders."

I pulled the packages of fish from the carriage and went to the kitchen without responding. Anders was handsome enough, but what did I care? I was going to marry Jens. His actions the other evening proved his love. I felt heat creep up my neck and hurried back outside.

When we emptied the carriage of the goods and had them all put away, Anders walked toward the door and stopped. "Good day, Frau Jensen, Berta." He tipped his cap.

I nodded. The morning had been long—an eternity—but my afternoon chores were left needing done.

"Anders, you are a good help. Thank you, ja." Frau Jensen turned to me with the hint of an idea brightening her expression. "Berta, dear, serve up Anders a piece of that leftover cake while

I begin preparations for supper." She smiled mischievously and set out two small, china plates of pale green with a delicate primrose pattern, the scalloped edges trimmed in gold. We would get our lashings for sure if Mr. Ilse found out.

"That sounds good." Anders came back and waited by the chopping table. "This is a rare treat. I haven't had cake since I left home."

"But shouldn't I help you?" I asked Frau Jensen. This seemed more like match-making rather than friend-making, and I didn't need a new beau.

"Nej. I won't need your help for hours." She wiggled her eyebrows playfully. "Now don't keep the young man waiting."

Anders smiled benignly, so I knew he thought nothing of her silliness. "You must come here, ja. Sit, and I will get the cake." I led him to the kitchen table. "It really is delicious."

"Serve yourself a piece as well." Frau Jensen worked some bread flour into her liquid. "You have also been a good help today."

My lips pushed together in disapproval. I would be in trouble if Mr. Ilse came; and she was being too obvious in offering cake to Anders and me in the middle of the day. Would Anders take the wrong impression?

My hands shook as I set each piece of cake on china and carried the dishes to the table. I placed one in front of Anders. Sitting across from him, I repeated the words I'd heard Mr. Ilse speak. "Frau Jensen is the best cook in the region." She was better, even, than Mama, though I wouldn't admit it out loud.

Anders smiled and took a bite of cake. "This is very good, ja," he said. Then he leaned over the table and whispered conspiratorially, "But it's not the best I've had." He took another bite and then leaned back in his chair and closed his eyes. "Mmm, it is the best that I've had in such a long time."

Where had he been that he'd had better? I took a bite of

the cake. It was Frau Jensen's special white cake, cream-filled with little bits of fruit, and frosted with a rich, white frosting. This was the best and most wonderful cake I had ever eaten. A whisper of delight escaped my lips as I pondered its goodness. "It's heavenly."

"It makes me miss home," Anders said between bites.

"Truly, you are no relation to Frau Jensen at all?" It was odd, but not surprising. After all, Mama's maiden name was Jensen, and I was no relation to Frau Jensen or to Anders. The Jensen name was common in Denmark. Perhaps she was a cousin or a dear aunt, though their features were not at all similar.

I placed my fork down, missing family and home.

Anders watched me. "My family lives far from here."

"So far away that you cannot return for a visit?" A lump suddenly formed in my throat at the thought of never seeing my own family again.

"The last I knew, they were immigrating to America. That was nigh on three years ago." He shoved a piece of cake in his mouth.

"But, shouldn't you find out if they stayed?"

"What if they haven't?" His expression appeared sad or full of regret. "Perhaps it is better not knowing." He took a bite of cake, his eyes down.

I also took a bite of cake to stop my talking. Who was I to judge Anders? Just because I missed my family, didn't mean he missed his. Perhaps his mother cooked well but was a horrible person, or perhaps his father yelled a lot, like Mr. Ilse.

We both faced our cake and ate our last few bites in silence.

"Frau Jensen, thank you for the delicious treat." Anders stood and took both of our plates.

"I can take those." I reached for them. "Let me wash them."

"Nej. I am perfectly capable." Anders took the dishes to the sink and got the hot water from the stove reserved for washing dishes.

Unwilling to be outdone in my servant duties, I grabbed a nearby towel. "If you are washing, I will rinse and dry."

"That sounds good, ja." He took the dry towel from my hands, held it by the corners and spun it tight.

"You wouldn't dare," I said, uncertain and stepping back.

"Oh, you think I wouldn't." He gave an evil grin and let the towel snap.

"You missed." I grabbed the towel from Frau Jensen's hand.

"That's enough, you two." Frau Jensen grabbed for her towel, but I darted away.

"I won't miss you, though," I said to Anders, and twirled the towel into a tight roll.

"You're a girl. I'm not afraid."

He stepped out of my way, but I let the towel snap. It hit its mark.

"Ow! You are going to pay for that!" He lunged forward and grabbed me and began tickling my ribs.

"Stop! Stop! Stop!" I laughed and squealed until I was breathless. "Stop, please."

"Do you say, uncle?" He spun me around, and I was facing him.

It felt so natural being in his arms. His eyes so blue and lit with good humor, it made me uncomfortable. I glanced down. "Uncle," I squeaked.

"Well, I must get back to work." He nodded to Frau Jensen. "I'm sorry if I caused you undue stress." He picked up his washing towel, cleaned up his plate and put it in the sink for me to rinse and dry. "Good day, Berta." He nodded to me and strode out the door.

Chapter 23

The hearty, beefy aroma of stew wafted to my nose. My stomach growled in anticipation. I placed the tureen on the table and then returned for the bread and butter. Helping Frau Jensen gave me a greater sense of achievement, and it helped her return to her husband sooner, though the extra duties left me exhausted. I stood near the set table, satisfied that I'd done an excellent job.

Mr. Ilse entered the room smiling. "Being out today has done you good." He strode to the table and pulled the chair out for me as was his habit.

"Thank you kindly," I said, holding back a yawn.

"Ahem." Mr. Ilse regarded me with raised eyebrow.

"I apologize, sir." I started to put my fingernail to my mouth but remembered my promise and thrust my hand under my leg. "The stew smells delicious. May I serve you some?" I started to stand.

"Nej." He put a gentle hand on my arm to keep me in my seat. "We've forgotten our manners. You must learn to give little niceties if you're to be the hostess of an estate such as the Larsens have."

Jens. Missing him and needing his encouragement, I swallowed back a sudden lump in my throat.

"Ahem," Mr. Ilse said again.

He wanted a return compliment. My shoulders slumped. I hated this exercise. We were not courting that I should compliment his appearance, and I did not remember ever once hearing the Larsens give any sort of compliment in my presence.

They were generally of an austere nature and not prone to participate in such silly things, in my opinion.

Mr. Ilse was not tall and slender, nor was he overly generous. I pressed my hand to my lip, contemplating as I looked him over. Perhaps I could compliment his vest—it seemed new.

"Honestly. Do you think me an ogre that you cannot give one pleasantry?" Mr. Ilse stood and glared at me. "You think because I'm wealthy that I have no feelings?"

I opened my mouth to speak, but nothing came.

"I'm done." He threw his napkin on the table and stalked from the room.

What had happened—had I honestly hurt his feelings? Would we not eat? I smelled the stew. It would probably be unforgivable to eat without him. Surely he would come back. He would want supper.

Frau Jensen's comment came to mind once again. I should try harder, I should do better, I should be more appreciative. I thought of his compliment to me. It had been nice, but not overly so. He had given an indication of my nice appearance without really saying as much. I scratched my neck, thinking. How could I do the same? I had grown fond of our evening meals, and I would mention how grateful I was for sharing suppers with him.

But he didn't return.

I felt the tureen. The stew was growing cold. When he said, "I'm done," did he mean for the evening—or did he mean done with me? An ominous feeling prickled over me, and I felt dread, true, real dread. I pictured myself sitting on a street in Odense, leering men walking past—and shuddered.

What had I done? Why shouldn't I give a small compliment to my employer and the man who kept me off the streets if it pleased him? Why hadn't I? I was acting the spoiled child towards a man who held my life in his hands.

It didn't matter if he slapped my hands—it didn't matter if he flogged me—it was nothing more than an insolent servant deserved.

I could not go to the poorhouse—I was in a different region from Aunt Thora and would not have her help or guidance. I would not live in the streets. And, why hadn't Jens proposed the other night? It only just dawned on me that he hadn't. Had these past weeks apart changed his feelings that much?

Feeling awkward and like a thief stealing through a stranger's house, I rose from my chair and walked across the room. From the doorway, I looked back at the tureen holding the cold stew and then peered out to the semi-dark manor. I knew what I must do.

I stepped timidly from the dining room. Frau Jensen was correct. I was foolish, to be sure. I needed to apologize, to let him know how much I appreciated all the help he'd given me. I needed to try harder, and I would start tonight.

My heart thumped as I walked down the corridor and toward the library. If he wasn't there, would I be brave enough to approach his bedchamber? Nej. I would die first of embarrassment. I could not enter his room after dark. He had to be in the library.

The glow of light shone from the doorway, and I placed my hand to my heart feeling great relief. I hurried the remaining steps and peeked inside. He was there. A half empty bottle of ale and a full glass of the drink was on the table beside him. Sitting on the sofa with his legs propped up and his shoes off with a book in hand, he watched me with a scowl on his face that did not soften as I entered the doorway.

Would he scream and yell and throw me from the premises? I'd witnessed his temper. Trembling, I waited. He kept his glaring eyes on mine while reaching for his glass and drinking it down.

"My lord?" My voice cracked and I held the doorframe for support. He wasn't nobility, but he was lord over his manor and held my fate in his hands. I needed him to bid me enter so that I might fully apologize. His expressionless gaze held mine as I tried pleading with my eyes and silently begging him to allow me entrance. My knees shook as I waited.

"Get on with it." He turned and sat with his feet on the

floor. "What do you have to say for yourself?" He regarded me, glowering.

"I came to apologize." I stepped into the room and paused. "I behaved poorly." I took another step.

When he didn't protest my taking yet another step into the room, I hurried to his side and knelt on the floor in front of him. "Please forgive my rudeness and my ingratitude!" I clasped my hands and touched them to my chin.

He continued regarding me stoically.

He had to allow me to stay and continue working for him. I had nowhere else to go.

"I am sorry. Ja?" I whispered. "I will do better. I know I can do better. I will work harder. I will try harder." I closed my eyes, and a tear slipped onto my cheek.

He still didn't respond. I looked on his face remembering I'd hurt his feelings. "I am so sorry that I didn't return your compliment." My voice quavered. "I was only thinking of the nicest thing to say." The Lord would have to forgive my little lie. "There are so many things I need to learn—and so many nice—nej, wonderful things about you. Which should I say first?"

"Tell me any that come to mind." His eyebrows lowered, his jaw clenched.

"You are very generous," I said. "You have taken me in, given me a nice room. You allow me to sup with you." More tears fell.

He patted the space next to him and allowed me to sit on the sofa.

"Thank you, ja. My knees were getting sore." I rubbed them and smiled through my tears. "You have given me a home," I continued. Giving voice to his fine points helped me to appreciate this man in a way I hadn't before. Another surge of tears came as I remembered my true situation. I tried blinking them away.

"There, there." He took the cloth from my hands and touched it to my face, drying it. "Let's not give it another thought."

I bit my lip and nodded.

"I don't know about you, but I've suddenly grown quite

hungry." He stood and then lifted me to my feet.

"I am famished as well."

He put his arm around my shoulder and led the way back to the breakfast room. Once there, I hurried from his grasp and to the tureen, lifting it. "I shall warm this in the kitchen and be right back."

"It's heavy. Allow me." He took the tureen into the kitchen, placed the contents in a cooking pot on the stove, and lit the burner. "Dorte and I used to enjoy an occasional supper in the kitchen."

With this mention of his departed wife, I smiled up at him. He had truly forgiven.

"So," he said. "Did you get a chance to visit with young master Jens the other night?" He took the spoon from me and stirred the stew.

"He did come to see me." My heart sank with the memory of my shameful behavior.

"Ah, I thought he might." He took a sip of the broth. "This is plenty warm. Let's eat. Shall we?"

"Ja, ja." I started to lift the hot tureen from the stove, but once again he took it from me and strode to the breakfast room.

"Do you have a proposal then? Will you soon be leaving me to wed your young man?"

"Nej." I wiped my face feeling tired again and no longer hungry. "He did not propose." His last words to me were spoken in frustration, though I felt at fault for leading him on.

"He'll be back. He kept stealing glances at you through the evening." Mr. Ilse served us both a bowl of stew and sliced the bread. "Meanwhile, shall we continue practicing for the time you become lady of the manor?"

"I would very much like that," I said, feeling more hopeful. Mr. Ilse must have had a talk with Jens.

"I am now hosting the activities for the young person's society." He took a drink of his ale. "You will be partners with Anders Jensen, my stable boy."

"What?" The spoon fell back into my bowl, and I began choking on the soup I'd just eaten. "Not A—" The venomous look on Mr. Ilse's face stopped me cold. I felt the color drain from my face. "I'm sorry, sir. I'll do as you please."

"Indeed you will." He finished his glass of ale and leaned back in his chair. "I hate explaining each and every motive, child. It's exhausting. Can you not trust that I am trying to do what's best by you?"

"It won't happen again." I watched as Mr. Ilse began to sway. Would he remember that he'd forgiven me on the morrow?

"In order to be the lady of a fine manor, you need to be educated on social manners." He filled his glass again and drank it down.

"Ja, ja," I agreed. Though the Larsen manor wasn't nearly as fine as Mr. Ilse's, they were not of peasant class.

"These social events will teach you much about the required etiquette. The Larsens, as you must be aware, have recently risen a notch in their social standing. They wouldn't even consider pairing their only son with one of my servants regardless of your previous relationship. Anders," he waved his hand toward the door, "is merely a convenience."

I sipped my stew while keeping an eye on him.

"It seems I've had too much to eat, and too little to soup." He hiccoughed. "I mean too little to drin—oh, I feel light headed."

He started falling toward the table. I hurried his plate and bowl out of his way and placed my hand under his head just in time to soften his landing.

"That's a dear girl," he mumbled when I pulled my hand away.

Oh, my! He had passed out again. And though I didn't want it, I needed Anders's help. I ran from the manor to the stables.

"Anders!" I opened the door and peered into the black building. "Anders!"

Chapter 24

"It seems his episodes are growing closer together." Anders pulled Mr. Ilse's socks off.

"What will I do?" I took a nearby quilt and covered him. "I can't stay here if he's going to start drinking himself silly each night." But I had nowhere to go until I received a proposal from Jens.

"What he needs is a wife." Anders took my arm as we left the bedroom. "He's terribly lonely."

"And, if he's to be important in his church one day, he should have a good wife by his side," I offered, wincing at the idea of Frau Olesen as lady of the manor.

"Exactly."

"Do you know if he has a lady friend?"

"Now, if he did, he wouldn't be so lonely," Anders replied.

I itched to tell him of Frau Olesen. We walked through the kitchen to the side exit with my observations on the tip of my tongue. I wouldn't have Anders think me a gossip.

"You are good to help with Herrer Ilse. He is lucky to have you," I said.

"He is generous with me, ja. And I love helping with his horses; it reminds me of home."

"Did you have good parents?"

"The best," he said. "Until they joined with the Mormons and wanted to move us all to America." A rueful smile twitched his lips.

"America?" My heart skipped a beat. His parents were Mormon. This was why he took my scriptures. "Did they go?"

Anders's shoulder lifted. "How do I know? I got angry and took off. I've been working for Master Ilse ever since. He's taught me a lot."

"Do you miss them," I asked.

"What?" He appeared startled, as though I'd interrupted his thoughts.

"Your parents." I pulled the locket from beneath my blouse. "Mama gave me this the morning they left." I opened it and showed him the image of my parents. "I miss them so much."

Anders leaned forward and looked at their faces. "Do you wish you'd gone with them?"

"Almost always," I replied. "Things have not gone how I'd hoped." I chewed on my lip, missing them so much it hurt.

"I apologize. Talking about your family is hard, ja. I also miss my family." He tipped his cap. "I'll see you in the morning."

"Ja, ja, and thank you very much for your help." I stood in the doorway, watching as he walked across the gravel, the lawn, and then entered the stable. I sighed in satisfaction. Anders was very nice. Though I felt certain that he had destroyed my Book of Mormon, I also felt the desire to somehow show my appreciation for his help.

"The way you stare after the stable boy makes me jealous." Jens came from the shadows. "Should I leave? He smiled crookedly.

"Jens!" I leapt into his arms, nearly sending him into the bushes, but he held me and twirled us in a circle. "I was afraid you wouldn't come back."

"I came as soon as I could. Work has kept me busy." He let me down but kept his arms around me. "Can I come in?"

"Herrer Ilse is asleep," I said. "And the others have retired to their rooms long ago."

He touched his forehead to mine. "I came this long distance.

Would you send me away?"

"Nej." I hesitated. "I am very glad to have your visit." But the others would know if I let him in. And I'd be in trouble. "The weather is nice," I said, "let's walk to the garden. Ja? We can visit there." The brief image of last time entered my mind but I shook it off. Jens had come to visit. Not kiss. I needed to talk to him about my religion, see what his plans for our future were.

"You are quiet," he said. "Do you wish me to leave?" He truly appeared sad.

"Please don't." I touched his arm. "I couldn't bear it if you did."

Jens put his arm around my waist and pulled me close to him as we walked. "I wouldn't want you to get chilled," he said.

I nestled into him, grateful for his concern.

"Your parents keep you very busy. They should hire someone to help." I brightened with an idea. "Papa knew a family near the Village of Neder Holluf. I believe their name is Nørgaard. They have plenty of children and not enough farm to support them. It would be a blessing to hire one or two of them. I know they have sons old enough to hire out."

Jens shook his head. "It is good for a man to work, and I need to know the family business."

"But ..." If he had more time, we could be together more often.

He touched his finger to my mouth. "You are much too pretty to be fretting over my family's business."

My cheeks warmed because of his compliment, and I did not respond, but my mind was a flurry of thoughts—of how, when he proposed and we married, it would be my business as well. Mama often had suggestions for Papa, and he was glad to have her as his partner.

When we got to the garden, we sat in the same bench as before. All I'd wanted to talk to him about, everything I'd wanted to share and say fell from my mind with his first tender kiss.

It seemed I had no will of my own, but my whole being surrendered to his divine kisses.

"We should talk," I finally whispered.

"About what?" He kissed me again.

"I mean it." I pulled away. "I stayed in Denmark for you. I love you." It came out as a pleading whine, but I didn't care. I stared him in the eyes with hopeful anticipation.

"I am so glad you stayed. I worried that I'd never see you again." He kissed the tip of my nose. "I've loved those cute little freckles since I was ten." Jens took my right hand in his. "And these fingers have been on my mind since I was twelve." He kissed each of them. "I love your cheeks." He kissed my cheek.

I sighed, disheartened. "I am serious, and you are making fun." How I wanted to give in to his desires, but I needed to turn my handsome wolf into a lamb, and pushed myself away.

"What?" He groaned. "What is it you want? I'll do anything."

I smoothed my apron in front of me. "I would like to talk to you about my religion."

"Religion?" He made a face. "You want to talk religion? Tonight?" He scooted near and wrapped his arm around my shoulders and drew near to kiss me. "I can think of better things to discuss," he said playfully.

I slipped away from his kiss and stood. "It is late and I must go in." I started down the path.

Before I'd taken five steps, he caught up to me and scooped me into his arms. "You are driving me mad," he murmured. "You temptress. I will hear about your religion if you will satisfy my desires." He placed me gently down.

My heart raced with anticipation. "I fear your desires cannot easily be satisfied," I said. "Perhaps we can come upon a compromise."

His face brightened with a playful expression. "I'm listening."

Chapter 25

"Berta! Berta Erichsen!" I heard the pounding on my door. "Are you ill?"

"I'll be right there." I groaned and pulled myself from the warmth of my quilt. My night with Jens had gone too long.

I went to the door and peeked out. "Frau Jensen, thank you for waking me. I will only take a minute to dress."

"You'd better hurry if you want any breakfast." She shook her head and walked back down the hallway.

I closed the door, hurried into my blouse and skirt, and ran to the kitchen. Frau Jensen handed me a small bowl of porridge. "This is all that is left. The others were hungry this morn."

"Ja, ja. Thank you." I grabbed up the bowl and ran to the empty table. The others had already gotten to work. "I owe you much, indeed," I said. "Jens Larsen came by last night. We went out to the garden." My face warmed with the memory.

"I don't want to hear the sordid details of your affair with the Larsen lad." She poured steaming hot water into the sink.

"Nej. There is no affair." I ate my last bite and brought the bowl and spoon to the sink. "There is nothing sordid." Why would she think this? "There is only the true love between a man and a woman." I took the cloth from her, washed my things and set them to dry. "He will come again tonight, I think."

"You forget that the window to Anders's room faces the garden." Frau Jensen dipped the pot into the water.

"Did he see?" I put my hands to my chest, horror-struck that

Anders had seen this private moment between Jens and me.

"He saw enough to make him concerned."

"Did he tell the others as well?"

"Give him more credit than that." Frau Jensen took my hand and guided me back to the table. "He's concerned, as am I. Dear, if you give yourself to him now, what does he need to marry you for?"

"Oh, I couldn't do that. I wouldn't," I said, though I needed to be stronger, for the both of us. "Mama and Papa warned me about such things."

"Your parents were smart. Ja?" She patted my hands. "If this is true love, he'll wait."

"Ja, ja. I told him only two kisses per night, but ..." I touched my hands to my mouth. "I didn't know it was possible for one kiss to last so long." We hadn't even gotten to talk about his becoming a Mormon.

"You're smitten, you are. And that Jens needs to cool his attitude. You'll be the one to suffer if you allow him to continue. Now off with you. Your chores aren't doing themselves, and I expect you back to the kitchen by four."

"Ja, ja, and thank you again."

When I got up to Mr. Ilse's room, sofa pillows were on the floor, his sheets were nearly pulled off, and there was a smudge of mud on the rug near his desk. What was going on? I set out to put things right knowing that Mr. Ilse did not do this. He was meticulous. Was it Helsa doing these things, or Frau Olesen? I intended to find out.

As soon as I finished Mr. Ilse's suite of rooms, I sought out the woman who was supposed to help me succeed. She wasn't even upstairs, and her duties lie upstairs. I found her in the formal dining room feet up, sitting on a chair, and talking to Helsa.

"Good," I said.

They turned a disdainful eye toward me as I went to face them.

"It is good you are here together. This way I only need to say it once."

"You're a little young to be my mother," said Frau Olesen. "I don't need a scolding from the likes of you." She turned her head as if to disregard me but kept watch.

"Well, you are the age of my mother and you should be a better example." My fists balled at my side. "Why do you torment me and make my work more difficult? We should be friends, comrades, and working together to make each of our duties lighter."

"I haven't a clue what you're talking about. Do you, Helsa?"

"Nej." Helsa made a face. "She goes on as though she owns the place though."

"I do not," I said. "Nor do I ever intend to own this manor. What's more, I have never given either of you cause to condemn me. What I do know is the Good Lord says an eye for an eye, and I don't intend to sit around idly while you sneak about putting mud to the floor and soot to the mirror frames." Satisfied, I turned and left them to consider my warning.

Once I finished the dusting and cleaning of the entryway, I went into the kitchen.

"You are getting quicker at doing your chores." Frau Jensen poured cream into the pot on the stove. "Let's hope they don't suffer because of speed."

"Nej. I am done sooner merely because I'm getting better at caring for this large manor." I stood beside her. "What would you like me to do?"

"We're making a light supper of it tonight. Herrer Ilse is in the stables with one of the mares. I've got biscuits in the oven. Go ahead and chop the rutabagas while I finish preparing the soup base. It'll be an easy night for you."

"The mare is having her colt?" I jumped up and down. "I must go and see." After seeing her concern, I continued, "I will finish my duties first, of course." I bobbed a curtsy and got to work on the rutabagas.

After they were chopped, and everything prepared, Frau Jensen gave me instruction on the rest of the meal as well as on the service.

"I'm off to my own supper now. See that you don't let things burn." She took up her scarf and coat. "I'll see you tomorrow."

I did as she instructed, taking care to follow her directions with exactness before hurrying out the door and racing to the stable.

When I got to the side door, I paused. Anders had seen me kissing Jens. I didn't know if I could face him. I'd been taught better than to kiss a boy like that. Those kinds of kisses were for after marriage only. What would Anders think of me? I respected him and his opinions, and regretted my foolish actions.

I'd have to talk to Jens. No more kisses. I couldn't trust myself, or him. Jens Larsen had all the affection he would get from me until our wedding day. We would visit and go on picnics. We would discuss our dreams and aspirations, and most importantly, we would discuss my religion. He had been interested before; he would listen now he saw how important it was to me.

At the sound of soft nickering, I pushed the stable door open and went inside. Anders and Mr. Ilse were beside Athena in a large birthing pen to the rear of the stable. She saw me and moved like she would get up. Anders and Mr. Ilse were there calming her, the colt's legs already visible.

"Is there anything I can do to help?" I asked, peering through the gate, my hands on the rail.

"Stay out of the way," said Anders.

"May I watch? I've helped with such things at home."

"Your animals were work animals and of no particular breeding," said Mr. Ilse. "This mare is expensive. The price this colt will fetch more than pays for the mother's care."

"Ja, ja," I said. "I will stay out of your way."

Athena nickered, her stomach contracted, and the colt slipped out and onto the clean straw.

"He isn't moving. Can he breathe? Is he alright?" I stood on tiptoes trying to make sure the little newborn was healthy.

"He is fine," said Mr. Ilse. "It's a lot of work being born. He's resting."

Athena lay limp for only a moment. Then she reached around and sniffed her baby. Before long, she was licking him clean, and the little guy seemed to enjoy the attention.

I watched as Athena got up, nudging her colt. He seemed to take her hint because he wobbled and stood. All this effort seemed to make him hungry and he knew instinctively where to find his meal.

"Well, this is the best part of it all, isn't it?" Mr. Ilse smiled and patted Anders's back.

"Ja, ja," said Anders. "It's best when things go along easily."

"Athena's and Aphrodite's colts should both be ready to leave their mothers before Christmas. A blessing, indeed." Mr. Ilse put an arm around Anders. "I've decided to start hosting the young persons' activities." They came out of the stall and stood beside me. "Berta here needs to learn some social graces, and I want you to be her partner."

"I'd be happy to help." Anders tipped his head, but I saw his jaw clenching.

How could he ask Anders while I was standing right there? How could he indicate that I needed to learn manners? I looked from one to the other not knowing whether to run and hide forever or to scream in frustration.

Chapter 26

I picked Mr. Ilse's pillows off the floor. The social gathering was tonight. Anders had made himself scarce since Mr. Ilse declared me socially inept. I tried reasoning why this mattered to me while rubbing soot smudges off the picture frames. The women hadn't relented their trying to sabotage me.

Their actions made me remember something Mama had said, "When a person refuses to get along, kill them with kindness." She had learned this tactic when working at Grandfather Jensen's mill as a young woman.

My demanding they treat me better hadn't worked, and it was not in me to seek revenge. I would try Mama's method next. I left the Master's room and snuck over to where Frau Olesen worked. She was running behind. As usual. I went in the next room, dusted with the busyness and silence of a scurrying mouse, and then hurried down the stairs before she saw me, while holding back a laugh.

I had to talk to Anders before tonight's gathering. We shouldn't be awkward. We shouldn't be at war. And, I wanted him to know of my sorrow for my shameless actions with Jens.

The thought of bringing attention to my private deed was hard. I stood, staring at the side door of the stable feeling quite afraid to open it. As I was gaining the courage to approach Anders, I heard, "May I help you?"

I jumped and turned around. Anders approached from the other side of the stable leading a horse.

"I came for a visit." I raised my eyebrows and smiled,

hoping for the best.

"I am working and have no time for afternoon visits." He tied the horse to a post and walked to the tack room.

"I actually came to help." I followed him. "I wanted to thank you for helping me with Herrer Ilse the other night."

"It is not your duty to tuck him into bed. Why should you thank me?" He frowned and looked me over. "What if this horse is spirited and does not accept your help?" He picked up a grooming brush and went back to the horse.

I took another one and hurried beside Anders. "This is Romeo. He is your gentlest horse. As you told me, he is a lover and not a fighter." I smiled, pleased with myself.

"You remembered." He brushed down the horse's flank.

I stood opposite Anders, brushing the horse's side. "I told you that I am good with horses—and by helping Mr. Ilse to bed, you were also helping me."

Anders raised an eyebrow. "Ja?"

"His not being grouchy from lack of sleep is a great help to everyone," I said, feeling defensive.

"Will you not get in trouble for being out here regardless of his mood? I heard about your punishment the last time you spent too much time in the stables. You should not neglect your own work to be with the horses."

"I am not neglecting my work. I'm free for half this hour, and I will be sure to get back so Herrer Ilse doesn't wait for his supper." I shook my head. Anders was full of judgments today.

He put the brush down, led Romeo to his stall, and started back outside. "On nice days I let the horses graze in the pasture." He shrugged his shoulders. "They enjoyed it, but now it is time to bring them back."

We walked together to the pasture, and I wanted to talk about my behavior with Jens. But I was embarrassed and couldn't form anything in my mind that sounded right. With the desire for an apology on the tip of my tongue, I remained silent.

The two colts, with a burst of energy, flicked their tails and bolted across the field. Anders gave a whistle. Zeus came and waited patiently while Anders put his bridle on. As we walked back to the stable, the horse held his head high.

"Zeus is a proud stallion," I observed. "I'm surprised he doesn't give you more trouble."

"Proud, ja. He is high-bred." Anders rubbed Zeus's nose affectionately. "Yet he also has manners and presence to accompany his royal status."

I stroked the spotted horse's neck. He was such a magnificent animal.

"These Knabstruppers are different from the Frederiksborgers my father had on our farm at home," said Anders. "Those horses are bred for hard work."

"Ja, ja," I agreed. "Frederiksborgers are hard workers." The Andersdatters had Frederiksborgers, and I knew a little about them. After helping groom Zeus, I scratched under his chin. "I should return to my work," I said, handing Anders the brush. "I have the added responsibility of helping Frau Jensen with supper each evening. This way she can get home sooner." I curtsied, feeling pleased to share this news. "She requested my help."

"She likes you." He made it sound like an impossibility.

I lifted a shoulder. "Ja, and I like her." I hesitated, wanting to voice an apology before leaving. I opened my mouth to speak, but no sound came out. It couldn't have been me out in the garden with Jens. A shudder crawled under my skin at the thought of Anders witnessing my indiscretion. Why was Anders even talking with me? I opened my mouth again. Nej. "I must go," I finally said, mortified of saying more.

Anders followed me out of the stable but did not offer conversation.

"Good day," I said, plodding toward the service entry angry with myself for not being brave enough to apologize. When I'd made it halfway, I heard him calling out. "I will see you tonight then, Miss Berta."

The young persons' guild. I forced a smile, waving, and walked into the manor.

Frau Jensen pulled a loaf of bread from the oven as I walked in. It smelled heavenly. "Did you enjoy yourself?" she asked.

"Ja." I shrugged. "Yet I did not wish for you to work alone."

"You are here now. Go ahead and set the table. When you get back, the bread should be cool enough to slice."

The everyday china was on a shelf, and I pulled down the dishes that we'd need.

"Hopefully things go how Mr. Ilse wishes tonight at the social." She spooned the herring in cream sauce into a serving dish. "Why he would insist on having the youth over for socials every week—" she shook her head. "Well, it's pure craziness to me.

Choosing to remain silent, I grabbed up the dishes and went to the breakfast room. When I came back, I sliced the bread, inhaling the aroma. I loved the smell of fresh bread. Wholesome was the only way I could describe it. "May I have a slice?"

Frau Jensen gave a nod.

Eating warm bread was a near perfect experience—nutty, buttery, heaven.

"You'll be there tonight serving up the drinks and the desserts that I prepare. It is your job to make sure the evening runs smoothly in order to keep Herrer Ilse in good spirits." She placed a bottle of ale into her apron pocket and then carried the platter of food out of the kitchen.

"Pardon?" I followed her to the breakfast room.

"He has been in a good mood since that colt was born. Don't spoil it with recklessness."

I had noticed his cheerful attitude. It was a blessed relief from his usual grumpiness. Come to think of it, he hadn't had as much ale either. Maybe worry over his horses had caused his drinking, though that hardly seemed like him.

"The other women, well, they wanted me to instruct you to mind your manners and keep him in a good mood." Frau Jensen fussed over the place settings I'd arranged.

"What do you mean?" I watched as she put the utensils she'd moved back to where I had placed them.

"They believe that, just like Inge, the maid before you…" She glanced up. "They're convinced Herrer Ilse wants you for his new wife."

Though the accusation was not funny, I burst into laughter and had to sit until I calmed myself. "This is the best amusement I've had in months," I said chuckling.

"You think this is a joke?" she snapped. "Why else does he pamper you so? He will either marry you or make you his mistress." She crossed her arms and glared at me.

This type of comment was not like Frau Jensen. I became concerned. Had she dipped into Mr. Ilse's ale?

"He does it for Jens Larsen," I said, all humor forgotten. "The Larsens are dear friends of his, and he is helping me learn the social graces that will please them." I sounded defensive by my own ears, but me as Frau Ilse? Ludicrous. That would be Frau Olesen's pleasure.

She pulled the bottle of ale from her apron pocket and sat it on the table. It appeared full.

"I am only trying to help, so I hope you will pardon my frankness," she said, her voice softening. "The Larsens will not allow their son to marry a servant." She held her hand to her hip.

"If I am not good enough for Jens Larsen, I certainly do not qualify as Herrer Ilse's wife." I took a deep breath. "This is why I sup with Herrer Ilse and why he is having the socials here. He is training me to take over as Frau Larsen." Could she not see it? "Mr. Ilse has no disreputable thoughts regarding me."

"Whatever you say," she conceded. "Just mind your manners this night. His reasoning for this nonsense is none of my business, but his mood is all of our business."

"That will be all, Tovi." Mr. Ilse stepped into the room, eyeing her. "You may return to the kitchen and prepare the punch and desserts for tonight's activities."

The color left her face, and I waited with baited breath to see if we'd both be kicked out to the road. How much of our conversation had Mr. Ilse had heard?

"Thank you, sir." She curtsied and hurried from the room.

Mr. Ilse pulled the chair out for me, and I sat down, my heart thumping in my chest. Was he angry?

He sat in his chair and regarded me. "I had just freshened up for supper when I heard a peal of laughter as light and pure as crystal bells." He unfolded the linen napkin, placing it on his lap. "Who was the owner of that delightful sound? Surely not Tovi."

"Nej." I blushed at his flattery. "It was me."

"Tell me the joke so that I might also have a good laugh." His head tilted, his eyes entreating.

"Herrer Ilse, it was a private moment with Frau Jensen, and you are too much the gentleman to insist I divulge the conversation." I served him his supper.

His eyes twinkled. "You have learned well, my dear girl."

"You are a very kind teacher." I nodded, pleased that I needn't say more.

"Let's change the subject then, shall we?" He poured ale into his cup and took a contemplative sip. "I've heard whisperings around the manor. The other maids think that I am treating you … too kindly." He raised an eyebrow.

"Ja, ja, they are jealous. I think." My heart skipped a beat. This was not a change of subject.

"It is because of your dreams and aspirations that you have caught my attention." He smiled gently and patted my hand. "I also know how deeply Master Jens's feelings lie. You are young and need to marry someone."

"Sir?"

"Like Jens Larsen, of course. Someone who can care for you. It's a simple solution for the right man."

"It's just as I told Frau Jensen." I was relieved to be correct in my assumption.

"Shall I have a talk with them?" He leaned back, interlocking his fingers. "Are the maids being unkind?"

"Nej. Please do not bother yourself." They were unkind, but things would only worsen between me and the others if he spoke to them. "It is enough that we know the truth."

"Indeed." He reached over. "May I?" He tucked a stray lock of hair behind my ear. I hadn't even felt it fall. "You'll need to freshen up a little before you meet our guests in the parlor."

"Ja, ja." I gulped at his lingering hand, feeling very awkward all of a sudden.

"I see you are nervous." Mr. Ilse pulled his hand away. "Don't let the other maids' gossip poison your mind."

"Herrer Ilse." Frau Jensen came into the room and curtsied. "I have done as you asked and am ready to go now."

"You may not leave." Mr. Ilse stared at her as though she was of simple mind. "It is you who will serve this night. Miss Berta is the young person who will host the gathering. Not I."

Chapter 27

Anders wore clean, brown woolen trousers, a long-sleeved shirt, a woolen cap, and well-worn leather shoes. His wooden shoes, along with everyone else's, were outside the front door.

I looked down at my feet, covered only with woolen stockings, a knot in my throat. Papa was going to buy leather shoes for Catherine and me when our feet stopped growing, but then we joined the Church. Instead of spending money on leather shoes for social gatherings, we had saved our money for Zion.

"Miss Berta Erichsen, you look nice this evening." Anders bowed and took my hand.

"Thank you, ja. Thank you." I curtsied. I'd known how to greet someone properly since I was ten. Yet, Mr. Ilse, playing the part of etiquette instructor, hovered nearby and insisted that everyone practice this most basic greeting.

The young people here were all clean and smart in dress. The girls wore woolen skirts in a variety of colors: blue, brown, or red. Their long-sleeved white blouses were adorned with plaid or striped vests, and some wore multi-colored aprons. Bonnets replaced their work scarves.

"Good, good," said Mr. Ilse from the head of the room. "You have all exceeded my expectations." He moved smoothly beside me, his grey hair greased and combed back. "I think you should try a little harder to elevate your compliments. Let's try, the two of us, shall we?"

I curtsied. "Herrer Ilse, you are so generous in allowing this gathering." I curtsied even deeper. "Your home is lovely, and I've never seen you look finer."

"Ah, that was most appropriate." He beamed and stretched out his hands, including everyone. "Let us continue."

In the corner of the room, a pianist started playing a lively tune, and the other couples made their way into a line of dance.

Anders leaned close to my ear. "What was that about?" he asked.

"Herrer Ilse is teaching me how to win favor with the Larsens."

A dark thought seemed to pass across Anders's face, but he bowed and led me into the dance.

"Herrer Ilse says that wealthy people give each other compliments." Now that I did not have wedding money or my chest of homespun wedding fabrics, my manners had to be perfect.

"You do it quite well, ja." Though the tune was lively, Anders seemed to stay closer to me than was custom. I found I did not mind.

"He's been teaching me almost since I arrived."

"Stop the dance!" Mr. Ilse bellowed above the music. The room became silent. Everyone watched, wide-eyed, as he strode toward Anders and me. "Excuse me. It's most difficult for Miss Erichsen to learn the proper form of the dance if her partner himself doesn't know it." He took Anders's place at the end of the line. "Music!" he said, and the pianist began playing.

"Notice the little variations of movement," he murmured. "These small nuances are the difference between upper-class civility and the dancing of peasants."

While he did dance differently, what I noticed was that all eyes were on me, none of them approving. Anders was in the back of the room, head tilted, appearing troubled. None of them understood. This was for my benefit. Mr. Ilse was right, I needed a husband. I needed a way to escape Mr. Ilse's licentious hands, and these people needed to stop their gossipy judgments.

When the music ended, he clapped his hands. "Thank you for allowing me this one indulgence," he said to everyone. His hand, like an anvil, weighted my shoulder, trapping me. He gave it a squeeze. "It does my heart good to be among such a lively group if only for a small moment." He bowed over my hand and kissed it. "I shall allow you to continue your festivities uninterrupted."

All eyes were cast on me as though I'd done something terrible. I wanted to rush from the room. I wanted to go home. But I had no home. Instead, I pulled my emotions together and curtsied deeply. "Mr. Ilse, thank you for your guidance this night. You've been most kind." I knew he expected these words.

The others in the room, six couples total, quit their staring at me and followed my lead in thanking Mr. Ilse. He sauntered to the doorway, turned and bowed with a flourish and left. I assumed he went to the library to read, as was his custom in the evenings.

The music started again, but Anders led me outside. The air was cool and crisp, having recently rained. I rubbed my arms.

He leaned against the manor. "It is a nice night, ja?"

A full moon shone between the clouds, the glow making his hair shine like combed flax. Anders was very attractive in this light, but I shouldn't think of such things while nearly betrothed to Jens.

"It is very nice." My toes tapped the music's rhythm as I looked out at the blue and shadowy landscape. On the opposite side of the stable, deer ate grass along the tree line.

Anders glanced at me. "This was all very awkward tonight."

"Ja," I said, not really paying attention. Baptizing and marrying Jens was taking too long. He hadn't been back for days. His parents must keep him too busy. "Anders," I said, wanting to apologize.

"Ja?" He took my hand between his palms. Their warmth unexpectedly melted into my heart.

I gazed into his eyes and couldn't speak. I wanted to tell him that I was not the kind of girl who kisses boys the way I kissed Jens Larsen. I opened my mouth to speak, and then took note of his lips. My heart did a little dance at the thought of kissing him that I did not appreciate. What was wrong with me?

"Berta."

"Ja," I murmured.

"The music is playing. Let us dance." He placed my hand in the crook of his arm and we strolled into the manor. At his touch, butterflies bounced inside my chest, but I silenced them. This would not do. Would I yearn to kiss every man who stood close? This was not Jens Larsen, the man I would marry. Nonetheless, Anders both calmed my soul and excited my spirits.

I danced with him for a moment, both of us quieter than usual, but I had to be true to Jens. "You dance nearly as well as Jens," I said. But, dancing with Anders while talking of Jens felt like a betrayal. I glanced around for an escape.

Upon seeing our cook still at work, I excused myself from the dance and went to the dessert table. "Frau Jensen," I said, "The food is delicious, as always." I took a plate with a small, fruity tart and plopped it in my mouth.

Anders stepped beside me. "I have something to discuss. Please come back outside with me," he muttered.

"Would no one come to help you tonight?" I asked Frau Jensen. I couldn't be alone with Anders while I felt so confused.

"It is not the other maids' duty to help." She handed Anders a cup of ale. "Would you care for refreshment?"

He took the cup, thanked Frau Jensen, and drank it down, all while watching me. He knew I did not drink alcohol, yet he took another cup. "Would you care to join me? It's very good, ja."

"Nej. Thank you." I curtsied, frowning.

"That is correct." His face held an ironic smile. "You are the Mormon girl." He held my elbow, guiding me toward the door.

"The one with secrets in the garden." He extended his elbow. "Come. Share with me your beliefs."

Though I had wanted to apologize for my shameful interlude, having him mention it frustrated me. "The music is nice. Let us stay here and rejoin the dance." He was seeking a way to mock me or my religion, to say I was unworthy. I would not give him the satisfaction.

"Of course," he said. We were already near the other dancers, and he led us easily in line. His quick acquiescence made me wonder if he had anything to discuss at all.

This was not how I hoped the evening would go. I was upset with Anders, upset with the other maids for their interference, and weary after having worked hard all day. I sorely wished Mr. Ilse would come and call it a night. I smiled feebly at Anders who seemed to have an abundance of energy. When the music was ended, he guided me wordlessly back outside.

"Berta, we are friends, ja?" He held my hand, probably to keep me from rushing away. Yet his hand on mine suddenly felt very personal. Like we were so much more than friends.

I gulped, and nodded. "Ja, ja. Friends. I hope we are." I offered him a weak smile.

"Tell me then, about yourself, because I do not understand." His eyes glistened, but my heart sank.

"What is the mystery?" My brow wrinkled in disbelief. "That I have no money? That I work as a maid rather than live on the street—or that I am anxious to marry Jens Larsen?" So that I can move away from here, I continued silently.

Sadness passed over his face and he momentarily looked away. "Tell me about your family. I know it's hard for you to talk about it." He turned his gaze to mine. "These questions are eating me inside. Were they unkind to you? Did you wish to be apart from them? Were you unsure of their religion?" He led me to an ornate bench.

Though I held out hope that Jens would convert and marry me, it was a mystery to me why I had stayed in Denmark as well. At the time, I'd been so certain it was the right thing to do. Only I grew more desperate to leave Ilse Manor with every day that passed. The anger, the inappropriate touching—nej, I could not stay much longer.

It was hard for me to think with Anders's hand placed over mine. "I love my family very much," I said, clenching my jaws together, forcing my emotion to stay hidden. "I am very committed to being a Mormon. But, as you know, I stayed in Denmark to marry Jens Larsen."

It felt wrong saying that to Anders, though it was true.

He smirked. "The fellow in the garden."

"Ja." His remark stung, but I deserved it. "Before my parents immigrated, he gave me this ring." I held out my hand and showed him once more. "He said that he wanted to share his life with someone he loved—with me." My shoulders lifted. "We made plans to meet at my aunt's the following week, and so I stayed."

"Did he come to your aunt's?"

"Nej." I stared at my lap. "I was never able to let him know that I had stayed for him. He only found out when Herrer Ilse invited the Larsens to supper."

"And now he forces you to work for Herrer Ilse instead of taking you to his home."

"Nej, that is not the case. Jens has not proposed yet, though he continues to assure me of his feelings."

Anders took a deep breath. "I see."

"Nej. You do not see," I said. Crossing my arms to calm myself, I continued, "My chest, my fabrics, my money, they are all gone from me and I have nothing to offer except a willingness to learn the special social graces the Larsens require. Since I am not willing to live on the street or in the poorhouse, I have no choice except to live with Herrer Ilse while he teaches me."

"You always have a choice." He took my hand in his.

The warmth of his hands was very distracting. *Marrying Anders would be the better choice.* The thought startled me, and I pulled my hand away. Anders lived in Mr. Ilse's stable and could not help me get away from Mr. Ilse.

"If I was this Larsen fellow," Anders continued, "and you were my lover, I'd not allow you to live here. I'd put you up somewhere safe."

"Lover?" My temper rose to the surface. "Put me up?" It was only by pure determination that I calmed myself. If I made a scene, Mr. Ilse would become involved. "I am no one's lover," I hissed. "And I'll not be put anywhere. For anyone." My fists clenched beside me. "You dare call yourself my friend all while supposing that I'd give myself away?"

"Many people who love each other can't afford to marry. This is nothing to be ashamed of."

"My mama and papa would not agree." I regarded him sternly. "The Larsens can certainly afford to pay for the wedding license, and I am a good girl," I said. "I will marry first."

He leaned back in disbelief. "I saw you in the garden with him."

"You are an eavesdropper and should mind your own business." My face heated from shame.

"This would be my great pleasure," he said, sounding irritated.

"Jens and I love each other, and we will be married." I touched my hand to Mama's locket and felt more calm. "This is what I wanted to explain to you."

"It is not my business." He touched my shoulder. His voice soft. "My only worry is over you."

"It will never happen again." I chewed my lip. "I promise." A tear fell to my cheek. "It is time for me to go in." Embarrassed, I walked away. Anders tried pulling me back into our conversation, but I jerked free of his grasp. "Please do not follow me inside."

Four of the couples were still there, visiting and laughing. Why had they not said their goodbyes and left? Frau Jensen still stood at the desserts table appearing tired and upset.

"Frau Jensen, I am ready to call it a night and you are tired as well." Feeling the catch in my voice, I poured myself a glass of cool water and sipped it. "What are we to do? Shall I find Herrer Ilse and ask him to send them away?"

"He has left you in charge." She sounded weary. "I would be most grateful if you'd put an end to this so that I might get home to my husband."

I nodded grimly. I'd never taken charge of a social gathering before. Standing in front of the serving table, I held it for support and cleared my throat loudly to gain their attention.

"Dear friends ..." I felt like a pretender, and my hands shook. "I regret that the time has come to say goodbye." They clearly questioned my authority, as did I, until remembering that I would be the lady of Larsen manor one day.

I took a cleansing breath and continued. "Our host, Herrer Jacob Ilse, bids you all a good night. My only comfort is the knowledge that we can resume our conversations at our next gathering."

When everyone had left, I helped Frau Jensen clean the room and put the remaining food away.

"Good night, Frau Jensen. Thank you, ja, for staying longer than was your duty."

"It is my duty to keep Herrer Ilse happy and well-fed." She left through the service door. Her husband was waiting to walk her home.

Having a home and a family—my heart ached for it. Before retiring to my room, I went to the library to bid a good night to Mr. Ilse.

"Did the evening go well?" He looked up from his book.

I tried to smile. "It was a lovely evening. Thank you, ja."

"Did you meet all of our guests and make them feel welcome?"

My shoulders drooped. "Meet them? Nej." I'd been too busy with Anders. "I will do better next time."

He leaned forward. "Did you at least walk them to the door?"

I shook my head. "Nej. Though I did thank them for coming. I bid them a good night, and I expressed an eagerness for our next meeting."

"*Min tåbelige barn.*" He stood and bid me to enter the room. "What were you doing all evening, entertaining yourself with the stable boy? Your foolishness has embarrassed me." He took a measuring stick from his drawer. "Hold out your hands."

I did not want him to hit me. My jaws clenched in determination, but when the vein in his neck bulged, I shoved my hands in front of me.

"This was the whole point of the exercise, for you to learn to play hostess." He smacked each hand with his stick.

It smarted, and I bit onto my lips to keep from crying out.

"You've wasted the entire week. All the things I've had to arrange. All the people I've had to schedule. All in vain on a worthless pauper who dreams of being a fairytale princess." He waved his hand toward the door. "Off with you now. I am too tired for this."

I curtsied, turned, and ran from the room, unwanted tears pooling in my eyes. Moonlight fell in through the windows lighting my way and making a lantern unnecessary, and I ran from room to room, down the hallway, through the kitchen and to my bedroom where I could finally have a good cry.

The window to my room was not large, but it gave enough light that when I stepped into the room, I saw that I was not alone.

"Jens!" I cried, and rushed to his waiting arms.

Chapter 28

"Berta, love, I thought you would never come." He stood and melted himself to me. "Your face is wet. You have been crying."

He must have let himself in through the servant's entrance. We were alone in my room, and I shouldn't allow him to stay, but I let him untie my bonnet and un-plait my hair.

"Come, ja, and tell me what has you so distressed." His voice was soft and comforting.

We would only talk. I would let him comfort me, and then he would go home. A home that would also be mine one day. He led me to the only place to sit—my small bed. He sat in the corner and pulled me into his arms. I rested my head against his chest.

What should I tell him, though, and how could he understand? I had disappointed Mr. Ilse while learning to be Frau Larsen and deserved punishment according to his rules. Though my hands still stung, I could not bear to tell Jens I had failed.

"There, there." He dabbed the tears from my face.

It wasn't uncommon for couples to seal their love outside of marriage. Jens would not comprehend why Anders's thinking I had done so would distress me. Jens might feel insulted. Nor could I tell him how Anders's touch had confused me. I wouldn't. The constant reminder that my lack of dowry or funds lessened my chances of marrying well made me feel more anxious than I should. Jens had already expressed a desire to grow old with me.

My only hope of making Mama and Papa proud held me tightly in his arms. "Except for you, I am all alone," I whispered.

Clutching him tighter, I closed my eyes, weary, lonely, and desperate. Only Jens knew me before—he knew of my talents and my potential. He knew that given time and money I could replace my chest of fabrics with more fabric I'd make myself.

Jens sat forward as if to get up. My heart raced. He couldn't leave. I clung to him, needing the reassurance of his love and needing him near.

He smiled softly. "I'm not leaving yet, my love." He held me away for just a moment. Then he kissed a tear on my cheek, and another. He placed his lips over mine, and I drank him in, thirsty for his passion as though this only was what kept me alive.

It delighted me when his lips left mine and trailed down to my neck. However, when he touched the collar of my blouse, the weight of Mama's locket thudding against my chest reminded me: once again I was doing wrong.

"I can't," I groaned, and sat up straight. "This is not right."

He reached for me and pulled me back, kissing my eyes, my nose, and then my lips. "This is good," he murmured. "I've never felt anything more right."

The idea that he loved me guided my response for a moment more. Then I stopped.

"I cannot disappoint my family," I said against his next kiss.

"Your Mama and Papa are far away and will never know." His passion filled my loneliness and made every touch, every kiss feel perfectly right. But Mama's necklace pressed between us told me this was not what I craved, as much as I wanted it to be so.

With desire filling every portion of my soul, I pushed him away and stood. "Nej. This is not right." My knees wobbled under my weight as I walked to the door. "You must leave. Come courting during the daylight, ja?"

He crawled forward on the bed, but he did not have the

expression of someone who intended to leave. I darted through the doorway just as he grabbed for me.

His curses followed me as I ran through the kitchen and left the manor. The stable loomed ahead, and I raced for the door. I didn't hear him following. He would calm down. He would leave.

Nevertheless, I opened the stable door and crept inside. Caesar whinnied at my intrusion when I stepped near. I rubbed his nose. "It is only me, and you've already had your oats. You won't tell on me now, will you?"

Caesar shook his head, and not wishing to discus my actions with Jens on this evening, I went to the back of the building just in case he surprised me by following. I waited, hidden behind the hay. It surprised and gladdened me when he didn't come.

Why would he curse me so? Was he merely using me? If not, where was his kind regard? Why had we not talked of marriage? His kisses screamed of love, yet his curses did not. Had his feelings toward me changed? I offered a silent prayer, wishing for the wisdom to discern his true feelings.

When I finished, my heart quit racing, and I thought of Anders. He was a true gentleman. If Jens loved me, he should treat me as Anders did—with kindness. This was the way Papa treated Mama.

Allowing Jens to stay for even a moment had been wrong. The more I thought on it, I had to wonder if Anders was right. It seemed that if Jens loved me the way he should, he would have proposed that first night. But why had he encouraged me to leave my family? Perhaps his family was interfering.

There was no time to think tonight. It was time to return to the manor. My eyes were droopy. Surely Jens had calmed down and gone home. It would give Anders a fright to see me sleeping in the hay when he came to feed the horses in the morning. As I started to get up, I heard a noise and went back to my knees.

The stable door creaked open. "Berta, love," Jens cooed. "I

have calmed down now. I am sorry for our misunderstanding." His footsteps crunched in the dirt.

My first instinct was to go to him. We needed to talk, because I needed answers. I started to get up, but my knees took me back to the ground. My heart encouraged my feet to get up again, but the Holy Spirit warned me to wait just a moment longer, to be sure. What if he talked me in to giving him more kisses right there in the barn?

"Where are you, my love?" His footsteps crunched again. The horses whinnied. "Come back to the manor. Ja? I will not hurt you."

He needed a chance to explain himself. I started to get up. Perhaps I had judged him harshly. But an uncertain feeling kept me still. I filled with worry and dread. My heart pounded. Would he find me? I closed my eyes, pleading with the Lord for safety. Why, I did not know. Jens wouldn't hurt me. I trusted him. I wanted to marry him. Or did I?

We needed to put an end to this madness once and for all. I made to get up.

"Berta, this is not a funny game you are playing." The frustration in his voice kept me hidden behind the hay.

"Hello?" Anders sounded groggy. "What are you doing in Herrer Ilse's stable this time of night?"

"What business is it of yours?" Jens snapped.

"It is my business," Anders said with authority. "Herrer Ilse pays me well to keep his thoroughbred horses safe and well fed."

"Jacob Ilse and my family are good friends. I've got business here. Now go back to your hovel," Jens growled.

"Herrer Ilse does not pay me to sleep in a hovel. He pays me to sleep here, assured that I'll allow neither friends nor strangers access to his stables."

I felt inexplicably pleased with the way Anders held his ground. Most servants would allow Jens to do as he wished while keeping an eye on him.

"If you'd like," said Anders, "we can go to the manor together and ask Herrer Ilse. He is the only one who might give you permission to be here at this unseemly hour. I will not."

"Forget it." I heard footsteps in the straw. "She's not worth the trouble."

I gasped, and put my hand over my mouth. Did he not love me?

"I assure you, Herrer Ilse's horses are worth every trouble." I heard more footsteps. Perhaps they were walking to the door together. "Next time, if you would like a tour of the stables, remember that it is only proper if Herrer Ilse is accompanying you."

Jens muttered something unintelligible, and then the door closed. If Anders found me here it would be embarrassing. I'd wait until he went back to bed before returning to my room, and so I hunkered further into the hay.

"Berta," said Anders. "Jens is gone, and you are safe now."

With an unwelcome heat warming my cheeks I stood up and peered around the hay feeling like a fool.

Anders was barefooted, his shirt barely buttoned together with the shirttail hanging out, and a nightcap fit snugly to his head. It amazed me that Anders, looking as he did, was able to convince Jens to leave.

"How did you know I was here?" I stepped beside the hay, still unsure.

"The horses told me." Anders gave me a lopsided grin.

"Ja, ja," I said. He would be able to read every movement of the animals he spent his life with. "Thank you for sending Jens away." I curtsied, unable to look him in the eye. He knew or suspected the reason of my hiding. I started toward the door.

"Sit with me a moment, will you?" Anders indicated a nearby workbench.

I trembled, partly because of the chill night air and partly because of distress, but he had helped me this night, so I went with him and sat beside him. "Ja?" I asked, apprehensive.

He remained silent for a time, wrestling something around it seemed, working out what he would say before he said it. It was oddly reminiscent of waiting for a scolding from Papa.

"I do not know all about Mormons, but I saw clearly how it offended you earlier when I assumed you and this Jens Larsen were lovers."

"Ja," I murmured, wishing to put the night's memories away. I still wore my blue frock from the social activity and pulled my handkerchief from the apron pocket. I twirled it between my fingers, thinking of Catherine.

"What I am saying is …" he gazed toward the horses and then at me. "Well, why do you suppose Jens came tonight?"

"I did not invite him here." I tilted my head, questioning. Did he think I had?

Anders' brow wrinkled. "Why does he not come to visit during the day?"

I chewed my lip, wishing I had an answer, and wondering why Jens hadn't proposed the first night, or the second, or even tonight. Jens had forever changed my life and so far I'd been left sorely wanting. He'd ruined my reputation to where I wasn't confident I could recover. I blinked back against the moisture welling in my eyes and dabbed them with my handkerchief.

"If you were my girl," he rested his hand over mine. "I would rush to you at my earliest convenience."

Did Anders want me as his girl? I searched his eyes, wondering, a hopeful feeling growing within my breast.

He touched my chin, and I felt like I could float with the clouds. "If you loved me," he cleared his throat, "I mean if we loved each other, I would marry you before you had a chance to change your mind."

"Would you?" Was Anders saying he loved me? I closed my eyes and leaned toward him.

"Ja," he said.

I blinked my eyes open and watched as he scooted back.

"This is a late hour for proper courting," he insisted. "I fear that …" Anders scratched around the edge of his nightcap. "Well, as a friend, I feel that I should warn you."

"What?" I stood. It was late, and I was too confused to think or behave in a rational manner. "I am tired," I said. We were friends and nothing more. Anders was merely trying to save my virtue. I started to leave, but I hesitated, realizing I needed a friend. "I fear that I will oversleep. Herrer Ilse will give me a lashing." I rubbed my hands. The pain held the truth of my situation.

Anders stood. "Did he hurt you?" His fingers trailed across the red marks. "I am so sorry." He kissed my hands. Touching my elbow, he escorted me to the stable door. His closeness, his touch, they were like fire to my soul. I didn't understand these feelings. Were they gratefulness for his friendship, or something more?

"Thank you again." I curtsied and turned to leave.

"I will see you safely to the manor." He led me through the grass.

I wanted to thank him for saving me this night, but my thoughts were a jumbled mess.

When we stepped onto the gravel roadway, he touched my hand as if to hold it. I winced and pulled away and then regretted being so hasty. Had he meant to hold my hand? I glanced at him hoping I was right. Had I made it up, or was he having the same feelings?

"Sorry," he muttered, and moved his hand away.

"It is well and good," I whispered, wishing for my hand in his.

The moon was nearly full and cast the grounds with light and deep shadow. The setting was perfect for a declaration of love, but we walked silently to the servant's entry.

"Tomorrow before morn's first light, I'll toss a pebble at your window to awaken you." He bowed.

"You would do that?" I asked, feeling a blush warm my face and wondering if he saw it in the moonlight.

"I shan't give Herrer Ilse a chance to display his foul temper on you again." He reached forward as if to shake my hand. Instead, he brushed his hands gently across my fingers, and then he turned and strode back across the gravel and the lawn.

He was so nice. So gentlemanly. Even though he had every reason to shun me, he took time to make me feel special. Anders waited near the stable entrance. I waved and returned to my room.

With my dress hung in the small armoire, my bonnet and shoes neatly tucked away, I lay awake on my bed. Anders's kindness baffled me. He'd been angry, or rather disappointed, with me at the social. I thought of his sullen mood as he drank down the ale. He knew my reputation was somewhat muddied, yet he didn't scorn me. He'd stood gallantly in my defense and chased Jens from the stable. Almost as though he cared in a way that had nothing to do with friendship.

Frau Jensen's words came back to me. "That Anders is a good catch." I agreed and had to wonder if anyone, with the exception of Sofrina and myself, had said the same about Jens Larsen. Had we been too caught up in our rivalry to see what was before our eyes?

On this moonlit night, I only knew two things for certain. Jens Larsen had not proposed to me, and, I could not stay here much longer. I felt it deep in my soul.

Chapter 29

It seemed that only an hour had passed before I heard the clink of a rock against my window. Heaving a sigh, I stretched and then stood peeking out the glass so that Anders would know I was awake.

He waved and then strode back across the lawn to care for the horses. A warm feeling overcame me as I watched. He was a good person, and I enjoyed our friendship.

The rising sun silhouetted trees near the horizon, and yet it brought a soft light to the lawn. I wanted nothing more than to plop back into bed and warm my feet on the oven wall. There was no time for comforts, however. I hurried myself dressed and ran to the kitchen, anxious for something to eat.

"Good morning." I greeted Frau Jensen with a curtsy.

"Herrer Ilse has already been asking about you." She handed me a bowl of porridge. "He is in a mood, and if I was you, I'd hide in the shadows until he left for the day."

His linens needed washing today; I could not hide in shadows. I rubbed my sore knuckles. If I hid, nothing would get done, and Mr. Ilse would rightly be angry. Again.

Anders wasn't at the table, and I turned to ask Frau Jensen if he'd eaten earlier, but she had already gone out to the garden. She liked to pick the vegetables fresh each morning.

Helsa looked a bit peaked, but she scooted over when I approached the table, and I sat beside her.

"Are you not well?" I poured cream onto my breakfast.

She gave a timid shake of her head.

"It is time to get to work." Frau Olesen stood with her

nose in the air.

Frau Claussen followed. "She thinks she can do whatever she wishes."

"You should not sleep so late," said Frau Olesen. "You are not the Little Cinder Girl."

"I will be right there," I replied. It was hard being nice when they were always so cross. Nonetheless, I started on my porridge.

Helsa went to the sink without a word. She was pale.

I gobbled up my food and washed my dishes, and then I put several large pots of water on the stove to heat. This nearly emptied the water barrel near the counter, which meant it needed refilling. It was an endless cycle, but it saved the effort of running outside each time water was needed. Frau Jensen would especially appreciate this. I completed that task and then hurried up the stairs wondering if it were possible to stay hidden from Mr. Ilse in his own home.

The doors to his room stood open indicating he'd already gone. A pleased smile pulled at my cheeks as I entered. I threw back his down comforter and grabbed up the sheets and pillow coverings, musing on the thought that the other maids hadn't yet had time to sabotage my work.

With the soiled linens gathered in my arms, I went to the bottomless cupboard and shoved them through. Although I'd done this many times before, each week I continued to poke my head in to watch them fall into a basket on the laundry room floor below. This bottomless cupboard was a truly brilliant invention.

"Servants generally use the stairs."

Startled, I stood abruptly, hit my head on the ceiling of the cupboard, and then fell to my knees. "Ow." I rubbed at my head then slowly stood. "Herrer Ilse." I curtsied. "It is a good morn, ja?"

"*Min tåbelige barn.*" He frowned. "We need to talk."

Oh, what would happen? Why did he call me foolish? Was

he still angry from last night? My heart thumped as I walked to him. "Ja?"

"I know what good friends you are with Anders." He led me to sit with him on his sofa.

"Has he been hurt?" I hurried to the window, though I don't know why.

"Come, dear. Come sit down and let's talk."

He motioned me over, but before I turned away, a wagon with passengers clopped into view.

"What is going on?" I gulped. I'd been here for the better part of the summer and no carriage had ever come here. Mr. Ilse had his own, nicer carriages, and the staff couldn't afford to pay for rides.

"This is what I wanted to discuss with you. Come sit down."

"I will do better." I knelt beside Mr. Ilse. "Please. Do not throw me out!" I heaved a ragged breath.

"You are not going anywhere, my dear." He patted my hand. "Anders has decided to go home—"

"Anders?" I darted back to the window. "We are friends. He cannot leave. Will he be back?" Anders came from the house. Had he wanted to tell me his plans before leaving? "Anders! Anders!" I pounded on the window knowing that if he cared, he would not leave without telling me goodbye.

"Come away from the window before you break it." Mr. Ilse guided me to the sofa.

"May I go and bid him farewell?"

"The carriage will not wait." He pulled me to the sofa and helped me to sit. "You've been on a carriage and should know this."

In truth, I felt too shocked to think. I'd taken for granted that Anders would always be here. Why hadn't he said something last night?

"This is actually good timing." His lip curved upward. "We need you focused on your duty."

What did dusting have to do with saying goodbye to Anders?

"Don't tell me you've forgotten?" He chuckled, but it seemed forced. "Your betrothal to Jens Larsen? I understand that Anders is a good friend, but let's not forget where our love lies."

"Jens has not proposed," I said.

"Now, that is a surprise. I understood he was going to just last evening. I know the hour was late, but didn't he come courting after the social?"

"Ja, ja," I said, feeling weary. "He came by, but he never hinted at a proposal."

"He talked to me after you'd run off. Hinted that you cared for the stable boy. It broke his heart. He left hurt and alone."

Was he telling the truth? Had Jens come to propose, and I'd ruined it? "What should I do?" I asked.

"We must keep up our lessons." He raised his eyebrows. "Anders's leaving you like this does pose a problem, however."

My hands were on my lap. He placed his hands over mine, watching for my reaction as he cupped them in his own and caressed them. I twitched with the desire of recoiling from his touch yet dared not flinch back.

"It is late in the season and everyone has their partner." He touched my hand to his lips with a kiss, his grey eyes piercing mine. "Would it be such a horrible tragedy if an old gentleman was your partner? Just for a few weeks." His lip curled upward as though at some private joke. "It will give Jens time to lick his wounds, and I am certain you will gain your desired proposal before the summer is over."

"Ja, ja," I said. "You are so kind." My voice cracked as he toyed his finger over the top of my red knuckles. Unable to take his attentions any longer, I stood. "Today is laundry day. There is too much work ahead for me to spend it lollygagging about." I curtsied. "Please excuse me." I turned and fairly ran from the room.

After last night's debacle, I considered Jens on my way down the stairs. Jens was the reason I'd stayed, and the desire to marry him had been the only thing sustaining me for these past months.

When I walked through the breakfast room I noticed that the lamps hadn't yet been filled. Helsa wasn't feeling well and was behind on her work. This would be my good deed for the day. I went to the supply room and gathered the can of lamp oil. Then, with a grin on my face and checking to make sure no one was near, I crept back and filled the lamps. A drop spilled onto the table, and I wiped it with my apron.

Lighting rooms with oil lamps was sometimes a good thing, and sometimes not so good. They lit the room, but the lamp shades turned black from the smoke and they left a layer of grime on the walls that required our constant effort.

Once I'd made it back to the kitchen, I saw the water was hot. I lugged a pan of it to the laundry room below, poured it into the washing tub, and then went up the stairs for another pan full.

"You have your work cut out for you today." Frau Jensen was in the kitchen making bread.

"It is a miserable job, ja? But I am happy to have work." Why should I be cheerless just because Anders had decided to leave? I wrapped a towel around the hot handle of the pan and hefted it off of the stove. "I will soon be ready to help in the kitchen."

"See that you take great care in doing your work well. Helsa was already dealt a terrible punishment for slacking in her duties today."

"I will, ja. Thank you." I hurried down the stairs with the pan of hot water.

Although Mr. Ilse lived alone, he made sure there was always plenty to wash. I pulled a sheet from the laundry basket and dipped it in the hot water, taking a bar of soap to it, determined for a job well done.

There were too many things to consider while performing my weekly labor. Jens's lack of chivalry, Anders's sudden departure,

Mr. Ilse's pawing over me, his anger with Helsa—were they all tied together somehow? It didn't make sense. I wrung the sheet through the wringer to squeeze out the extra water, draped it over the drying racks, and then started on another.

❧

"Have you finished your chores for the day?" Mr. Ilse stood over me, his hands lifted to the stray hairs at the nape of my neck.

"Frau Jensen expects my help in preparing suppers," I reminded him. "I enjoy helping in the kitchen and hope to cook as well as she does someday." My hands fidgeted, wishing to interrupt his toying with my hair, and yet not daring to do so.

"The lady of a fine manor doesn't cook her own meals." His hand trailed down my arm. "Missing one day in the kitchen will not do you harm and may actually be of help."

"Pardon?" I took a casual sidestep to straighten a doily.

"The weather is nice. I've worked hard today arranging the affairs of the manor, what with the sudden departure of Anders." He took my hand and placed it in the crook of his elbow. "I shall be rewarded with a diversion." He strode to the kitchen with me stumbling behind.

"Your supper." Frau Jensen handed him a basket with a cloth draped over the top.

He released my hand and lifted the cloth. "This is perfect. Very good as usual." He extended his elbow toward me. "Tovi prepared our supper in picnic style. Shall we go?"

I looked at Frau Jensen wondering what was going on. How long had she known about the picnic? Was it only Mr. Ilse and myself? We exited out the servant's entry, and I saw that Mr. Claussen stood in the gravel with Mr. Ilse's stallion, Zeus, and the roan, both saddled and ready to ride. A lump rose in my throat as I realized I wished it was Anders standing there.

"Are we meeting someone? Is Jens coming on the picnic?" It seemed unlikely, but Mr. Ilse had mentioned Jens wanted to propose. A picnic was a good way for that to happen.

"The lad is very busy learning the management of his father's properties, but he has promised to try." He took Zeus's reins from Mr. Claussen and said, "Help her onto her horse. It's too tall for her."

"Ja, ja." Mr. Claussen tipped his head toward Mr. Ilse and then made a cup out of his hands for me to step on as a way to mount the roan.

Although Mr. Ilse had said Jens wanted to propose, he'd been upset the last I saw him, and I'd not easily forget the last words I'd heard him speak. "She's not worth it." But it seemed Mr. Ilse had reached out to him, and Jens wanted the opportunity to try again.

"Can you keep up?" Mr. Ilse mounted his Knabstrupper. The horse took a couple of anxious steps before Mr. Ilse gave him a firm nudge with his heel and the steed took off on the run.

"Of course I can keep up," I said to his retreating frame. I kicked the aging mare and hurried after. He led by a long way, and I never caught up until he had traveled to the small lake we'd been to before.

He stopped his horse, dismounted, and then walked to the garden bench before I caught up. "You've got an exceptional horse," I said.

"I would have nothing but the best."

I jumped down and joined him.

"The horses won't wander while we're here." He sat down and put the basket on the bench. "Sit with me, and let's see what Tovi has packed for us."

"Ja, ja," I said, not wishing to displease. After his behavior this morning I was hesitant to sit too close, but the bench was wide enough for the both of us with the basket between.

"Ah, she prepared for everything." He handed me a plate and

silverware. "There's some good roast beef slices. They're still warm." He put some on both of our plates. "Jens had better hurry up if he's coming. I'm famished."

There were rolls, baked potatoes, fresh peas, and apple slices with sugar and cinnamon.

"It is all so delicious," I said. "I wonder why Jens hasn't come." Perhaps he was still disappointed with how things ended. I was. But I needed to make things right between us again.

"I know if I had the opportunity to spend time with a pretty girl like yourself... well, you didn't find me absent." He smiled congenially and continued eating. "The flowers are beautiful this time of year, are they not?"

"Ja, ja, the gardener does a good job with them." I loved summer with all its beautiful flowers.

"A gardener? Nej. I planted them myself, and I care for them myself." He touched his hand to my knee. "It brings me pleasure to be among such beauty."

He meant the flowers, surely. I nodded and continued my eating.

He tore a piece of roll and tossed it to the lake. A white swan glided toward us with several fuzzy brown cygnets following behind. "Swans are such graceful birds. You'd never think it by looking at their young."

I had to agree. We ate with easy conversation. This was one lesson I'd learned from Mr. Ilse, the ability to spend hours talking without saying anything meaningful.

"Hans Christian Anderson's story of the Ugly Duckling reminds me of how you are a peasant girl growing into a well-mannered lady of the manor."

With no polite response to his comment, and with the sun lowered toward the horizon, I merely said, "It is getting late."

"We will head back soon, but first, there is a slice of cake for dessert." He pulled a piece from the basket and handed it to me.

"Frau Jensen makes the best cake." Forgetting my manners,

I took a bite without waiting for Mr. Ilse to get his.

"My dear," his voice stern, he gave me an icy glare. "Do you ever think of anyone other than yourself? How shall I strip you of such impulsive and careless behavior? It's a good thing Jens didn't choose to come tonight." He took my cake and flung it to the swan. "Will you ever be ready to run an important household?"

"I can do better. I promise." I was shocked with his sudden change of behavior. "What can I do to make it up?" It was only one bite of cake, after all.

"What you can do is to take consideration for someone besides yourself for once." He put the basket under the bench. "Over my knee."

"Sir?" How could he ask me to do such a thing?

He slipped his belt from around his waist. "That's one. How many will it take for you to learn your lesson?"

I threw myself over his lap, clenching my teeth and steeling myself for his belt, but when it came across my behind-side, I cried out.

Mama and Papa never treated anyone thus.

"There, there," he said. Helping me up, he dabbed at my tears and embraced me. "I do not wish to be the bearer of punishment," he said, and held me at arm's length, "but the good book says, 'Spare the rod, spoil the child,' and we cannot have that." He held me again, caressing my back. "I have a healing balm at the house if you need it."

When I tried pulling away, he behaved as though he did not notice, but held me firm until I panicked and said, "Herrer Ilse. Shall Jens come and find us thus entwined?"

"Dear child, nej. We must be heading back." He took his piece of cake from the basket and took a bite. "However, there's no need in wasting good food." With a slim smile etched on his face, he took another piece of cake on his fork and put it to my mouth. "Here, have a taste. It's delicious."

With my bottom still smarting, did I dare refuse? I did not, but took the bite and thanked him for it. This effort did not come without a price however, for at that moment I loathed the man.

"I suppose you'll need to use the bench as a stool." He rose and mounted his horse. "Hand me the basket."

I handed it to him and then stepped up on the bench and mounted the horse.

"I'd have thought a picnic and the nice fresh air would have brought a smile to your face, yet you act as cross as a rooster without any hens."

"I am merely overtired," I lied.

He kicked his horse and took off for the manor uninterested in my reply. He knew full well the reason for my sour mood. A whipping would do that to a person, but perhaps he didn't know how it felt on the receiving end.

Anders hadn't been gone a full day and life at the manor had already taken a drastic change. But why should his leaving have any effect on Mr. Ilse at all?

I felt an urge to also leave, as Anders had. But where would I go? I had no friends or family who could put me up, and I had no money to make it on my own.

When I approached the manor, Mr. Ilse stood near Zeus and Mr. Claussen just outside of the stables. He didn't acknowledge me when I arrived. I hadn't raced home as before, but I hadn't dawdled either. Was it my fault his horse was bigger and stronger? Nej.

"Tomorrow is the Sabbath. I'll expect you ready by mid-morning."

"The People's Church will always have a place in my heart," I said, my nerves skittering like a mouse in the coffee bin. "And my grandparents are buried there, but I have been baptized a Mormon. Now that I am settled, I wonder if I might meet with others of my same faith."

I saw the anger flash across his eyes. It was a bold request, especially given the punishment I'd received for being too hasty in eating a bite of cake. I held my teeth together, awaiting his response.

"Those who wish to remain in my employ will worship as I do. It brings me great satisfaction supporting Pastor Østergaard in this way." He turned and strode toward the manor.

Pastor Østergaard was a good man. I didn't know many better. But his preaching no longer held the key to my faith. I needed more. Nonetheless, I was not foolish enough to express my feelings aloud.

"Good evening," I said to Mr. Claussen. I picked up the basket that Mr. Ilse had left behind, walked to the servant's entry, and let myself in.

I heated a small pot of water for washing the dishes and then emptied the picnic basket. There were only place settings for two. Had Mr. Ilse merely been sparing my feelings when he said Jens would try to join us? I was too tired to worry about that tonight and set myself to washing and cleaning the kitchen.

On many occasions, Mr. Ilse had me come to his library after supper. He loved to read in the evenings, and I think he did not enjoy being alone. I was too tired to read, but I did not desire another spanking with his belt.

I peeked into the library. "How are you doing? Do you need anything?"

He looked up from his reading. "Have you finished the book I lent you?"

"Nej." I shook my head. "It is very good though. Thank you, ja."

"Reading is not only relaxing, it is good for the mind." He patted the sofa beside him. "Sit down for a while."

Clenching my teeth, I did just that, and read two pages before daring to beg my leave.

"I am much too tired to enjoy the book more on this night." I covered a yawn with my hand. "I laundered all of the upstairs sheets today."

"A grueling task indeed. Off to bed with you." He waved his hand toward me. "I'll expect you awake for tomorrow's services."

"I will be ready." I bobbed a curtsy and left.

How could I attend services tomorrow without Anders? I hadn't known that I'd miss him, but I did. We were similar in many ways, our love of horses and of the land, our enjoyment over simple pleasures. Only now, where I'd held Anders's friendship, I felt a hollow ache inside.

This had been a long and cheerless day. I extinguished the kitchen lantern and walked to my room with the near-full moon lighting the way, and yet feeling the gloom of darkness pressing its way into the creases of my soul.

Something small and dark lay on my bed. I picked it up, puzzled. My Book of Mormon! I'd been right. Anders had had it all along. I clasped it to my chest, uttering a prayer of gratitude for its safe return.

My bookmark was moved. Had Anders read the book? I stroked the cover, clasped it to my chest again, and then opened it. Underneath Mama's name was an address. What did it mean?

Flipping past the title page, I started at the beginning and read like a starved child until I fell asleep.

Chapter 30

Morning light shone through my window. I felt my face—the book had left a crease along my cheekbone. However, being able to read my scriptures at last, I'd woken up with such happy spirits. I went into the kitchen and sat at the servant's table waiting for Mr. Ilse. My being ready for church would please him. Rather than dirty a pot and dishes to make porridge for one, I passed up the idea of breakfast altogether and simply waited, since he usually left through the side exit when bringing me along.

He came to the kitchen earlier than I'd expected and held some kind of package. "You look nice today, but that blue dress is threadbare and it is also too small. I cannot have you attending church on my arm dressed as you are."

His statement shocked me. "This is my only dress. I haven't another." I stood, sweeping my hands across it to show him. "This is the same dress I've worn every Sunday." Did he wish me now to stay home?

"Do not be upset, my dear." He chuckled. "Knowing of your humble origins, I took it upon myself to remedy the situation." He placed the package on the cutting table. "In my visit with Olaf the dressmaker the other day, he mentioned that he'd made a dress no one had yet come to buy. I felt it was a terrible waste when you needed clothing so badly."

My mouth opened and shut as I tried to respond. How could he think to buy clothing for me? He was not my father. "Thank you, sir, but I cannot accept such a fine gift."

"You have not even seen it." He smiled and opened the package, pulling out a dress like I've never seen before.

There was so much lace on it. Papa could never have afforded such a dress, and the fabric was my favorite color—a delicate safflower blue.

"I felt it the perfect color to show off your eyes. It will highlight your pretty blonde braids and accentuate your cream-colored skin." He lightly traced my cheek and down to my chin with his fingers.

"Herrer Ilse." I gulped. "This is too generous. I cannot afford such a dress."

"It is a dress that Jens Larsen will appreciate. It was made for a woman and will perhaps entice a quick proposal. Let's just call it a betrothal gift."

"But—" Weren't betrothal gifts between the betrothed? Yet I knew that impatient glare and changed my comment. "But, it is still very generous, and such a beautiful dress. I hope I can do it justice."

"I'm sure you will. Hurry now, the pastor is waiting." He gave a light push in the direction of my room, and I scurried away.

I looked down at my bosoms. The dress, tailored for a more mature woman, showed more of me than I liked. I held my hand over the gaping neckline. Then, with a desperate idea, I got my handkerchief and placed it there. It wasn't the best cover, what with the old fabric up against the new, but it was the best I had, and now that I felt more decent I went out to a waiting Mr. Ilse.

"You look beaut—" He strode forward and pulled the handkerchief from its resting spot, his hand inside my dress. "What is this?" He shoved it near my face.

"The neckline is too low for me." I covered the area with my hand. "It is the only cover I have."

"Nonsense. I told you it was cut for a woman. You are planning on marrying wealth. Married women don't dress like children." He took my hand and marched toward the door.

My heart pounded as I followed, and I held my hand over my bare chest while stumbling forward. Mama did not dress like a child, and her necklines were never this immodest. Frau Andersdatter always dressed well, but her necklines never plunged, and neither did Frau Larsen's. What would everyone think of me?

"This is not right," I squeaked.

"We do not have time for such nonsense, and I won't be tempted to spoil your dress, but you will pay for your insolence." He thrust me in front of Mr. Claussen, who was standing near the cabriolet. "Is the dress indecent?" He pulled my hand away from the neckline and held it firmly in his.

A lustful gaze crossed over Mr. Claussen's face. "'Tis a charming gown, sir."

My teeth began to chatter, but not from cold. I clenched my jaw tight.

"Then we are ready." Mr. Ilse smiled as though it were a glorious day.

Frau Claussen already sat in front, her husband climbed up beside her. I started for the other side, to squeeze in beside Frau Claussen.

Mr. Ilse put a staying hand to my arm. "Allow me." He took my hand, directing me to the back of the cabriolet, and helped me in as though he were a proper gentleman.

He climbed in beside me, touching his hand to my knee. "You may feel a slight discomfort for now, my dear girl, but when you see the spark in the men's eyes and the jealous reactions from the women, you'll know the dress is a perfect fit."

I tried to smile, for I knew he required it. Perhaps if I did well enough he would forget the threatened punishment. "You know best," I murmured, trying to meet his eyes but not quite making it.

"Indeed." He grinned like a tomcat with a mouse. "I feel more revived of spirit than I have in such a long time. The weather is as nice as any July day I've ever experienced, and I've been blessed with the company of a beautiful woman." He took my hands and pressed them in his. "The dress has made all the difference on you," he said as he gazed on my open neckline. "Your gentleman would very much appreciate seeing you today."

"Do you think?" I asked. Would Jens approve? I thought of his treatment of me in the garden and had to think he would very much like seeing me in such a dress. At the same time, I did not believe that Anders would. "Will Jens be at services today?"

"Jens?" He acted as though the thought took him completely by surprise. "I know of no reason why he shouldn't be there. Oh, there, you are shivering." He put his arm around me and leaned closer. "Let me help."

"Sir. Truly, I'm fine. I am not a bit cold." I scooted closer to the side and patted his hand, thus untangling myself from him without causing offense. I hoped. "The weather truly is remarkable." I put my hand out the side and felt the breeze flow through my fingers.

The whole time Frau Claussen paid no attention to me, or anyone. She and Mr. Claussen sat like statues on the front bench and never moved. Had I fallen from the cabriolet I don't know that she'd have noticed.

When we arrived at last and stopped down the lane from the small white-stucco church, Mr. Claussen helped his wife from the front bench. Mr. Ilse leapt from the cabriolet with the spry energy of a gentleman half his age. "My dear," he said, and extended his hand for me as though I were the queen.

It was so opposite of how he usually treated me. I felt heat flush through my cheeks.

"You glow with the innocence of youth," he said. "Will you join me beside the pastor?" He extended his elbow.

This was not a question as it seemed, more of a polite demand. Still, I had to ask, "I like to visit my grandparents' graves before services. May I?"

He frowned. "Services will start soon. We do not have time for such sentimentalities." He indicated his arm. I took hold and followed him to where Pastor Østergaard and his wife greeted their congregation.

"Jacob," greeted the pastor, and then peered at me with wide eyes. "Miss Erichsen?"

Mr. Ilse took his usual place in greeting the last few parishioners as they came and pulled me to stand beside him. It was humiliating, I tried standing sideways to cover myself. The men approached smiling and looking me over as they murmured a greeting. Their wives nodded at me with a scowl and nudged their husbands toward the church as though prodding a wayward bull.

Time came for services to start, and Pastor Østergaard and his wife led the way. Mr. Ilse took my arm and escorted me into the church. It all seemed very formal. Frau Jensen and her husband sat near the back. I started toward them, but Mr. Ilse kept my arm firmly in his. Frau Jensen watched me, and I could tell that she wondered, as did I, what was happening.

When we got to his bench, he sat beside me, but not too close. He left a respectful distance between us. That gave me time to take a breath, though I did not relax, but rather felt as though the eyes of the congregation were upon me. Each whisper and disturbance I felt was directed toward me, and my plunging neckline grew and grew until it filled the whole building for all to see and to gawk.

Pastor Østergaard gave a lovely sermon and talked about

letting the light of our faith shine. Afterward, the whispers and tittering got to me. I wanted to cry and run from the old church never to return. Mr. Ilse made that impossible. However, he was in a most pleasant mood on the way home, and I hoped his mood would continue.

"The meeting was most instructional, don't you agree?"

"Ja, ja," I said. "I love the story about not keeping the light of our faith under a bushel. It gives me a lot to think about, like how I can be a better person. Pastor Østergaard is a wonderful speaker." It was what I always loved about him. He brought the scriptures alive for me and made them feel more personal.

When we got home, Mr. Ilse climbed from the cabriolet. "See that you change out of the dress until supper. I don't want it soiled." He then walked to the manor without me as he usually did, though it made me wonder if I had overreacted to his behavior these past two days.

I went to my room and changed back into my old dress. Threadbare it may be, but it covered me well. I came out to the kitchen and found Frau Jensen preparing Mr. Ilse's meal.

"What can I do to help?"

She was chopping carrots and potatoes. "A fresh green salad would be nice," she said. "You can pick the lettuce. Ja?"

"Oh, ja, ja. I will get it." I rushed out and picked lettuce for a small salad and came back.

"You'll need more than that. The Østergaards are coming for supper."

"The pastor?"

"And his wife." Frau Jensen took a roast of pork with a nice layer of fat and thick skin and put it in a pan. She was preparing *flæskesteg*, my favorite. It was a pork roast, that when finished, would have a wonderfully crisp skin. "They should be here in an hour."

"I'd better hurry then." I went out and picked more lettuce

and washed it at the well before coming back.

Frau Jensen and I were busy making ready the dinner she had planned when Mr. Ilse came to the door. "The Østergaards should be here soon. I'll expect you to be wearing your new dress." He turned and left the room.

"That's some dress," said Frau Jensen. "Where did you get it?"

With a nod of my head I indicated the door that Mr. Ilse had just exited. Then, in low tones I said, "He brought it this morning and insisted I wear it for Jens, but the Larsens were not at services. I have not seen them there this whole summer."

"When their fortune changed for the better they began worshipping in town."

"Oh." Why hadn't I known that?

"Does this dress give any indication of Herrer Ilse's feelings toward you?" She worked at the sink without looking up. "Do you think perhaps the others were right?" She continued to speak quietly so as not to be overheard.

I kept my voice quiet as well. "He has behaved so strangely since Anders left, but I do not understand why." I joined her at the sink. "And when we went on that picnic the other evening, he said he had invited Jens, ja. When I was cleaning up, I discovered there were only settings for two all along. What his thoughts were, I do not know, but if he thought of romance, he ruined it by getting angry. One bite of cake, and he whipped me with his belt."

"He took you over his knee?"

"Ja, ja." I heaved a breath. "It has all been too much."

I stayed in the kitchen helping with the final touches of the flæskesteg, vegetables, salad and an apple pie, until Frau Jensen insisted I get changed. "These are all things to worry about another day. Today you must be ready to greet his guests in any way that he wishes."

I dressed and went to the entryway expecting this night to be like the night the Larsens came for supper, but nothing was the same. I pulled at my neckline trying to get it to cover me better.

"Stop that. You'll ruin the fabric." He slapped my hands down.

When the doorknocker sounded, I started toward the door.

"Don't worry yourself," he said. "Your duty tonight is to look pretty and keep your mouth shut as much as possible." He answered the door himself.

"Pastor." He bowed. "Ingrid." He bowed over her hand and then kissed it. He indicated me with a flourish. "You both know Berta Erichsen. She will be joining us for supper."

So I did not help Frau Jensen serve. I sat at the table like an ornament, wearing a dress more expensive than any I'd ever imagined, and yet feeling uglier than I ever knew I could.

I looked down at my meal and saw Mama's locket against my bare chest. I knew she would not be proud of this moment. Papa would also be disappointed. I needed to leave Ilse Manor before I became this person.

But I had nowhere to go.

Chapter 31

I sat in the wagon next to Frau Jensen. It was our first time going to town since Anders left. The traitor. How could he leave without saying goodbye? Why had he taken my scriptures? And, did he think that giving them back made up for taking them in the first place? They could have brought me so much comfort.

The address on the inside cover of my Book of Mormon. Who had written it there? I didn't remember it being there before. Hadn't Ringe been the town where the carriage horse had gone lame? That family I'd stayed with—they'd been so kind. Hadn't their surname been Jensen? I'd known them for such a short time, yet they'd seemed like family. I had no travel money however, even if Mr. Ilse would allow me to visit.

"I miss him too," said Frau Jensen. "He was like the son I never had."

"What? Who?" I folded my arms. "I don't miss anyone."

"It's that bad, is it?" She chuckled.

"I have no idea what you're talking about," I said. "Anders and I were barely friends." I thought of our many disagreements.

"Someone is in love." She jerked the reins.

"I am not in love," I said, and then I remembered I was supposed to be in love with Jens. A shudder prickled the hairs on my arms. I glanced at her furtively and then watched the countryside. Going to town made me nervous. It didn't matter how often we went.

"A pond can deny it is water," said Frau Jensen, "but at the end of the day, the swan still glides across its surface."

"Ja, ja," I said. "I admit it. I am in love. With Jens Larsen." I could barely speak the words. "I stayed in Denmark for him."

In my last conversation with Mr. Ilse, he insisted that Jens would soon propose. It seemed ironic, really, now that I didn't care to become Frau Larsen, I would. I thought of my promise to Mama and hated to break it, but the mere thought of Mr. Ilse and my life here filled me with an ominous dread that I had no hope in making sense of.

Were his intentions honorable? If he was somehow thinking of me in a romantic way, as Frau Olesen and Frau Claussen accused, the thought made me sick in my stomach. But if it were the case, why would Mr. Ilse be so helpful in matching me with Jens? Nej. It could not be true. Mr. Ilse was merely a lonely old man who hadn't learned to control his temper, or his hands.

Jens would change. He had to. I would marry him, and he would once again be the person I'd fallen in love with. He was my only hope.

When we got to town, we went straight to Mr. Petersen's shop. It was Frau Jensen's favorite.

"Berta Erichsen," greeted Mr. Petersen. "I understand that you are working for Herrer Ilse. A better employer you couldn't find." He smiled and patted my head. "What I wouldn't give to live on an estate such as his. You are a lucky girl."

"Ja, ja." I curtsied. I had admired Mr. Petersen as a child, wanted to be smart like him. No more. No longer did I admire his intelligence. No longer could I tolerate being in his store. "Frau Jensen," I said, "may I help gather the things?"

When she agreed, I gathered items from her list and put them on the counter while Frau Jensen visited with Mr. Petersen. We would go to the meat market next, and then to Larsen's mill for flour. Perhaps Jens would be there. Perhaps he would propose before we left. This thought did not hold the same charm as it had months ago. But Anders was gone, and Jens would make me happy enough.

As I walked through the store, I overheard snippets of their conversation, "Herrer Ilse came in ..." said Mr. Peterson. And then Frau Jensen replied, but I could not hear. I tried to listen harder. Mr. Peterson said something about a ring, and I heard the word, "engagement."

It must be true. Jens would propose. But why would Herrer Ilse be making arrangements for the ring?

"Berta, take these things out to the wagon, ja." Frau Jensen motioned.

"Allow me," said Mr. Petersen. "They are much too heavy."

Frau Jensen put a hand on his arm. "Berta is young and perfectly capable."

"It is my pleasure," I said, picking up a block of soap. "I will take these to the wagon, and then I will be back for the rest. This way you two friends can visit." I scooped up an armful of merchandise, feeling much kinder toward Mr. Petersen, and hurried outside. My heart thumped with the anticipation of being engaged by nightfall.

After I set the items into the wagon, I saw someone up the street. It was Jens, and I started to call to him. But I didn't want to appear as a lovesick cow calling to the bull in the next field. As I watched, hoping he would come this way, I wondered, was it he? He went into Olaf's dress-making shop, and I knew it wasn't Jens. It must be someone else, for why would Jens go into the dressmaker's shop? He hadn't proposed yet.

I shook my head and went back into Mr. Petersen's store.

"Did someone move the wagon?" asked Frau Jensen. "You were taking a long time, and I wondered if you had gone on ahead."

"Nej." I curtsied. "I am so sorry." I grabbed up the remaining items and hurried away.

As I got to the wagon, I turned toward Olaf's dress shop.

The person I'd thought was Jens was not there. I gazed around, searching the streets while putting my load into the wagon, ever hopeful of seeing Jens. Because of this, my foot missed the curb and the cold mushy feeling of mud sloshed into my wooden shoe and through my woolen sock.

"Why is this happening to me?" I grumbled. Though I knew why. Mama always warned to watch where I was going. I lifted my foot from the puddle, and looked up as Frau Andersdatter, Sofrina's mother, went into Olaf's shop. How strange, I thought. Not that she didn't have plenty of fine dresses, but that she entered soon after I'd thought Jens had gone in.

I hobbled to the side of the wagon. Sitting on the sidestep I removed my shoe and sock, and twisted the sludgy brown liquid from my stocking. Some splashed onto my apron, which made a bigger mess when I tried to flick it off. Mud was on my hands and fingers. Mud was on my apron, my sock, and my shoe. It was also on the hem of my skirt. The more I tried to clean it off, the more it spread.

I was horrified, knowing I looked as though I'd wallowed with the pigs, and I brushed at my apron all the harder. While absorbed in the mess, two pretty leather shoes stopped within my view.

"Berta Erichsen?"

Slowly I stood, eyeing the person who had addressed me. "Sofrina Andersdatter," I replied, trying to smile.

"It is you!" She clapped her hands as though happy to see me.

I knew better. We'd both vied for Jens's attentions since we were old enough to like boys. With the pulse of competition racing through my veins, I stuck my hand into my apron pocket and slipped Jens's ring from my finger.

"Has your whole family stayed, then?" Sofrina leaned in and gave me a quick hug, missing every spot of mud on me. A lock of

Sofrina's golden tresses fell into her face.

"It is only me," I said. "My family is in America." She could not know Jens and I would be married, nor could she know Jens was my second choice. The whole town would know by sunset and ruin my chances. "You look very nice," I said. She wore my blue Sunday dress, though it was not Sunday.

I wanted to escape, and turned to do so, when Sofrina tucked her hair back into her bonnet, a gleam of amber shining from her finger. I gasped. It appeared similar in style to mine, though larger and more expensive.

Frau Jensen saved me from further comment. "We need to get to the fish market and then we're off to the flour mill. That should please you, ja?" She stopped upon seeing Sofrina. "Oh, is this one of your friends? It is a good morning, ja? Please excuse us, we must finish our shopping." She placed her hand to my arm.

We bid our goodbyes and started walking across the street. "Oh, my. I've forgotten the vanilla. Stay here, and I will be right back." She took her leave and hurried back into Mr. Petersen's store.

I smiled at Sofrina, feeling awkward, and not wishing to visit at all.

"This is good. I am so glad you stayed." Sofrina beamed with joy. "This gives me a chance to share my good news." She let out a squeal and leaned in to tell her secret. "Jens and I will be married." Sofrina clapped her hands together, and then showed me her ring. "Isn't it beautiful? It is so clear and perfect."

My legs wobbled. I clutched the wagon. The ring was beautiful. "I ... I ..." I didn't know what to say. I couldn't think above the pain in my heart. The sun's heat felt unbearable. I wiped at the sweat near my hairline with shaking hands.

"You'll come to visit, ja?" Sofrina smiled as though innocent to my pain. Yet, how could she be?

"Of course," I muttered, barely able to speak.

Frau Jensen came, giving me a quick, concerned expression. "It is time we leave." She gave a polite nudge. "We don't want Herrer Ilse impatient for his supper."

The time for leaving had not come soon enough. I rushed to the front of the wagon barely able to keep from sobbing.

"Are you working as a maid for Herrer Ilse?" Sofrina asked as we pulled away.

I cringed and pulled at my bonnet, wishing I would just die and refusing to voice an answer. While Frau Jensen purchased fish and meat, I sat in the wagon numb and unable to move. The wagon started moving again and I realized she had gotten back in.

Jens was marrying Sofrina. He had lied to me. Used me. He'd tried to make me his, though he'd never given me his heart. He never loved me.

It shocked me in a way that I could not shake off.

Frau Jensen drove to Larsen's mill. I saw her checking on me occasionally, but she didn't say anything until she'd stopped. "Will you be all right here, or would you like to come and help carry the flour?" she asked.

"How could Jens do this?" I'd been so foolish to hold on to his empty promise. "How could he lie like that? Why I almost ... I almost ... He wanted ... Oh! What will happen to me now?" I sobbed. "And with Sofrina!"

Frau Jensen patted my arm and climbed down. Before I had time to consider her absence she came back lugging a sack of flour.

"It's a good friend who carries the flour by herself when men are around to help." Frau Jensen dropped the flour into the back and then took control of the reins.

"Jens was there?" I asked, blinking.

"Ja, and his father." With a flick of the leather straps the horses started down the road.

I drew a long shuddering breath. Sofrina had to be lying. I pulled the ring from my pocket, toying with it. Sofrina had lied before.

"Now, that's lovely," said Frau Jensen. "May I have a look?"

"This is the ring Jens gave me when he said he loved me and wished I would stay in Denmark." I thought on the moment, realizing he had never said he loved me. He'd indicated it on numerous occasions. I thought of his kisses. "Sofrina lies. She stretches truth to suit her fancy." It had to be a lie. I had behaved shamefully. "He wouldn't kiss me like that if he didn't love me."

"The young lass in town? What did she tell you?" Frau Jensen pulled the wagon to a stop on the side of the road.

"She said..." I placed my hand over my chest. The enormity of Sofrina's implication made breathing difficult. I heaved an unsteady breath and tried again, "She said... Oh, what if it's true?" I sighed, feeling hopeless. "She has a ring similar to mine, except much finer, and she claims that Jens Larsen will marry her soon."

Frau Jensen nodded. "There has been talk in town." She placed her hand on mine resting on the bench. "I'm so sorry."

It was not a lie. My hopes plummeted.

"Was I not good enough?" This is what the gaping hole in my chest screamed at me. And now I was not fit for Anders. He was gone without a word, probably ashamed by the way I'd behaved with Jens.

"You must never think that, dear. You are a wonderful girl with a lot of good possibilities." She handed the ring back. "I know it's hard to hear the truth, but it is Jens Larsen who is not good enough for you." She gulped, and continued. "Herrer Petersen said Jens and the Andersdatter girl have been promised for more than three months now."

"More than three months?" I started weeping again. Not

because I desired Jens, but because of his lies, the loss of my family, my shame. Most of all, because of him I had ruined my chances with Anders.

"If Jens loved Sofrina all this time, why did he give me the ring and pretend to love me?" Something told me that he didn't regret choosing Sofrina. "Was it for our secret interludes?" I patted my face with my handkerchief, and watched Frau Jensen. "Why didn't Jens spend his efforts trying to seduce her?" None of it made sense to me.

"Now stop your fussing and focus on the positive." She lifted my chin with maternal concern. "He was never good enough, and now you know it. And a nice ring like that would buy a pair of leather shoes."

"This is an idea," I said, and then drooped my shoulders. "But what would I do with leather shoes? Mr. Ilse will know of Jens's betrothal to Sofrina soon enough and will send me away." Though he might still keep me on as the maid. I'd learned my duties well enough. My soul prickled at the thought.

I could not stay.

"I know you're not keen on the subject." Frau Jensen gave a sideways glance. "I only mention it now because I've grown fond of you."

"There is more?" I clenched my teeth.

"Herrer Petersen let me know that Master Ilse brought in a ring for cleaning. It should be back from Odense in a week." She watched me.

"What does this mean? Why do I care if Herrer Ilse has his jewelry cleaned?"

"It was an engagement ring."

Chapter 32

"You are quiet tonight." Mr. Ilse tore a piece of his roll and ate it while watching me.

"Ja. I think I am coming down with a summer cold." I wiped my brow hoping to convince him. "It has been a difficult day. After I clean the dishes, I wonder if you might allow me to go straight to my room rather than accompany you in the library."

It had been hard acting as though I suspected nothing each day. Each moment I stayed, the darkness loomed thicker. But I had no home. The stress of it etched in my soul.

"Is your throat sore?" He touched my arm. "Should I make you some salt water to gargle with?"

"Thank you, but I am capable of doing it myself. You go ahead to the library. I know how you love to read in the evenings."

He nodded thoughtfully. "You know me well."

I responded with a weak smile.

"You have had a lot of troubles this week. First overtired, then a stressed ankle, a sore headache, and now a summer cold." His eyes narrowed. "I'm beginning to think you've grown tired of me."

"Nej," I hurried to say. "It is not that at all." What was it? "I ... I ... I'd really like to rest up for the social activity tomorrow night." I closed my eyes and took a deep breath.

"Well. About that," he said with an ominous tone.

"Ja?" I peered at him, waiting.

"I've decided that tomorrow will be our last gathering of the young persons' guild here at the manor."

He knew of Jens's betrothal. I frowned.

"You do not care enough to ask the reason?" He watched me with his grey eyes.

"It is only out of respect that I wait so you might tell what you wish." Let him take that and do with it what he wanted. I would not be bait for his anger. I dabbed the napkin to my mouth and returned it to my lap.

He nodded, again regarding me. "If you must know, the strain of it is too much. I am not as young as I appear. Nevertheless, you have learned your manners quite well since Anders left. He was a bad influence on you and I am glad he's gone." He waved his hand as though waving away a pesky fly. "You might be pleased to know that your manners have improved to the point that I'm quite certain you will make a fine wife." He cleared his throat. "For young Jens Larsen, of course."

"Ja?" I gulped. My insides battled me, itching and whirling and anxious; my toes nervous, anxious to run. I put my fingers to my forehead and rubbed.

"You appear a bit peaked. You should rest. Tomorrow will be a big night."

I stood. "Thank you kindly," I said, and turned to leave.

"Berta, dear. You mustn't forget your kitchen duties."

"Oh, of course." My heart fluttered as I returned to the table. He picked up a few dishes and walked with me into the kitchen.

"Since you aren't feeling well, I will delay my reading, *Min lille kære.*" He reached past me to light a fire under the stove. "You're not offended by my pet name, are you?

"Nej." Hadn't he called his deceased wife his little dear? I shuddered at his nearness, though afraid of a scene I tried to act normal, stacking, rinsing, and preparing to wash. "Shall I go and wash the table?" I lifted a shaking fingernail to my mouth, and then remembering he despised such behavior, awkwardly slid my hands down my skirt, pretending to smooth it.

"Wash the dishes first. I want to talk to you, to let you know you're safe here. There's no need to worry any longer."

"I don't understand." I pulled a plate from the wash water with a nervous hand.

"Remember that my windows face the front and the side." He looked down at me. "The night before I sent Anders away, I heard quite a ruckus and got to the window in time to see a shadowy figure on horseback. It was some time later when you hurried from the stables with Anders by your side."

"But..." I was not afraid of Anders.

He took the plate from me and rinsed it. "Now, I'm not going to judge your little tryst, but I have let the new man know that Anders is not to come back onto the property. And, I've requested the gate be shut each night."

"Anders never harmed me." It was Jens who had acted inappropriately.

"There is no need to defend the lad. He isn't here to appreciate it. You'll never see him again to let him know of your gallant words, and your continued defense will only anger me."

"Of course." I began drying the silverware, my hands too jittery to attempt drying the plates.

He stood behind me and placed his thick warm hands on my shoulders. "It will comfort you to know, I'm sure, that I am a restless sleeper. I'll hear if anyone comes, or goes." He spoke the words in a whisper, but the threat of them gave me chills. There was no escape. "When my beloved Dorte was alive, that wasn't the case. Once I remarry, I'm sure I'll eventually return to nights filled with peaceful slumber."

"Herrer Ilse." I barely kept my voice from shaking. "I must thank you for helping, though I've never felt in danger here." I curtsied. "I really am feeling unwell and must bid you a good night." My insides twitched and crawled and I couldn't wait to get away.

"You must truly be under the weather. The color has left your pretty face." He grasped my hands before I could escape. "Before you retire, I want you to understand that this has all been my pleasure. It's been years since I've felt the warmth of a woman beside me—the dancing, your company. It is very pleasurable to me, and I hope to you as well."

"Ja, ja, of course." I attempted a smile. "My only regret is that we cannot continue."

"If you like," he said, "perhaps we can have a more formal occasion with a few of my friends instead of the peasants I've hired." At that, he pulled me into an embrace.

"Herrer Ilse!" I tried to push him away. "Herrer Ilse! This is most inappropriate. You said you were a gentleman."

"Min lille kære, of course I am." He released me and chuckled. "Forgive a lonely old man his indulgence." He looked me over with a lustful gleam in his eyes, caressing my neck. "Young master Larsen has informed me that you are a woman of virtue and would not give in to passion before you were wed." He bowed slightly, took my hand and kissed it. "I beg your pardon." He turned and left.

I rushed to my room and closed the door, my heart pounding as though I'd run to town and back. Had Jens's coming here been some trap or test by Mr. Ilse? That seemed ridiculous, but why else would Jens tell him such things?

With Mama's locket pressed to my heart, I tried to think. What should I do? From the warmth of my bed, I reached under the thin mattress and pulled out the Book of Mormon.

I ran my fingers over the cover and thought of Anders. I'd been so angry with him for taking it, though it wouldn't have made a difference with Jens at all. If he'd asked Sofrina for her hand in marriage over three months ago, he'd been engaged to her that day on the hill. And every night since then.

It was then my heart filled with pity for the woman I'd so recently despised. Though we'd been rivals for Jens's attention, she deserved someone better.

Anders had been kind and caring. Jens had taken advantage. He didn't love me. And, I realized, he never had. Though I'd been brought up not to take stock in appearances, I'd been deceived by Jens's handsomeness and his charm.

After reading a few pages of scripture, I knelt on the floor and opened my heart to my Heavenly Father. He alone could save me from this mess.

Instead of feeling the comfort of the Spirit, an overwhelming fear enveloped me. My heart thudded this truth: I needed to leave. Tonight.

Where should I go? How would I escape? With no answers to these questions, I pulled my travel bag out from under the bed in quick desperation. There were not many things to pack. I only owned two spare outfits. My Book of Mormon and Grandmother's quilt went on top. Mr. Ilse's fancy dress would stay here. Before I got my bag latched, a quiet knock came upon the door.

It was late. Who could this be? Had Mr. Ilse come back? Not knowing if it was the right thing to do, I timidly went to the door. "Who is it," I whispered.

"Helsa," came the quiet reply.

I peeked out into the hall. It was Helsa. Mr. Ilse needed to believe I'd gone to bed. I pulled her through the crack in the door, and into my room. "What do you need?" I asked.

"You really do not wish to marry Herrer Ilse?" She bore a puzzled expression.

"Nej, I cannot marry such a man." I shook my head. "Do you wish to marry him?"

"For me, that is not an option. I am not pretty like you. Herrer Ilse—he sees a pretty face and thinks he is in love. He cannot see that Frau Olesen would be his perfect match. She is more

Tina Peterson Scott

his age." She glanced at the packed bag. "Just like Inge. She ran away too. He will not take it well. This is what I came to tell you." She handed me a bundled cloth. "And I came to bring you this."

"Please sit down." I moved the bag and offered my bed. "Tell me what I should do." I sat beside her and opened the cloth to discover a slice of cheese between two slices of bread. I wouldn't have stolen food, but this gift would be cherished. "Thank you, but how did you know?"

"I have seen your nerves and distress. It gets more each day. I think Herrer Ilse sees it as well, ja? This is why he has started locking the gate." She indicated the cheese and bread. "You will need something to keep up your strength." She offered a brief smile. "I know it was you who filled the lamps the day I was ill."

"It is nothing. I wanted you to see that I was not the enemy."

"Though we treated you as one."

I patted her back. "But you are here now."

"You cannot leave out the front gate. He will be watching."

"This is true," I murmured.

Her voice lowered. "There is another way. At the back of the manor the fence is low. If you take a straight course, keeping the rising moon to your left, you will come upon the highway. You have family, ja?"

"Ja," I assured her. If they let me be a part of theirs.

"Wait until Herrer Ilse has gone up to bed before leaving. Stay close to the manor and go silently to the back property. There will be the devil to pay if he catches you."

That was true. I nodded. "Your help is most valuable." I rummaged the ring from my pocket. "I want you to have this."

Her eyes widened. "I've never owned a ring before."

"I don't know what it's worth, but you can keep it or sell it for something else. I do not mind."

Chapter 33

I snuffed the candle and opened the door a crack. "It's safe for you to leave now," I said.

"I wish we would have been friends." Helsa gave me a quick hug, left my room and made her way down the dark hall.

I slipped the door closed and waited on the bed with my bag on my lap, staring at Catherine's chest and wishing there were some way to take it with me.

The only way to keep the chest was to become Frau Ilse. That would not happen as long as I remained free to choose. After what seemed like hours, I lifted the curtain and peeked out the window. The moon had traveled across the sky sufficiently.

It was time to make my escape. I donned my coat and took my wooden shoes in hand, my bag on my arm. I opened the door and crept down the hall and through the kitchen.

A cloudy sky muted the moonlight, but I knew the kitchen well enough that I made no noise. My heart pounded as I opened the door, slowly, quietly, hoping not to make Mr. Ilse aware of my leaving. I'd just backed out the door and closed it silently behind me, when I heard a noise and turned. My heart skipped a beat.

"What are you doing?" Jens demanded. "Where do you think you're going?"

"I ... I ..." I squared my shoulders and looked him in the face. I didn't owe him an explanation. "How did you get here? Herrer Ilse said he closed the gate at night." I hadn't much time to make my escape.

"I couldn't wait another moment to see you, my love," he said smoothly, dropping his horse's reins, stepping near and leaning forward for a kiss.

That I'd ever longed for him sickened me. I evaded him in one smooth step and moved beside the horse. "That will no longer be a problem." I thrust my bag to his chest, quite unsure of what I was doing. "I've become tired of waiting for a proposal and was on my way to your house this very night. The pastor can marry us in the morn." With reins in hand, I put my foot in the stirrup and thrust myself up and into the saddle. "Hand me my bag, please."

He handed it over, slack-jawed.

As soon as I had possession of my bag, I kicked the horse. "Come on, boy. Let's get out of here," I said, amazed with the ease of my escape.

"Wait a minute, now." Jens leapt forward grabbing the stirrup. The horse whinnied and pranced.

Mr. Ilse stormed out the door. "What is going on here?" he demanded.

"She is stealing my horse!" Jens tugged the stirrup.

I took advantage of the horse's upset and kicked him solidly. He reared back. Jens lost his hold on the stirrup and fell backward.

Mr. Ilse ran forward screaming, "Get back here, you ungrateful trollop!"

Amidst the sounds of Jens and Mr. Ilse's screaming and chasing, I kicked the horse again and we galloped to the back fence.

I dared not look back but kept the horse at a steady pace, my heart beating in rhythm. Helsa had suggested that I go in a straight path through the newly thatched hay. This would leave me an easy target. Mr. Ilse would follow. His temper made no question of that. Jens would be his companion.

If I followed the line of ash and oak trees that grew along the borders of his property, it would keep me hidden. I leaned forward, letting the horse gain more speed, and veered to the right.

I could hear them. Full speed, and gaining ground, the pounding of the horses' hooves echoed in my ears. What would happen to me if they caught up? I did not want to know. I leaned in closer, kicking the horse again. His nostrils flared, steam puffed out and into the damp night air. The horse and I were one as we galloped harder toward our shelter.

It wasn't until we pressed between the first line of trees that I dared slow. Yet the birds, distressed by our interruption, flew into the sky with a shriek. In the middle of the field to my left, two dark figures started toward me. I kicked the horse and he lurched into a run.

I hadn't gone more than a mile, their shouts growing more pronounced, when I heard a distinct voice, *"Jump off and roll to the right."* Without stopping to consider if this was good advice, I threw myself onto the ground and rolled down a sloped edge. As I rolled, my bag flew forward and out of my hands.

My action spooked the already stressed horse. He whinnied and raced away. How would I ever get where I was going on foot?

I landed in some type of shallow hole, damp with moss, yet counting myself lucky that I'd suffered no broken bones. The men drew nearer. Vibrations of hooves pulsed the earth. Jens gave a shout upon spotting his horse. He wasn't far away. I pressed myself to the moist earth and stilled.

"My horse bucked her off, she's got to be close by."

"I swear, when I find that impudent little wench, she'll regret toying with me."

"You'll not coax her out of her hiding with a tone like that," said Jens. Sweetening his own voice, he cooed, "Berta. Love. I think there's been a misunderstanding. There was no need for you to steal my horse." His syrupy sweet tone might have been comical if I didn't fear for my life.

He stopped not even a stone's throw from where I lay. I closed my eyes and offered a silent yet fervent prayer. *Let them tire of chasing me and go home. Please. Do not let them find me.*

"Maybe she got knocked out when she was thrown," Jens said.

"She'll get knocked out when I find her," Mr. Ilse growled.

"I agreed to test her faithfulness. I even agreed to chase her down for you. But my help stops now if you plan on beating her half to death."

"I'll do as I please. And you will help," Mr. Ilse said. "I'm sure the Andersdatters would think differently on you marrying their daughter if they knew I'd seen you in the arms of another woman. And a peasant at that."

"It was your idea," Jens said.

"Bah! It wasn't my idea back in April. There you were in your father's field having your pleasure when I rode past—and engaged to my good friend's daughter. Nej. I've spent too much time grooming her for success to let her slip through my fingers like Inge." Mr. Ilse clucked his tongue and the horse stepped away. "*Min lille kære,* come to Papa," he sang.

I listened to the sound of their horses' hooves padding along in the grass, their muted conversation becoming less distinct.

Rain began falling in gentle sprinkles. I prayed for it to disappear, but the storm continued with a breeze that grew increasingly dramatic, chilling me. I pulled my coat over my head. Shivering and wishing I dared move somewhere drier, I hugged closer to the earth. Nevertheless, the cold wet ground was no good for keeping me warm.

The sounds of shouting men kept me still. I couldn't tell their direction.

As I waited for them to discover me, not knowing whether I'd live or die, my heart formed a prayer. I'd been foolish. Would Heavenly Father forgive me? Could he? Could I ever forgive myself, and could someone ever overlook my foolishness enough to marry me? Would I ever again in this life have a place I could call home?

Before long, the rain came in torrents. By then, I was less concerned with the rain than I was the saving of my soul. I prayed to my Savior for forgiveness. I hadn't behaved as well as I'd been raised, and thinking that if need be, I might pray for days or weeks, or how-ever long it took to cleanse my soul.

Chapter 34

I awoke with a start in the hazy light of early morn. Someone had touched me. I felt it again, the slight stroking of my ankle. Had they found me? I sucked in a breath and sat up.

No one was there.

I glanced down. A family of adders rested over and around my legs—their venomous tongues licking the air, hissing at my movement.

A scream rose to the tip of my tongue, but before it escaped, a voice whispered over me, "*Be calm.*" It felt like a warm glass of milk, calming my soul. I offered a prayer of thankfulness. Screaming would have only gotten me bit—and there were plenty of fangs for biting. If I didn't remain calm, I'd die before the sun went down. Instead, I continued praying for my safety.

My jaw clenched. My eyes squeezed shut. I held still, barely daring to breathe as they started moving across me, probably looking for a nice rock to sun on as they were known to do. I watched them slither over my legs, the hair on my arms and neck prickling as they moved away and into the rushes.

Once I was out of danger, I heaved a shuddering breath and took in my surroundings. Long grasses and cattails hung over me, causing a type of canopy. The hole I'd landed in wasn't deep at all, more like a recess in the earth. It opened out into a nearby pond. Mr. Ilse's pond. Fog floated up from the cold water. My bag lay beyond me and near the water's edge.

There were no sounds other than the sounds of early morning: frogs, ducks, birds, insects, all eager to start their day. Why did I feel so ill at ease? Had my tormentors camped nearby? Or would Mr. Ilse return for me this morning? That probability caused an impatient thump in my chest.

A previously hidden little adder crossed the pathway, hissing as though in protest to the beating of my heart. When it slithered into the grass, I rose to my knees, peeking through the rushes for any sign of human danger before tip-toeing to my bag. I was soaked through and chilled to the bone but there was no time to change. And, though I wanted to read my scriptures, hoping for guidance, this was not the time.

The prompting came to go. I grabbed up my bag and ran. My head ached, my eyes watered, my whole body throbbed. But I ran. The rushes hid my escape as I hurried to the other end of the pond, the grass covering my tracks.

A jumble of oak, elm, and ash trees was near what I hoped was the highway. Between me and the trees, a large open field. There were no workers working, no horses plowing. Odd, I thought. No Jens, and no Mr. Ilse chasing. No one. I hesitated only a moment before dashing into the field, keeping watch to my left and to my right, hoping to make it through without getting caught. I ran, nearly tripping on the uneven ground. Straightening myself up, I ran harder.

The sun had brightened the sky by the time I'd gotten to the middle of the field. My lungs screamed with pain. I surveyed the horizon in every direction. Why was no one here working? The hay lay in long rows upon the ground, waiting for peasants to gather and stack it. But no one was here. The hair on my neck twitched. Were they waiting for it to dry? I sneezed. It was the hay, I told myself. I refused to be sick, and again I started on the run.

My heart beat from exertion. Anxiety coursed through me. I ran. I stumbled. I ran. My gloom lifted as I drew closer, and I was hopeful. Perhaps I would make my escape.

However, as I neared the stand of trees, Jens pulled out from a hiding spot, smug satisfaction slathered across his face as he met me.

"I knew you'd still be near the pond," he said.

"Let me go, please." I bent over, hands on my knees, wheezing. "I cannot go to Herrer Ilse, and I mean nothing to you."

"You do," he said, frowning.

If he was unwilling to give up his ruse, I would help him in that regard. "There's no need to pretend. I heard you and Herrer Ilse talking last night." I folded my arms. "You were engaged before my family left for America."

He scratched his forehead. "I'm sorry I got carried away. All I wanted was a kiss."

"We talked about you coming for me. About growing old together." I pressed my hand to my chest. "And it was more than just a kiss to me."

He kicked the dirt and glanced back toward the road. "I had no idea you'd leave your family and stay in Denmark."

"But I did," I said. "And what about the ring?"

"I was going to give it to Sofrina, but I found a nicer one." He shrugged his shoulders. "I had it in my pocket, and when you came, I thought it would make a nice going away present."

"I thought it was your promise to marry me. That thought only is what has kept me going since April." I clutched my stomach, the hurt washing through me.

"I'm glad to have obliged." His face brightened in some hopeful expression.

"Don't count yourself gallant," I snapped. "You should not have treated me like this if you did not love me." I shook my head. "What were all those nights in Herrer Ilse's garden?" I couldn't believe I'd been so foolish. Shame burned my cheeks.

Jens didn't immediately answer, lost in thought or trying to come up with a good excuse. "Herrer Ilse is a good man," he finally said. "He just needs a good woman. And, when he mentioned that he was interested, I agreed to help." He kicked at the ground. "Why shouldn't it be you living on his estate? Then I wouldn't feel so guilty." The corner of his lip quirked up.

I did not know what to make of his confession. Had he honestly thought he'd been trying to help me, or was he lying to excuse his fiendish lust? "What are your plans now that you've found me? Are you intent on taking me back? Because I'll tell you right now, I do not want to marry that man." I would not.

"Are you headed to your aunt's?" He hedged.

"Ja, ja," I quickly agreed. I'd mentioned her being taken to the poorhouse. If he hadn't cared enough to pay attention, I would not correct him now. "She will let me stay with her."

"Are you sure?" he asked, his head tilted. "Perhaps you are on your way to meet up with Anders Jensen. Master Ilse felt threatened by your friendship."

"He stole my scriptures," I said, looking him in the eye. "Even if that weren't the case, I have no idea where he went. He thought his family immigrated to America." I picked up a moist clod of dirt and crumbled it between my fingers. "Nej. If Aunt Thora is busy, I have another aunt," I lied. "I will stay with her."

"I didn't know about another aunt. Where does she live?"

"Do you plan to leave Sophrina and come calling?" I shook my head. "Nej. We've had enough chat." He was probably stalling for Mr. Ilse. "It's time for you to decide what you will do. Will you be a gentleman and let me go, or will you be Herrer Ilse's puppet and subject me to a life of misery?"

Jens's jaw worked around some thought, his eyes solemn. "I never meant to hurt you, Berta."

"And yet," I said, "this is what you have done. Will your hurting end now? Today? Or will it continue?"

"It ends today," he said. "Here." He thrust his horse's reins toward me. "Take my horse. I will walk home."

My eyes narrowed. "Nej. Thank you." He'd probably have me arrested for horse thievery.

"Let me take you there, then." He stepped closer. "Your aunt lives so far from here. Vejstrup, if I recall correctly. It is too far for you to walk."

"Oh, you think because I worked for Herrer Ilse that I have no money," I scoffed. "You will be comforted to know that Papa left enough for transportation and a wedding dowry." If only I still had it. I put my fists on my hips. "Don't think me a skeptic, but I've had enough of your brand of help." The longer he held me here, the greater the chance that Mr. Ilse would come. I began walking toward a westward-traveling road in hopes of throwing him off.

Jens chased after me. "This is not the road to Vejstrup," he said. "Let me show you the way."

"I know perfectly well where this road leads," I said. I turned to hide a sneeze. "I've decided to stay with my father's sister. She lives well away from Herrer Ilse's influence." Mr. Ilse was on his way, I sensed it. I took my damp coat off, draped it through the handle of my travel bag, and started in the direction of Jutland. I would have to backtrack after Jens left.

He continued following me like a lost puppy.

I turned and glared at him. "Go home, Jens. Go home to your family. Go home to Sofrina. Go home to Herrer Ilse. You have done your duty. You have helped me enough for a lifetime, and quite frankly, I've grown tired of your company." I waited, unmoving, hoping he would leave—demanding he leave with my expression and stance.

Jens waited too, and I began to fear he wouldn't leave when he nodded once, mounted his horse, and cantered away.

Chapter 35

I hastened down the road, walking in the grass to the left, keeping an anxious watch behind me for Mr. Ilse.

It was amazing what I'd said and done to Jens, how I'd stood up to him, made him think I was traveling toward Jutland, Denmark's peninsula. The night before, I'd so coolly taken his horse and spoken my mind.

As I contemplated the Lord's hand in my delivery a smile rose on my face, and, walking a little further off the road, I knelt for a prayer of gratitude.

While I prayed, I got an uneasy feeling. *Run!* I gathered my things and ran south. Though there was no road there, a shallow recess between two rolling hills provided limited cover as I ran.

When I got to the top, I bent over, my lungs screaming for air. A grouping of large rectangular rocks that were said to serve as a Viking burial marker was nearby. I stumbled forward and took cover behind them. At the sound of galloping horses I pressed myself to the rocks as though hiding from a vulture overhead. Though I was far enough away, the rocks barely visible from the main road, I waited with bated breath.

When I no longer heard the horses, I wasn't sure if they'd stopped or if they'd ridden on, or even if it was Mr. Ilse. Had I left tracks behind me? Was he climbing the hill this very moment, ready to snatch me back? I shivered.

When I realized how silly it was to sit and wait to learn if they were, indeed, climbing toward me, I peeked around the rock. It was clear to the left and down to the road, though I didn't dare move on. Not yet. What if it had been Mr. Ilse, and he came back? If I was on the main road, he would take me back to his manor. This thought left me no alternative. I could not follow the highway any longer.

I shivered again. It was ironic, actually, to get a summer cold after having pretended I'd had one. However, a foggy head and runny nose could not stop me from my course. I needed to get away from Mr. Ilse and Jens, to find a home where I would be safe. The Lord prompted me forward. I couldn't live in an open field.

What I really wanted before moving on was clean, dry clothes. I had a change of clothing in my bag, and looked around uneasily. There was no one here, no farmhouse. There were also no trees for hiding behind. I hesitated. It felt completely wrong changing my clothes out in the open. But when a breeze whispered off the rocks, chilling me further, I gave it more serious thought.

Unable to bring myself to strip down, I unbuttoned my blouse and draped it across the front of me while I wriggled through the sleeves of my petticoat. I grabbed my dry petticoat and tugged it over my head, followed by my dress. Then I stood by the tallest rock and kicked off my wet skirt and petticoat. My fresh clothing tumbled into place.

I stared at the bread in my bag with longing but needed to save it for tonight. Having something in my stomach would help me sleep. It still didn't feel right to leave yet, so I waited under the cover of the rocks. Afraid of moving, I pulled the scriptures from my bag.

As I read, I prayed for forgiveness and guidance. More than anything, I wanted a home. And someone to love me. I realized that someone was Anders. It didn't matter that he'd taken my Book of Mormon and that he'd left home because he didn't like his parents' new religion. All that mattered was Anders. He was a good person. But would he be able to love me?

Occasionally I heard travelers on the road and peeked out. They weren't Mr. Ilse. I'd begun thinking that I'd overreacted. Why would Mr. Ilse spend all this time and energy chasing me? I was no one. Still, I understood he had done such a thing with Inge.

Perhaps Jens had done something noble and pacified Mr. Ilse. They wouldn't hunt me down after all. And then I heard again the pounding of hooves, and I peeked around the rocks.

Mr. Ilse and Jens sat in front of the wagon that Frau Jensen and I used to take to town. Had they thought they'd bind and gag me and throw me in the back? I bristled at the thought.

The wagon stopped.

I slunk down to the ground, shaking, and draped my damp blanket over me.

"Berta, dear!" shouted Mr. Ilse. "Where are you?"

My spine tingled.

"I know you are lost, but do not fear," he called out, "I have set watchmen out to help you find your way home!"

I waited and when they did not leave, I crept up and peeked over the hill. Mr. Ilse was on the other side of the road walking around, alternately searching the ground and surveying the tree-lined countryside.

And then Jens's gaze lifted to mine.

Oh! I dropped to the ground, heart pounding. Had he seen me? He'd looked straight at me. I rocked back and forth. What was the right thing to do? Run? Stay? They both had risks. My foot jiggled as I rocked. I was a bundle of pent up anxiety, a rabbit waiting for the fox to pounce.

He didn't pounce.

Moments later, I heard the wagon leaving. I couldn't believe my good fortune. If Jens had come up the hill, I could not have outrun them. With shaking knees, I peered toward the highway. Near a turn in the road they started the process over again;

the shouting, the searching for clues, and then travelling closer toward their home. Had I run, they'd have seen me. Mr. Ilse crossed the road, bent, and studied something. Jens looked my way, threw me a kiss and waved.

I leaned against the rock, eyes closed, and let loose a nervous chuckle. The constant evidence of the Lord's hand in my delivery from Mr. Ilse humbled me—especially since I didn't deserve the Lord's help. I hadn't been obedient, hadn't gone to Zion. I'd been fooled and tempted.

Thoughts of Anders filled my mind. I longed to see him, tell him I loved him and ask his special forgiveness. Would the Lord allow this to happen? I was yet to discover. But, I decided, I would find Anders or die trying.

My head felt like a cow had sat on it, not that I would know, but it ached. My nose ran, and, I felt my forehead. It was hot. Too exhausted to move, I lay in the sun. Just for a moment, I told myself.

The grass was cool against my face.

The sun was at high noon when, once again, I became conscious of my surroundings. My spare clothes were still damp. I hadn't hung them anywhere to dry, so I rolled them up and put them in the bottom of my bag, my scriptures to the side. Oh, they might ruin against the wet clothing. I took them out and put them in an outside pocket, and placed my quilt and the sandwich on top in the main compartment.

Would Mr. Ilse know where Anders went? Would he and Jens wait for me there? I'd have to keep on the watch for them. I started my journey due south, with hopes of finding the Jensens' farm near Ringe, and praying that these Jensens had a son named Anders.

By evening, I knew only one thing: I was incredibly lost—lost on an island I'd lived on my entire life. But that was my plight. Since the surrounding farms weren't aligned in a straight row, I found myself dodging to the right to take cover among the trees that divided one smallholding farm from another. Then, it seemed I was headed due west, and so I tried making my way further to the right until I had no idea how far I'd traveled. All I knew was I hadn't yet found the Svendborg Sound, or any other large body of water, indicating that I'd walked across our island of Fyn.

The Jensens, if I pictured correctly, were situated somewhere in the center of Fyn. It would take a miracle to find the Jensen family while avoiding the roads. It would be another miracle if Mr. Ilse was not there waiting, and yet another miracle if Anders, indeed, lived in their home. And, another miracle altogether if Anders loved me the way I had finally realized I loved him.

I shook my head. That was too many miracles to expect the Lord to perform on my behalf.

With no other option, I trudged on while forming a plan to walk all the way to Svendborg. Once in that southern city, I could travel the highway back up to Ringe. It would probably take several extra days but I could find the Jensens' farm from there, providing Mr. Ilse hadn't set guards on the southern road as well.

If only I could find Svendborg and not starve first. My stomach growled, but I shushed it and walked on.

A flock of geese honked overhead in the early evening, and I watched as they extended their wings, let their feet down, and landed on the other side of a wall of shrubs. There was water over there. Thirsty, I headed in that direction.

The shrubs were too thick, but I held to them, making my way around until I came to a beautiful lake. I knelt at the water's edge and splashed the cool water to my face and then drank my fill. It felt good, but I was hungry. This was a beautiful area with no threat of Mr. Ilse finding me, so I opened my bag and retrieved the bread and cheese.

Once finished, and feeling slightly revived, I started on my way again. A shiver coursed through me, but I demanded that I not be sick. After my unseemly behavior with Jens—going after him like a dog for a fresh bone—how could Anders ever forgive me? With all of my past, I was sure he wouldn't allow me to stay if I caused his family undue worry and expense by being ill. I needed to be able to pull my weight. That was assuming he even lived in Ringe.

I trudged through the farmland to the line of trees and shrubs in the horizon. The shrubs would make a good shelter for the night and I mustered my remaining strength, forcing myself to continue walking until I made it there. The grass under an oak tree was inviting. I dropped my travel bag, and then in the distance I saw a half-timber farmhouse.

My heart skipped a beat. It had a thatched roof and was a traditional three-winged home like ours. I picked up my bag and stumbled closer, and then smirked at my silliness. This wasn't our house, I reminded myself. Mama and Papa were no longer in Denmark. They couldn't come to my rescue.

Then I noticed the horses beside me. Anders had talked about his father's field of Frederiksborgers. These were the Jensens' horses!

Though I'd walked past several fields this day, many of which had horses, these had to be Anders's. Why, I didn't know. I hobbled farther into the field, giving my best effort to run, to catch one and to ride it to the farmhouse. It was the Jensen farm, it had to be.

The horses scattered. They didn't know me, didn't know I needed their help. I could make it to the farm if I could just catch one, and I chased after first one and then another. While trying to corner one, the graceful movement of a stork caught my attention.

It swooped from the sky, and then with wings outstretched and its spindly red legs hanging, it came to land atop a nest of twigs nestled over the chimney of the half-timber farmhouse. I stumbled and fell, hitting my head on something hard. The horses whinnied. It was as though they laughed at me. But I couldn't get up. I pawed the ground, trying to move, and then fell limp.

※

Music filled my senses. The room was bright. Grandfather Erichsen sat in a straight-backed wooden chair with a harmonica to his mouth. He winked at me and continued playing.

My mother's parents, Grandmother and Grandfather Jensen danced into the room. Grandmother Erichsen clapped her hands, her toes tapping.

I opened my mouth to call them. I was so tired. So cold. "Help me!" I tried to shout. But they kept on dancing. Uncle Erik joined them, and in his arms, my dear aunt Thora. They were younger. "Aunt Thora," I murmured. I was so sorry she had passed into the eternal world.

Someone tugged at me. I didn't want to leave, and resisted. I was home. I was safe at last. I felt another tug. The room darkened, the music quieted.

"Berta?" Anders put his face close to mine. "Berta!"

"I love you," I whispered. I'd waited so long to tell him that.

Chapter 36

"You're awake!" Sister Jensen stood in the doorway. "I'll get you something to eat. You must be starved half to death." She disappeared.

I wondered, vaguely, if I was dreaming, but my head hurt. A patchwork quilt covered me in its warmth. It wasn't my quilt. What had happened to mine? I sat straight up, or rather tried to sit. My head throbbed. "Oh," I moaned, and started back down.

Hands held me, helping me lie comfortably. "Don't go overdoing it."

"Anders?" I tried to think how I'd gotten here. "Where am I?"

"You're home, if you'd like." He took my hand in his.

"There'll be time enough for that another day," Sister Jensen said. "Let the girl eat. She's had quite a spill and I'd wager a touch of pneumonia as well. She needs to get her strength back."

Sister Jensen shooed Anders out of the room, and then took the seat beside the bed. "Let's get some food in that stomach. You haven't had a bite to eat in three days." She raised a spoon of broth to my mouth.

It didn't take much coaxing. I was famished. She watched me eat with an amused expression. "I'm sorry," I said, licking the spoon. "I truly was hungry. How long have I been here?" It hadn't been three days.

"Anders brought you from the pasture three nights ago last eve," she said. "It was touch and go there for a while, what with your fever and then banging your head against a rock. You gave us quite a scare. Especially Anders." Her expression took on a glow when she said his name.

"But..." I winced. "Why is Anders here?" I touched my hand to my forehead. "Just last night... Anders..." What had I said to him? "It was just last night," I insisted.

"Oh, sweet girl, Anders is our son."

"Your son?"

"Our oldest. And just last night you were chatting with your grandparents." She patted my hand. "Telling them goodbye, I reckon."

I did remember something about Grandfather Jensen. He was always such a tease. He had said something about Anders, and I had thought he was joking at the time. I closed my eyes, trying to think of what it was.

"Do you feel up to visitors?" asked Sister Jensen. "I've a whole household waiting to call on you. Hmph!" she said. "Like you were the queen."

Before I had a chance to respond, Greta and Kirsten came into the room. "Are you really going to live with us?" They sat beside me.

Kirsten stroked my hair. "Anders said—"

"Enough of that," interrupted Sister Jensen. "The girl hasn't even had a chance to get out of bed yet."

There was a loud commotion at the door. We all turned toward the sound. A hand gripped the doorframe. Someone tugged it away. There were sounds of struggle—a loud thud on the ground and the scraping of a chair on the floor. Nathan jumped into the room, his hair tousled, a wide grin on his face. "Are you going to marry my brother? He's been pining away for a—"

Anders lunged into the room, putting a hand over Nathan's mouth. "Someone needs to learn to mind their own business," he said and tugged him out of sight.

"Those two have been making up for lost time," Sister Jensen said. "They used to wrestle like this ..." She shook her head, smiling. "I thought they'd tear the house down back then. Now that they're grown, they just might."

Young Hans came into the room. "Hello, Berta. Are you feeling better now?"

"Much better, thank you."

"Have you fed the chickens and milked the cow?" asked Sister Jensen.

"Ja, Mother."

Sister Jensen stood, touching her hand to the bed. "Do you feel like getting dressed?"

"That would be very kind. Thank you." I'd never had so many people see me in bed before. I was beginning to feel uncomfortable.

"Everyone out." She motioned toward the door. "Kirsten, it's your turn for the morning dishes. Greta, the rugs need a good pounding. Hans, take the bucket out and feed the pigs."

Kirsten patted my cheeks. "I'm so glad you came back," she said.

"It's like having an older sister." Greta smiled. "It will be great fun."

Nathan and Anders slipped into the room as their sisters slipped out.

"Nathan, you have too much energy," said Sister Jensen. "Go out and chop a couple of logs into kindling."

"What about Anders?" he protested.

"He can go with you. I expect the box full of good kindling wood when you're finished."

"But, Mother—" Anders started.

"The girl will still be here when you're through. There'll be plenty of time for talking after she's dressed."

Anders kept his eyes on me while shepherding Nathan through the door.

"What was that for?" he complained. "I can walk on my own."

The front door slammed shut.

"I washed your clothes," said Sister Jensen, crossing the room. "Here you go." She placed my clean clothes on the bed. "Do you feel well enough to freshen up? I have some warm water on the stove."

"That sounds wonderful. Thank you." I sat up on the bed, waiting.

She came right back with a pitcher and basin. "If you need any help, give a holler. I'll hear you."

※

It was good to be clean and wearing dry clothes. I sniffed the sleeve of my blouse. Nothing smelled better than sun dried cotton.

I sat on the bed, feeling too timid to go out and face them, and yet this is what I'd dreamed of. Being here. They were all so accepting. I pinched my cheeks. Was this a dream?

There was a quiet knock at the door.

"Come in," I said.

The door opened, and Anders walked in. "I've been waiting forever to talk to you." He sat beside me.

Sister Jensen loomed in the doorway. "No son of mine will court a young woman in her bedroom. Out!"

"I've watched over her in this very chair for three nights." He motioned to the chair by the bed. "You had no problem with it then."

"That was then. This is now." She gave him a stern look.

Anders stood, but he held my hand. "Do you feel up to a walk outside?"

I gazed up into Anders's smoky blue eyes and nodded. Was I dreaming?

"Let me know if you get tired, ja, and I will bring you back." He led me outside.

Kirsten and Greta tagged along behind us. When we got outside Nathan joined us as well. "What are you doing?" they asked. "Where are you going?" "Are you going to kiss?" The way they pestered him reminded me of Mary and Ana. I gulped back the thought.

Brother Jensen came from the barn leading a team of horses pulling a wagon. "If you want any privacy, you'll need to go farther than the chicken coop." He handed Anders the reins. "The lake north of here should do the trick."

"Thank you, Father." He handed the reins back. "Let me help her into the wagon."

"I'm fine," I said. "I don't need help." I started up, but my head became dizzy and I felt myself falling backward.

Anders was there in an instant, holding me, taking my hand, helping me into the wagon. He jumped up beside me. "We won't be long," he said. He clicked his tongue while jerking the reins, and we started down the road.

We drove in silence, the awkward tension mounting as we neared the lake. I had so many things to say. What should I say first? My confession hung in the air between us.

Anders pulled to a stop under the shade of some trees and helped me from the wagon. He took my hand and we started walking around the water, still silent. He wanted me to explain myself. I owed him a lot of explaining.

"I've been so wrong," I started. "I have prayed this past month for the Lord's forgiveness." I watched for a change of expression in his handsome face. "Will you forgive me? But, how could you ever? I was so... so..." I choked on the words and turned in shame. He knew my transgression. He'd seen me in the garden. How could he ever love me or want to kiss me after that unseemly display?

Anders's hand rested on my shoulder. "Berta."

I was filled with guilt and pulled away, rushing along the side of the lake. Exhausted, I sat near the bank, hiding my face in shame and sobbing my remorse. If only I could take it all back. Make it go away somehow.

Anders was there, lifting me to my feet though I kept my face hidden, my hands soaked with tears. How could he ever love me?

"Berta, you are not yet well." He took off his jacket and spread it on the ground. "Sit on this. I have my own confession. Ja?" He helped me back to the ground and sat beside me, facing me. His sober expression piqued my curiosity. What would he confess?

"I have loved you since I first met you at your home." He raised his eyebrows with a hopeful expression and then dropped his gaze. "But I was angry." He took my hand, toying with my fingers. "I was angry with my parents for joining your church, and then they insisted on immigrating to America." He looked out over the lake, contemplative.

"Is that when you went to work for Herrer Ilse?" I prompted.

"Ja," he said. "I left not knowing if they had immigrated, but I was angry with them as though they had." The corner of his mouth quirked up. "I should have known they would not leave without me."

He held my gaze for a moment before continuing, his eyes fierce with emotion.

"I took your Book of Mormon," he said. "I determined that without it you would be free again to choose the Church of Denmark." He ran his fingers through his hair. "The problem is that before you came to live with Herrer Ilse, I'd read it and knew for myself that it was true." He stared down at my hand as though noticing it for the first time. "Where's your ring?"

"I gave it to Helsa."

"It was expensive." His brows furrowed.

"I couldn't stand the reminder." I gazed at him through my lashes. "It was a bad token, representing lies and shame."

After a pause, he continued. "I intended to give your scriptures back to you, but that Jens fellow is such a cad." He looked out over the lake. "I was jealous," he said, "and I couldn't bring myself to do it. I knew you'd give him the book. I knew he'd dump it in the rubbish." He took a deep breath. "Because of that, I kept it much longer than I should have. Will you forgive me?"

I'd been angry that he'd taken my book. Their words could have strengthened and guided me. Perhaps I might have discovered Jens's nature sooner. None of it mattered anymore. I was here. Anders looked at me with what I hoped was a look of affection. His lips were so close. All I could think of was wishing to feel their touch on mine. Yet I could not make so bold a move. It had to be Anders's choice.

He chewed his bottom lip, awaiting my reply.

"All this time I thought I'd stayed to marry the Larsens' son." I couldn't speak his name. "I was slow to realize the truth."

"What truth?" he asked, pulling my hands into his.

"Heavenly Father let me stay in Denmark to meet you."

He gazed on me for the longest time. I wanted him to kiss me, but would he ever be able to without thinking of Jens Larsen? The thought saddened me. And then I remembered what Grandfather Jensen had teased me about. I hadn't believed at the time, but now I knew it was true. "You were baptized," I said.

"How did you know?" Anders watched my mouth. "It hasn't been that long ago, and I swore my family to secrecy." He touched my face almost reverently.

"My grandfather Jensen," I whispered, almost afraid to hope that Anders loved me. "He was such a tease, I didn't believe him at first. Why did you do it?" I asked, immediately regretful of the silly question.

"I came to know for myself," he said. "The Church is true." He tilted his head and quirked a smile. "Besides, I knew you wouldn't marry me otherwise."

"Oh, we're getting married?" I said, though my heart leapt with joy at the prospect.

"Well." He rubbed his chin. "You did say you loved me."

My memory flashed to the whispered confession. My face heated, and I looked away.

"Is it true or not?" He touched the side of my face, bringing me to see him once more.

"It is true," I murmured, watching my shoes.

"I love you, too." He leaned forward, his hand on my neck, bringing us together. The kiss he gave me was pure, and simple, not greedy or anxious.

He let me go too soon. Was he sorry he'd kissed me? I watched in surprise as he sat back, reaching in his pocket.

"It's nothing fancy." He knelt in front of me. "But I understand that the American Pioneers use it as a symbol of their affection, and so I made one for you, hoping you'd come."

I was dying to see the object and hoped it was a ring, but I had one more question. "Was it you who wrote the address in my Book of Mormon?"

Anders tilted his head, his brows furrowed. "How else did you know to come here?"

"Did your parents not tell you? I met them before. They were so kind. I had hoped they were your parents, and that you would be here." I glanced anxiously at his closed hand. "It is the only place I knew to come."

"The Lord sent you to me." He cleared his throat, taking my hand in his. "Berta Erichsen, if you'll allow, I will love and cherish you for the rest of my life." He opened his hand. A ring rested in his palm.

I took it and turned it over in my fingers. It was a nail, one generally used for shoeing horses, and curved into a ring with a flower etched into the side.

"Berta, my sweet Danish rose, will you marry me?"

"Ja, ja!" I said, a little too eagerly. I cleared my throat. "Ja," I repeated in a more subdued tone. "It will be my pleasure to honor and adore you for the rest of my days." And then I felt too giddy with joy to quit talking. "I will be a good wife. I know how to cook and clean, ja. And I will bring you lots of children. Ten of them, if you want. And we will raise them together. You will never doubt my love or my—"

His lips were on mine once again, his kiss gentle and loving, but also careful and respectful. It was exquisite, and when it was over he didn't let me go. He held me close. I rested my head on his shoulder breathing in the scent of him, my heart filled with joy.

I was home at last.

Because of the careful ministrations of Mother Jensen along with Anders's loving care, I made a full recovery. A week later, Anders and I were married by the local authority—Bishop Jensen, Anders's father. The following year, on the 28th of April, 1864, Anders, me, the Jensen family, and 974 Mormon Saints immigrated to America together aboard the *Monarch of the Sea*. I was most anxious to find my family and introduce them to my beloved husband and our new little son.

Please dear reader, if you enjoyed this novel, it would be greatly appreciated if you would add a review to Amazon, Goodreads, or your preferred social media site.

Thank you,
Tina Peterson Scott

Book Club Questions

This story took place in Denmark. Did the author succeed in giving a general feel for the area?

Do you have Danish ancestry? Is it a place you might like to visit?

Did you learn anything new about Denmark?

Do the characters seem real and believable?

Have you ever been on your own, without family? How did you feel?

Was there a time in your life when someone who you loved betrayed you?

If you met Berta or Jens or Anders, what would you say to them?

How might Berta have behaved differently in her relationship with Jens? Has there been a time when you behaved a certain way only to later regret it?

There were times when Berta followed a prompting or listened to a voice when it didn't seem a logical course of action. Have you ever had a similar experience?

How might the book have been different if it had taken place in a different era?

Has this novel changed you or broadened your perspective?

Did you find the ending of the story satisfying? Why or why not?

Author's notes:

Starting in 1852, thousands of Mormon Pioneers began emigrating from Denmark and other Scandinavian countries with hopes of dwelling in Zion. Many of these pioneers left loved ones behind, for one reason or another. Those left behind often came to America at a later date.

Though there are sure to be inaccuracies and inconsistencies in this historical novel, every effort has been given to ensure the reader a feeling of the time period and lives of the common or peasant class Dane. Some of the details and research are as follows:

The author's ancestors lined their petticoats and trousers with money to keep would-be thieves from taking it.

Faroese horses - http://www.equestrianoutreach.com/Equestrian-Outreach-Faroese-Horse-Page.html. Because of their size, Faroese horses are more commonly classified as ponies, standing at between 11 to 12 hands.

Faroese wool - Knowledge obtained at the Viking Museum in Roskilde, Denmark.

Kerteminde, Fyn. In this charming town and others, many homes are long rows with each residence painted differently. The long-armed mirrors are still on a few of the homes.

Books mentioned in the novel by Berta:

I Sverrig (In Sweden) was written by Hans Christian Andersen and published in 1851. It is a poetic yet journalistic account of his travels to Sweden. Hans Christian Andersen Museum, Odense Denmark.

Eventyr, Fortalte for Born (Adventures Told for Children), by Hans Christian Andersen was published in 1835. Hans Christian

Andersen Museum, Odense Denmark.

Danish names and terms: http://www.sa.dk/content/us/genealogy/genealogical_dictionary http://www.sa.dk/content/us/genealogy/danish_names/danish_female_names

Viebaeltegard in Svendborg wasn't built until 1872. It was a four-winged building, and it served as a public poorhouse and workhouse until 1974. It was for the deserving poor, old, and sick, and for fit men and women without employment who would have otherwise survived by begging or prostitution. It included provisional accommodations for people with mental illness, a lock-up for drunks, a wash house for vermin infested clothing, a chapel with a mortuary, and a few rooms that were originally used as the local hospital.

The king giving gifts of land was mentioned on a boat tour in Copenhagen, Denmark.

Food culture of Denmark: http://www.copenhagenet.dk/cph-eating.htm

Danish peasant life – knowledge was gained through a personal visit to Den Fynske Landsby.

Young persons' guild – knowledge obtained through literature at Den Fynske Landsby.

The tack room and carriages as mentioned in Ilse Manor are similar to those at Egeskov Castle.

Horse stalls similar to the ones described at Ilse Manor are located at Tranekær Castle, Langeland, Denmark

The custom of wearing the wooden shoes to the door of a social gathering and then slipping into leather ones, as well as the custom of fabrics in the hope chest is found at: http://www.quest2europe.com/id30.html

Storks in Denmark: http://www.birds-of-denmark.dk/stork-hvid.htm

Birds and wildlife in Denmark: http://www.fugleognatur.dk/wildaboutdenmark/specieslist.asp?id=1&sort=2.

Birds in Denmark: http://www.birdlist.org/denmark.htm

Images in the locket: http://www.europepress.com/history/

photography_history.htm. "During the 1860's the common type of photography was the Daguerreotype. It was in use from 1851 – 1880's when the Ambrotype was invented."

For a history of white, rye, and whole wheat breads: http://www.foodtimeline.org/foodbreads.html

The Evangelical Lutheran Church and the Parish Council: http://denmark.dk/en/society/religion/, and http://www.lutheranchurch.dk/faq/

The Evangelical Lutheran Church was established as the official church of Denmark with the Reformation in 1536, and reaffirmed as such in the religious revivals of the 1800's. In the 17th century the king prescribed the use of the white ruff (chasuble) that pastors still use together with the black robe.

Of Danish Ways, by Ingeborg S. MacHaffie and Margaret A. Poulsen "Compulsory religious affiliation continued in Denmark until 1849 when Grundloven granted complete religious freedom to every citizen of Denmark."

Frederiksborg Horse: http://www.frederiksborger.com/

"The Frederiksborg horse was used as a coach horse as well as a riding horse. The breed became so popular that too many horses were exported to other countries, and by the middle of the 1800's, the population was too small to continue the success of the breeding. The stud farm was closed around 1871, and after this, the breeding of Frederiksborg Horses was continued on a private basis by the farmers."

The three stages of foaling: http://www.drsfostersmith.com/pic/article.cfm?aid=1583, and http://www.shiredalefarm.com/Foaling.html

Knabstrupper horse –

http://www.knabstrupperforeningen.dk/sider/english-knabstruphistory.htm Spotted horses were bred in Denmark since the late 1600's, and were used in the Court Riding academy of Christiansborg Castle. Unfortunately, this Royal line found its demise in 1750. Then, in 1812, the spotted horses returned to Denmark through a new bloodline.

Danish money and Stamps: In 1653, the postal service was privatized and mail coaches were introduced to deliver mail to nine main routes in Denmark. In 1854 currency changed to the skilling and rigsdaler. http://www.apta.com.au/SubMenu/Brief_Postal_History_of_Denmark.aspx?id=122

General information on Denmark: http://www.everyculture.com/Cr-Ga/Denmark.html

Alcohol consumption and Danes: http://alcoholcultureindenmark.webbyen.dk/

Wedding rings: http://en.wikipedia.org/wiki/Ring_finger- "In some Orthodox Christian, Roman Catholic and Protestant countries such as Russia, Greece, Georgia, Poland, Austria, Germany, Norway, Denmark, Spain, Chile, Venezuela, Colombia and India, the wedding ring is worn on the ring finger of the right hand."

The icebox: http://www.thevintagefridgecompany.com/history-origin.aspx There was an 'ice safe or refrigerator' at the 1851 Great Exhibition, in Europe.

Harmonica: Musical instruments resembling the modern harmonica were popular in Europe in the early 1820's. http://www.musicfolk.com/docs/Features/Feature_Harmonica.htm

Cross Adder – venomous snake in Denmark: http://vipersgarden.at/PDF/M.Wirth.pdf

The Monarch of the Sea: http://mormonmigration.lib.byu.edu/Search/showDetails/db:MM_MII/t:account/id:932/keywords:william+morris

"On April 13, 1864, the English steamer 'Sultana' sailed from Copenhagen, Denmark, carrying 350 emigrants. Thurs, April 28, 1864—The ship, Monarch of the Sea, sailed from Liverpool, England, with 973 Saints, under the direction of Patriarch John Smith. It arrived at New York on June 3rd."

About the Author

Tina Peterson Scott was born and raised in Mesa, Arizona. For much of her childhood she could be found nestled against a branch high in their pecan tree and reading a book. Her favorites were fantasy and mystery, and it delighted Tina when her mother read to her from Grimm's Fairytales and the stories of Hans Christian Andersen.

Tina and her husband have seven children and a growing number of grandchildren. Other than large family get-togethers involving lots of food and fun, she enjoys writing, watercolor painting, long walks, ice cream, and traveling to Europe—especially to her father's ancestral home of Denmark.

Tina writes freelance for a few select publications, has won awards for her writing, and loves best to write about ordinary people in extra-ordinary circumstances.

Connect with Tina:
Connect with Tina on social media:
http://www.facebook.com/TinasWritingAdventure/
http://www.pinterest.com/tinascott161214/
www.linkedin.com/in/tinapetersonscott
Twitter: @authortinascott

Other Books by Tina Scott:
Farewell, My Denmark
Surviving Denmark on a Bag of Peach Rings
Menopausal fairy Mischief

Made in the USA
Middletown, DE
11 December 2018